MW01596316

The Unexpected Unseen

Book 1: Learning the Ropes

Hamid Rafizadeh

ARCHWAY
PUBLISHING

Copyright © 2018 Hamid Rafizadeh.

All rights reserved. No part of this book may be used or reproduced by any means, graphic, electronic, or mechanical, including photocopying, recording, taping or by any information storage retrieval system without the written permission of the author except in the case of brief quotations embodied in critical articles and reviews.

This is a work of fiction. All of the characters, names, incidents, organizations, and dialogue in this novel are either the products of the author's imagination or are used fictitiously.

Scripture taken from the King James Version of the Bible.

Archway Publishing books may be ordered through booksellers or by contacting:

Archway Publishing
1663 Liberty Drive
Bloomington, IN 47403
www.archwaypublishing.com
1 (888) 242-5904

Because of the dynamic nature of the Internet, any web addresses or links contained in this book may have changed since publication and may no longer be valid. The views expressed in this work are solely those of the author and do not necessarily reflect the views of the publisher, and the publisher hereby disclaims any responsibility for them.

Any people depicted in stock imagery provided by Getty Images are models, and such images are being used for illustrative purposes only.
Certain stock imagery © Getty Images.

ISBN: 978-1-4808-6408-5 (sc)
ISBN: 978-1-4808-6407-8 (e)

Library of Congress Control Number: 2018906716

Print information available on the last page.

Archway Publishing rev. date: 06/19/2018

Contents

1

The Watcher

It seemed like any other weekend.

He sat in a dark corner of the room, invisible to anyone peering from the outside, and pointed his sound-locating shotgun microphone at the house across the street. He was listening to another weekend party of the people he had come to suspect. None looked American. He listened intently to the conversation. The shotgun microphone could not pick up the sounds well, but over the years he had gotten used to the accents. From the party's murmur, he could distinguish specific voices. Only occasionally did he use the binoculars to see if anything was happening other than what he heard.

He knew them all by first name. That was how they addressed each other. He had never heard their last names and had made no effort to learn them from other sources. The house belonged to the man whose name sounded like "roughie." Another, a tall, long-haired man with a beard, was called "so long." He had always wondered if un-American names were proof of guilt. No American would name his child Roughie or So Long.

"But then there is the Texan who named his boy Sue!" he said to himself as he smiled. He loved that Johnny Cash song.

He'd retired from the police force four years earlier. It wasn't that he was old or had not done well. One day he just could no longer do the same routine. He had to get out, and he did. Then he had felt the true misery of having nothing to do but watch cable television from morning to evening. Yet the pain had produced no urge to go back to his previous job. He was stuck in a purgatory of his own making.

Then, in his moment of greatest desperation, the 9/11 catastrophe had happened. Suddenly, everyone with a foreign face had become a potential enemy. Concern about the neighbor across the street had become a must. This was much easier than anything he had done previously.

He had always thought the wrong mix of people meant the potential for wrongdoing. On the police force, he had come across many groups involved in criminal activities. Watching Middle Easterners fly airplanes into the Twin Towers had suddenly made him recall the group that met regularly at his neighbor's. A shotgun microphone had cost him $150 and let him listen to conversations that could reveal what the neighbor and his guests were up to. But despite hours of recorded conversation, he had nothing outside the ordinary friendly chitchat.

He had never met the neighbor and never wanted to. On rare occasions, he had had to wave and exchange curt greetings on the run. The man was small and swarthy. Why did he keep that weeklong growth of hair on his face? Couldn't he shave like a normal human being? On top of his odd appearance, he did not mingle with the neighbors. Instead, he threw parties, regularly, for others who looked just as strange.

He sighed. Today seemed no different.

The windows of the neighbor's guest room and TV room were partly open to let in fresh air, and with the shotgun microphone he heard everything they said. For months he had thought the party was just a facade for outsiders. He honestly had believed that at some point sinister plans would surface, and he was there to nip them in the bud. But after months, he could no longer suppress the thought that perhaps nothing out of the ordinary was to be expected from the weekly gatherings.

Looking through the binoculars, he muttered, "What the hell?"

in utter surprise. He moved closer to the window, oblivious to the possibility that he might be seen pointing the long, black microphone and binoculars at the neighbor's house. What amazed him was the separation of men and women. It had not happened before. The women continued to stay together in small groups in the guest room and TV room, but the men were all disappearing.

"Where the hell are they going?" He put the microphone down, threw on his shoes, and went into the yard, where he pretended to look for something, all the while watching the windows of the house opposite him. Then he noticed shadowy movements across a small, dark window in the basement. He all but ran back into the house, got the binoculars, and tried to peer through the small basement window.

He could see little.

The movements came to a halt and steadied into a picture in which he could recognize the head of one man sitting with his back to the window. It was the tall man with the long hair and the beard. He had listened to him many times and suspected he was the ringleader. He spoke most charmingly with the women, but with men, he knew nothing but the worst of the four-letter words.

He put the binoculars down, adjusted the microphone's sensitivity to the highest level, and turned the volume way up. But no matter how he aimed the shotgun microphone through the basement window, he heard nothing but garbled noise. The surreptitious meeting he had awaited for years had begun, but he had no way of finding out what was being said.

He dropped the microphone, cursed his luck loudly, looked through the telephone book, and started dialing.

"Expert Surveillance. How can I help you?" the voice said softly.

"This is John Reagan. I have an account with you. I need a DetectVoice. Do you have one in stock?"

"Let me check." After a short pause that seemed an eternity, the voice said, "Yes, we do. It's 608 dollars. With tax, shipping, and handling, it comes to 662 dollars."

"Send it next-day delivery."

"That would be 692."

John rushed back to the window with his binoculars and the microphone. The women were chattering as if nothing had changed, and the men were huddled in the basement, where his eyes and ears could not reach.

He felt a strong urge to sneak into the neighbor's house, hide near the basement, and listen to the conversation, but instead he got a cold bottle of beer and watched cable television.

He could not bear to look at the tiny basement window.

2

The Need to Know

Arjuna and Khufu were my best friends. Both had already lived long lives. Arjuna was Indian, and Khufu was Egyptian. Though they lived in the United States, they thought and acted in the ways of ancient India and Egypt.

Arjuna was born and had lived most of his life in southern India. When his wife died unexpectedly, he had moved to the United States to be near his grandchildren. Khufu had lived many years under the shadow of the Giza pyramids. Countless times he had seen their imposing silhouettes in starlight. He had immigrated to the United States because he was unable to bear the tyrannical rule of the Egyptian government. These days, his most remarkable feature was being hairless, the battle scar of a cancer he had fought and beaten.

Enoch and Solon were two other friends I had chosen to burden with my zeal for prehistory. They were not so old as Arjuna and Khufu, but they were as intelligent. Enoch was a Jew who took immense pride in his Hebrew heritage. He had lived most of his life in New York City, but his heart belonged to the rolling hills around Jerusalem. Solon, who was Greek, was a university professor who taught philosophy. His appearance and attitude befitted a hippie who rejected conventional values and was prone to using marijuana and psychedelic drugs to alter reality. I had known him for just a few years. He had mentioned once that instead of drifting through hippie communes, he chose to express hippie ideas through philosophy. His long hair and beard still recalled the defiant youth who had sought to single-handedly challenge the world. Despite a predilection for foul language, in his heart he was still a flower child of the sixties, constantly seeking an excuse to rebel.

For a long time, I had been searching for people with whom I could share my radical ideas on prehistory. I ultimately had set my mind on a few candidates, a select few with whom I had hit it off right from the start. These were people I had regularly met up with for years so that we could enjoy each other's company. But could social relations, even among close friends, last when radical ideas were entertained? How would the challenge of radical views of prehistory tint our deep friendship?

I also faced another problem.

My close friends did not cover all the disciplines needed for our group to discuss and analyze my radical prehistoric ideas. I needed others who were not my close friends. So I asked George, whom I had known distantly for years. We'd gone to the same school, where he had been just another odd kid. Today, he would have been labeled a nerd. He'd always loved science. Without him, our group could compare only cultures, ideas, religions, and myths. There would be no science. George would bring the math, the equations, the tools of science. He also wouldn't be burdened by any deep sense of friendship.

George cared for neither religion nor culture, having reached the unwavering conclusion that experiments and theories could explain everything. For him, the myths and sacred texts meant dreams, hallucinations, and mental disorders, subjects to be studied by science. I knew he would be a constant source of agitation, but I found the contradiction appealing. What if he proved that my views of prehistory had nothing to do with science and everything to do with the large pizza I'd eaten before going to bed?

A swift scientific kick in my family jewels would rid me of my prehistoric obsessions.

3

The Public Encounter

In appearance, it was just another weekend when I asked everyone over for lunch. But everyone knew I had a special announcement for the men and needed a few hours of their time. They were warned that the discussion would last into the late afternoon. The women did not mind. They could talk about more intimate things in our absence.

Before the weekend, Enoch and Solon tried hard to find out what was happening.

Enoch moaned, "Is everything okay between you and your wife?" His parents had divorced, and he hated the separation of loved ones. I assured him it was not a family matter.

Solon probed other possibilities. "You didn't get fired, did you, you moron?"

The day of the meeting, lunch went quickly and quietly. None of the men seemed interested in social conversation, though their eyes constantly bespoke concern. I felt sorry for them. They were friends, some quite old and not ready for lengthy suspense.

After lunch we went to an unusual gathering place—the basement, small and somewhat dark but dry. They all looked around as if facing an impending disaster, but no one objected. The place smelled of the old broken furniture that cluttered every corner. At some time in the future—only God knew when—I was going to fix the pieces. Opposite the entrance, two small windows beamed a dusty glow over shelves of bottles and cans whose previous or potential use I could no longer remember. A light fixture adorned each brick wall. In the center, seven old chairs, a sofa, and one large square table formed a rough circle. The chairs were comfortable, the walls thick. We could argue and yell as loudly as we wanted. We would disturb no one. My wife brought tea, coffee, and some cookies. We were ready for action.

Avoiding the inquisitive, concerned eyes of my friends, I said gently, "I am going to be very frank. It's the only way to get to the bottom of my problem and force you to be direct."

They nodded in agreement. None could hide his anguish.

My voice betraying agony, I said, "I have developed a radical model of prehistory." I stopped and studied the faces before me, expecting an outburst, or at least an expression of derision or disbelief. I had imagined the encounter so many times in so many scenarios—at the very least, their faces would harden in astonished indignation—but they sat as though I had asked whether they preferred tea or coffee. They remained stoic, unchanged, their eyes glued on me.

Solon broke the dreadful silence. "Am I hearing you right?" He looked at me probingly. "Are you declaring yourself as the one who will shatter millennia-old thoughts and beliefs on human origin? When did all this happen? Not having talked to anyone until today, how do you know you're on the right track?"

Arjuna motioned to Solon to be silent and asked hesitatingly, "What is it that you have discovered?"

Enoch chimed in, "Yeah, what model? What theory?"

I saw a chance to explain. "I know, everyone is prone to foot-in-the-mouth disease. My only hope is the simplicity of my model." I swallowed nervously and said, "Through years of research, I have come to the conclusion that all of humankind's prehistory, all of the myths and sacred texts, originate at the human experience of a large comet colliding with Earth."

George raised his eyebrows and said softly, "*That* should be easy to check. We know so much about comets, much more about Earth. If it hit Earth, we'd have the footprint."

Solon groaned audibly. Gazing at me, he said, "Are you sure your theory is pointing at the right agent—a comet? Do you know what you're saying? You're saying that the social and personal behavior of every human, for thousands of years, has been dictated and directed by a comet. You're so off the wall! People are not that dense. In the Stone Age, maybe. They saw comets and took them for gods, but not in recent times. The Greeks abandoned a lot of hocus-pocus gods with a single application of logic. That's why there is no Greek religion, only myths. Their societies would have discarded comets much earlier."

George murmured, "Yes, if a comet hit Earth, science would have found the scars hundreds of years ago."

Solon threw an apologetic glance at Arjuna and then at Enoch and said, "I am sorry, but the whole ancient mythical and religious scene is a pile of dirt. Who cares if a comet or the deficient human mind produced myths and religious thought?" He then smiled at me and said, "To be honest, I think you've been having too much baklava and vodka!" He laughed and got up, did a few steps from his favorite Greek dance, and sat down, still smiling.

Enoch tried to hold back his smile and said, "I agree with Solon. Your model would make every Hebrew a comet-worshipper. Yet they have analyzed the text of the Torah for thousands of years, and not once has there been the slightest hint that Yahweh was a comet or had comet attributes."

"My friend," Khufu boomed, "I think I have gotten over the surprise of your announcement. Regardless of the years I have known you, this one was a fast one. You, claiming to know the single factor that determined the prehistory of humankind! You know, you just don't come across as one. I agree with George and Solon. You have to come down from your messianic perch. No one will take you seriously." He paused, fiddled with his cup of tea, and said, "Since I know you, I accept your research efforts as exceptional and real. But that doesn't guarantee you developed your model right."

Solon said, "Even if you have the right model, you have a fat chance of getting the community of scholars to abandon their established ways of seeing the prehistory."

George brushed the back of his index finger across the tip of his nose and muttered nervously, "I said it before and will say it again. We know a lot about comets. All we need is to line up comet characteristics with things that definitely took form in prehistory, such as the sacred texts and myths." He cleared his throat. "Why don't we start with a comet tutorial? I can put one together. As a starting point, we can comb through myths and sacred texts for similarities. If we find something positive, I can then go through scientific literature and see if someone has discovered your comet's footprints."

As friendly faces contemplated me, I said, "We would not be here if this idea had happened yesterday or last month. It has evolved over years of research. Until today, I had told no one. My first reaction was to make sure I had all my marbles. You know that I have always been a straight arrow. I shouldn't be prone to false views of human prehistory. I—"

Solon interrupted sarcastically. "So you want *us* to walk the plank with you so you don't have to do it by yourself!"

I looked down at my feet and said, "I need you to make sense of my experience. I agree with what you say. I'm not going to individually prove a radical model of prehistory, nor do I want to hide behind you. That's why for years I have been studying comets, sacred texts, and myths by myself. I genuinely thought that knowledge was the way out of my dilemma. But the more I learned, the more I became troubled by the whole thing."

Arjuna said, "From what I know, a true discoverer has to be a master of the hard sell. *That* you're not."

Solon nodded and added, "Yeah, you're shitty-soft."

Arjuna glared at Solon and then continued, "But you're not alone.

Moses could hardly speak two sentences right, but he delivered a message. He delivered it right. He lived to be a very old man."

"How can I face the fanatical believers and scholars who want none of our view of prehistory changed?" I asked.

Arjuna said, "People develop religious beliefs without any deep examination of why they do. Even scientists often get trapped in structures of stagnated thought, which they call paradigms."

Solon interrupted again and said, "Something really bugs me. Tell me point-blank. Are you pulling our legs? Should I expect hidden cameras or a practical joke? Shit! You shouldn't be able to tell us this story with a straight face. We're your friends."

I smiled without joy and said, "I wish it were all a joke. I wish I could deliver my findings publicly, come hell or high water. But I am mostly scared."

Solon looked at me in disbelief and said, "I expected you to say you were just shoveling the dirt, but you're serious."

"Though I believe my model of prehistory is true," I said, "I see little value in it. For thousands of years, in myths and religious texts, humans haven't seen a life-altering comet—no signs either in the halls of science. Why would they want to see one now?"

"I see your point," Enoch agreed. "Moses faced a similar problem. Instead of comets, his message was Hebrew freedom. You have to make a personal choice. Moses faced the pharaoh, armed only with a divine message. Not even the Hebrews liked his message. Getting to the masses of people to deliver the message of seeing life in a new way has never been easy."

Solon said, "We do have a leg up on radical views of life. We already know a lot. Moses wasn't alone. Jesus had the same problem. He had the nerve to talk about the coming of the kingdom of heaven. What was that? Even today, no one knows what he meant by 'the kingdom of heaven.' No one understood him. Instead of listening and asking for more, they told him to zip his lip. When he didn't, the top dogs silenced him. No one will ever know what he wanted to say. On the plus side, your model of prehistory is more physical. It's a crappy comet that supposedly everyone should have seen. But you have a bigger problem. Historically, when people look at a messenger of change, they tend to see a person claiming to be the next controller of the ways of the world."

George bristled. "But *that* is stupid. I don't accept the mail based on whether the mailman is a Nobel Prize winner or not."

Solon shook his head and said, "It may be wrong—in fact, it *is* wrong—but messengers have always been competitors to the established views, not just delivery boys."

We had gotten deeply into the fate of those who dare to develop radical alternatives to established ways of human life. Khufu talked about Mohammed. The Islamic message had been foreign to Arabs at first. Mohammed affirmed one God, not many. But the Arabs already had many gods and were comfortable with what they had. They first tried to convince Mohammed to shut up voluntarily. After all, he was a wealthy, popular businessman. He belonged to a powerful tribe. Killing him would not be easy. But Mohammed, undeterred, pushed his new model of life, so they tried to kill him. He survived a number of attempts on his life. Finally, he chose war and put together a group to fight and spread his way. Those who lost had to adopt the victor's way of seeing the human life.

"I don't think that's an alternative for you or any scientist," Khufu observed.

"No, my warrior days are over."

Enoch said, "Something similar happened to Moses. No one in Egypt listened. His only choice was confrontation."

"True," said Khufu, "but Mohammed relied on war to spread his model; Moses relied on divine intervention. God fought on the side of his model." He turned to me and said, "Now if you have someone powerful to fight on your side, you'll have no worry in this world or perhaps even in the hereafter." He giggled.

"The problem is not exclusive to prehistoric views of myth and religion," said George. "The same happens in science and politics.

Messengers don't have to come from God to become targets. Martin Luther King had a human message. When he said it too loudly, he was silenced. Galileo used his telescope to see Jupiter's moons and proved that Earth was not the center of the universe. That information did not become fully public in his lifetime because he was told to shut up or die. He chose to shut up. It will be the same if you tell people that a comet sits at the prehistoric origin of religion and many aspects of the social structure. The response could be the same: shut up or die."

"That's my point!" I said. "How do I find out the degree to which the new way of seeing prehistory is offensive? When do I walk away and let someone else worry about how prehistory looked?"

Arjuna leaned back nervously, as if to increase his distance from me. "Perhaps you have to ask if people have a *need* for your model of prehistory. Otherwise, it would be like the most skilled snake charmer in India trying to teach your wife to handle cobras. The way your wife abhors snakes, it wouldn't make the slightest difference if he were the world's supreme snake charmer." Arjuna paused, studied our faces, and went on. "I learned a simple lesson from knee surgery. The doctor told me I had a torn ligament. I had to have surgery. After I had it, I thought about the experience. Would I ever let him do the same to my uninjured knee? No way! Not even if he brought to the operation the best arthroscopic surgeons on Earth. Even if he offered to do it for free, I would never let him. My healthy knee would have *no need* for surgery."

Solon said, "Logically, let's assume you're the real McCoy. We can also assume there are a lot of bad things in the prehistory of myths, religions, and social organization. Furthermore, talking seriously about any aspect of established religious beliefs would bring on a kind of blah feeling. So I'll reverse the roles and use a simple example. Assume that someone is at the door, offering to tell you the prehistoric origin of religions. Forget about everybody else. Just concentrate on us, the guys in this basement. Would any of us need it? It is the simple supply-and-demand question. Do any of us go through the day dreaming and creaming about someone with news of the origin of religions and myths? From everything I know about us, we will all answer no. If *we* have no need and are not searching, why should anyone else?"

I laughed. "Before talking to you, I did send to a dozen publishers an account of my model of prehistory. Only one asked to see the manuscript. He returned it so fast, it felt I had never sent it."

"Publishers and editors," Arjuna said, "are judges. They ape and mirror what humans *need* to read. Today, the need is to read about the president fondling someone in the Oval Office. I agree with Solon. Nobody wants to read about the prehistoric origin of religions. It has nothing to do with right or wrong, only preferences. People love sexual scandals, but they don't want to hear about theories and models that change the already-established views of the human past."

"Why is the human so lopsided?" I asked. "Isn't our origin as important as a national leader's sex life?"

"Pardon me all to hell," Solon interrupted. "In human societies, even something as important as God is a settled matter. Everyone knows it. God was taken care of thousands of years ago. All we need is to accept the Bible-thumping ways of our fathers. Reopen the question of God, and you pose a challenge to people. No one wants to revisit God. That's why they'll go crazy on you and wreck your life if you claim their prehistoric view of God is some cometary illusion!"

Khufu said, "For me, five daily prayers and a Friday visit to the mosque take care of God. For someone like George, perhaps it's an occasional Sunday at church. An hour here, another there, and we are done. For Enoch it is a weekly temple visit and some dietary restrictions. We already have a simple, efficient system to deal with God. Now you bring a comet into it, and—how does Solon say it?—you fart up the whole pissing thing!"

Laughter visited every face.

Encouraged, Khufu continued to mimic and butcher Solon's way of talking. "Your buttocks will make the natives restless, and they will nail your pecker to the wall!"

Everyone laughed louder.

"You'll have to part the Atlantic to get away!"

As they laughed and teased, I wondered why anyone would want to know a more accurate picture of prehistory. I did not need to look at human social organization to develop an understanding of human orientation. Religion was more than enough as an example of how humans related to new flow of knowledge about the past. Religions were about God. Every religion claimed to have come from divine experience. But if they were all based on divine contacts, why did people adhere to just one religion, especially an old one from thousands of years ago? Why not seek a more recent connection?

Why did every believer lose his cool when his beliefs were challenged? Whenever a new divine message was announced, the believers in previous messages tried to prove it false. No one looked for a new messiah. They all wanted to hang on to what was already there. Was every believer a prisoner of fossilized experience from thousands of years ago?

Fact or not, his arguments would be considered fighting words. Believers would not stay calm, listen, and learn. As Solon had once said, "When it comes to fanatical belief, humans have shit for brains."

As the others talked, I continued to review the simple historical picture. If I said that people were really comet worshippers, I would distinctly imply a disconnect from God. Would that make any difference? How could I or anyone else argue that a more recent and more proper link to the creator, different from what we already had, would be more advantageous?

I had no notion of what was right. I knew only what was not right. What arrogance—to interfere in established ways when I knew so little.

People saw their view of God as the proper model for relating to the most powerful being in the universe. How could a weakling like me deliver a model that would radically alter all previous views? That could not be right. Yet what was the big deal if a cometary phenomenon of tens of thousands of years ago lay at the root of every religion? So what if religions were linked not to God but to a comet? The comet's majesty would adequately represent the majesty of God. Was not God the comet-maker?

The laughter and jokes had died down. The silent smiles demanded a response. Arjuna pointed a finger at me and asked, "What are you going to do?"

"For years I have straddled the fence," I said. "This isn't something the cat dragged in. Doesn't matter how you or anyone else sees or interprets it. I have to deal with the information I have discovered. So I'm in a tight spot. Worse yet, you could be stuck with me. I fear for you as much as I fear for myself, especially since few if any would want to know about a new view of prehistory of humankind that alters almost every established view. Just from the perspective of religion alone, no redefinition of God is needed anywhere. Furthermore, I'm not geared for confrontation. I am not ready to face the music. Acting or not acting on my discovery of a comet-riddled prehistory has been my choice. If I choose against it, there would be no need for a new look at myths, human social organization, or even God. No one has to hear about my comet model of prehistory."

Solon was not pleased. "What are you trying to say? You *quit*?"

"I think I can put my model to better use. Rather than talking about a prehistory in which humans were primarily comet worshippers, I can tell the story of a comet that once visited Earth."

"You totally miss the point," George hissed. "You're jumping to all sorts of unwarranted conclusions. Listen! Many comets visit Earth regularly. We know all about them. Unless you link comets to something exotic like prehistoric origin of religions, there is nothing new. There's no new comet story to tell. When you quit as defender and promoter of your radical model, you quit as a storyteller."

Coming from George, this was a surprise. He had stopped believing in God a long time ago. He had looked deep into the universe. Not once had he seen God. Everything was matter and energy in constant motion. Life as we knew it could exist and sustain itself without ever having to utter the divine name. He should have been the first to reject the significance of how humans construct gods out of their physical environment. He would be the least interested in tearing the religion down. He thought religion was already a goner. Science had torn religious beliefs to shreds. Everyone but George approved of my retirement from prehistoric model building. What was it that George could not walk away from?

Then I saw it in his face—the possibility of an exceptional experience, one that could be demonstrated with earthly evidence. He would challenge me about the significance of developing a religious model out of a cometary experience, but the challenge would stop if I showed an exceptional, natural, earthly phenomenon. His mind, attuned to the exceptional stuff of science, would see the panoramic view of the religious texts becoming scientific evidence. However wrong the religions might be about God, their sacred texts might be scientifically right about an exceptional comet. The religious texts would join science and show unequivocally that without them science did not know everything about comets. Not every comet story had been told.

I should have kept my mouth shut. Only later would I recognize that at that moment I tore up my resignation as a prehistory model-maker.

I felt compelled to challenge George, to show the weakness of the scientific understanding of life. All I needed was to point at a few features of the exceptional comet. At that moment, I saw George as the only remaining barrier to my retirement from pursuit of radical models. He had to be subdued. I had to do it to get through my dilemma.

I looked at George fiercely and said, "You may *think* you know a lot about comets, but you don't. Tell me, Einstein, how does a comet create a penis thirty thousand miles long?"

Solon grinned from ear to ear.

"Stop joking!" George mumbled. "How can I make you people focus?"

Calmly, I replied, "I'm not joking. The thirty-thousand-mile penis is a fact. I can prove it. I can show that you and your science don't know everything about comets."

"I love this," Solon murmured. "You don't mean inches or feet? You actually mean miles—and thousands of them?"

"Yes, miles. Fit only for God. At least that's how the ancients felt."

"What's your point?" George said loudly.

"My point is, instead of talking about prehistory of religion, I can talk about a comet. I can use the sacred texts to show comet characteristics, all without any reference to how things like myths and religious thought emerged out of the prehistoric cometary experience. Later, if someone sees today's life as a story of comet worshippers, it's his problem. He can do it on his own time. I'd be out of the picture."

Enoch eyed me and said, "That is not how it works. Reveal any piece of the sacred text as a thirty-thousand-mile penis, and you'll deal with every believer's wrath. They'll stick that celestial penis up your you-know-what!"

I was pleased: more reason to quit. "So we're back to the inevitable. Either way, I will be dragging the masses kicking and screaming into a radically new view of prehistory. Yet I have no desire to do so."

"You may twist the sacred texts into a sexy, action-packed story," said Enoch, "but you cannot avoid contradicting the stories already told by the same texts. Your comet story will negate deeply established religious stories. You'll find out the hard way that the belief of a fanatic is big enough to choke a horse."

"So religions have robbed the fanatic's rational mind blind. But that is not the key. *This* is the key: whether you come out as a scientific storyteller or a radical changer of the social structure, you're going to face the same audience."

"So I might as well deliver the radical message of my model about prehistory rather than tell a scientific comet story," I said.

"That's right."

"Or I can shut up and say nothing."

"That's also a prudent choice." Enoch sounded more approving. "The Torah tells of many prophets who chose silence. They lived long lives. You'd be in good company."

Solon brought his head close to mine, as if afraid others might hear him. He said, "Forget about science. If the damned comet was impressive enough to be imagined as God for tens of thousands of years, it would be the key to the human psyche. It would be a window to everything humans have built in their screwed-up minds. It would explain all the symbolism and imagery that seem to have no place in reality today."

Khufu looked like he had been bursting to speak. I desperately hoped he would advocate my silence, but he built on Solon's idea and said, "Symbolism and imagery are not limited to religion or the past. Today, we see people operating powerful machines. We see them in flying machines. So we imagine the superman, the most powerful machine, a godlike man-machine combination. And that's just *one* example. We use telescopes to peer into deep space. There we create symbolic human presences, galaxies into which the Starship *Enterprise* travels faster than light—so many godlike attributes. Do you see? Do you see what I'm saying? We humans want to extend our lives symbolically toward a godlike destination. So as Solon would say, how do you like them apples? We constantly create godlike imagery out of things around us. Yet if our ancestors saw a comet and called it God, we call them brain-dead. That's hypocrisy. Let me ask you: how would we extend our lives symbolically today if something unexplained entered our world? How would we describe and relate to something exceptional? If my ancestors saw all sorts of unexplainable cometary features in the sky, they had to incorporate those sights into their lives—no different from the galaxies that enter our lives through telescopes. I am least troubled by a comet God. If the ancients portrayed an exceptional celestial phenomenon as God, we should see it as the human way."

George shook his head vigorously. "There you go again, equating God with the unknown. When are we going to understand that God is the biggest unknown in human life? We know absolutely nothing about Him. What's wrong with you? We know nothing about faster-than-light travel. Do you see me worshipping it? Something's got to give. At some point we must stop bowing before unknowns, stop making them God."

"Aren't you guys jumping the gun?" Enoch asked. "We don't have the smallest sliver of proof of an exceptional comet. We don't know if it ever existed, or if it was impressive, or that people took its features to be gods. In a pinch, we can abandon all this for lack of evidence. Yet you talk as though it were all true."

Arjuna said, "That's human imagination. It would be nice to have the facts, especially about God. The truth is, we don't. Yes, we give Him attributes—all-knowing, all-powerful, omnipresent, eternal—but how did we come to know such attributes? We imagined them. We have no facts to back them up. They all emanate from our imagination of God, not from facts about God."

George said, "Here's another attribute, a perceived fact: God has balls."

We smiled, confused.

"Who has seen God's genitals to say *He* is male?" George asked. "What if He is *She*? What if He is *It*, no sex whatsoever?"

Now we understood. Everyone assumed God was male. George wanted a testicle as proof.

It was Arjuna's turn. "We all need *facts* in our lives. If the findings of your research experience are real, then you have brought us a new fact of life. Humans can no longer continue to imagine, as they have for thousands of years. Imagination is not the same as fact. It is a grave mistake to imagine God. People need facts. I don't know how and can't prove it, but my gut feeling says an imaginary God is harmful. It may more likely destroy humankind than change it for the better."

Solon got up, knelt beside Arjuna's chair, and said, "I see the logic— preferring facts to imagination. But facts are scarce. Imagination is often the only thing available. Why not use an imaginary God until enough facts are gathered to see otherwise?"

Arjuna looked down for a while and then threw me a quick glance and said, "Not that I mean to put down your idea, but what about one of my stories—a quick story?"

We always dreaded his lengthy storytelling, but nodding heads prevailed.

Arjuna began telling his story, and surprisingly, it did not start in India. Instead, he pointed to the automobile as today's popular way of meeting the human need to go from place to place.

"At new car dealers, people buy brand-new automobiles. Others go to used car dealers and get a car that has already taken others to places. Few go to auto graveyards; there they find only ruined bits of metal and plastic. Yet if somebody spent a lot of time repairing and rebuilding a graveyard automobile, it is possible that it could take him from here to there."

Arjuna saw all such possible automobiles—new, old, solid, or rusting—as *facts*, physical facts.

"We can touch them. We can feel them. They satisfy a daily need. They take humans from place to place.

"But what if people *imagined* automobiles? They can imagine a brand-new car. They may imagine a luxury car. They may imagine a sports car." He looked at us defiantly and asked, "Have you ever driven an imagined car? If you have, you know it doesn't take you anywhere. It cannot physically move you from one place to the next. It cannot because it is not a fact. You cannot touch it. You cannot feel it. It doesn't exist anywhere but within your mind. To become a fact, it has to exist outside of your mind."

Khufu exclaimed, "But I can feel and touch my imagined car in my mind."

"You can *imagine* you touch and feel it, but you *cannot* touch and feel it. It is not a fact."

Arjuna went on, noting that not every car was the same. "They all take you from one place to another, but they do it differently. A car put together in an auto graveyard is not the same as one in a used-car lot. The one in a used-car lot is not the same as one in a dealer's showroom. In what fundamental way do they differ?"

George shrugged his shoulders and said, "You've already said it—speed, reliability. Only you haven't brought up price, but that is obvious."

Arjuna threw up his hands in exasperation. "Pay attention to what I am saying. In what fundamental way do they differ?"

No one understood where Arjuna was leading us. He smiled, gloating, and said, "They differ in their distance from their creator. The factory is the creator. The closer an automobile is to the factory, the shinier, faster, and better it looks. The farther it gets, the junkier it becomes. Eventually, the link to the factory is severed. The factory no longer provides it with anything. It ends up in the graveyard."

"That's the life cycle of the things we make and use," George said. "With age, everything gets distanced from the factory."

"Again, you are missing the point. It is not that they are aging. They are becoming distant from the factory."

"Why the hell is the factory linkage so important?" George blurted.

"Because the factory is all-knowing when it comes to creating cars. The knowledge of every aspect of a car is at the factory. Every day, the creator improves the car. The creator wants its knowledge to flow constantly into the automobile. Being distant from the factory is being distant from the source of knowledge that brings the car to life."

"Arjuna," George hissed, "can you tell me where you are going with this car theory of yours? I thought we were talking about human beings imagining God."

"The human need for God is no different from a car's need for factory knowledge. God is of value because He has all the knowledge a human needs to remain brand-new. Unquestionably, His knowledge can improve human life. If we know Him and stay close to Him, we will be like a new automobile. If we don't know Him or we become distant, we will be like a used car. When we totally lose track of Him, we turn into junk. But whether we are broken down or brand-new, the relationship is based on facts. Only facts get us from one place in life to the next. A total disconnect from God would happen when we only *imagine* Him, especially if we imagine him wrong, confusing him with exceptional things around us. God then becomes like an imaginary car. He cannot take us anywhere, regardless of how hard or how well we imagine. I tell you, factually, an imaginary car does not exist. Nor would an imaginary god."

"It would have been a lot quicker," George bellowed, "if you had said an imaginary god is not the same as a factual god. This automobile comparison was a complete waste of time."

"But you did get my point," Arjuna rejoined.

"It's obvious. If I eat and drink imaginary food, I'll be dead in a few days. If there is a god, which I do not believe there is, it is foolish to relate to an imaginary surrogate that has nothing to do with the factual one."

"*That* is my point."

"Okay."

It was getting late. Night was not far off. We all would have stayed longer, but we knew the signal. My wife had walked a few steps into the basement and retreated. Everyone had to leave so that I could spend time on domestic assignments.

I smiled and asked gently, "What about next week? Same time?"

Heads nodded. My friends were showing rudimentary interest in the possibility of prehistoric comet worshippers.

4

Heartache

The DetectVoice arrived the next day, and John was elated. It was an expensive piece of equipment that promised pinpoint accuracy even at three hundred yards, and it had a three-band equalizer that adjusted to specific sound frequencies. Its twenty-inch-diameter dish was not easy to hold by hand to focus on a target, so he ordered a tripod to aim it precisely at the basement window.

By the weekend he had tested the parabolic dish on the neighbor's house with excellent results. He could hear the conversations much better than with the shotgun microphone, but still he worried about effectiveness in penetrating the tiny basement window. The device's high degree of directionality could also be a problem. It might capture the voice of the person it was aimed at but not those of the others scattered around the basement. He nonetheless impatiently awaited the next meeting.

The Sunday came, and the pattern repeated.

After lunch the men proceeded to the basement, and John listened to his surveillance device with anticipation. The long-haired, bearded Solon again sat with his back to the window, the only one in line with the parabolic dish.

"Damn it!" he groaned. The sound reception was not good. "It must be the window size."

He also cursed the neighbor for not cleaning the window. Since it was close to the ground, rain had splashed the window with a layer of dirt. He played with the tripod adjustments to find the best fix on the basement.

At least I'm getting something, he thought positively. With the shotgun microphone he had not been able to hear a word. So he concentrated and listened as carefully as he could.

Though the barely audible words hardly reached him, he noticed a repetition of the word "commit." *What are they committing to?* he wondered. The fact that they were so focused on commitment in the initial stages of their meeting implied they were up to something big that required substantial personal commitment. Then his heart sank as he heard words that sounded like "dirty fireball," "many kilometers in diameter," and "gaseous cloud."

"Oh God, they are talking about making and using a dirty bomb!" he whispered.

He knew a lot about conventional bombs wrapped in a radioactive blanket. The explosion vaporized and released radioactive material over a wide area, making it uninhabitable. Although the loss of life would not be large, the economic damage would be substantial.

He couldn't tell who was talking.

For the first time his investigation of the situation disappointed him. For years he had sat in the house and had not tailed any of the basement people. He easily could have conducted such an investigation to produce a database of where they lived and what they did. But instead all he had were the first names of men who went to surreptitious meetings.

For a moment he thought of contacting the FBI, but he quickly rejected the idea. He knew he lacked solid evidence. Moreover, what he was doing was illegal. If he had heard wrong and the men in the basement were doing nothing but smoking cigars, he would be in a heap of trouble. The neighbor and his guests could sue him for everything he had for violation of privacy. He needed to build a solid case against them before bringing in outsiders.

He listened more.

"Hundreds of thousands to millions," someone said. This time he was sure he had heard right. They were talking about things of very large size and effect. He wondered if the numbers meant fatalities. Then the conversation switched to more specific topics. He heard "seal in there and swarm." That sounded like a plan for a terrorist attack.

He agonized as he clearly heard, "Nothing would be alive." Though he couldn't understand the rest, he sensed a sudden increase in energy levels. The voices grew excited about something that sounded like "can OP." What was the "OP" they were excited about? Did OP stand for some sort of "operation"? He did not think so. There had to be more.

The excitement died down, and the tone returned to normal. But the words "can OP" were repeated and seemed to be associated with the earth. Whatever the basement group was planning or considering doing now surfaced as "can OP earth" statements. Whatever the idea was, it had worldwide implications, and the basement group sounded quite confident of OPing the earth.

John could tell the meeting was nearing its end. He left the DetectVoice's recorder on. He could listen later to the whole conversation to see if he could identify other words. But for now he had to get ready to tail So-Long. He had to find out where he lived and worked.

John parked his car three blocks away at the corner, pretending to check the map. He knew So-Long would have to pass him, no matter where he was going. There was no other outlet. Twenty minutes later, a string of cars started to pass him, and he readily recognized the occupants. He had never seen So-Long driving and quickly realized he had no respect for stop signs or traffic lights. John wished he were still on the police force and could stop him for traffic violations. That would have made learning his address and workplace so easy. But for now, he followed So-Long at a pace that reminded him of chasing suspects on the run.

Finally, after a few miles, So-Long pulled into a driveway near the university. The house was small but in a nice part of town. He wondered why So-Long lived in a place that did not match his personal appearance of rebellious chaos.

The rest was easy.

He scouted the area and determined the spot where he would park and wait to follow So-Long to his place of work the next morning. In his mind, he made a similar plan for everybody in the basement.

That night John has a hard time sleeping. He constantly dreamed of chasing the letters O and P through busy streets named Roughie and So-Long.

5

The Sting

John had planned to be near So-Long's house at 6:30 a.m., but he was late. The previous day, chasing after So-Long at high speed and running red lights had given him a wrong perception of the distance. Not only was So-Long's house farther than he had imagined, but it also was Monday morning. He faced a build-up of rush-hour traffic.

By the time he arrived at the designated scouting point, it was 7:30 a.m. He cursed his planning and wondered if he should call it a day and start the next day. Then he decided to wait for a while, just in case going to work late was part of So-Long's counterculture makeup.

A few drivers and a man walking a dog studied him with suspicion as he pretended to check a map. As he was about to give up and move on, So-Long's garage door jerked upward. John started his car and readied himself for another chase, but So-Long came out dragging a garbage can to the sidewalk. Then he went back inside and closed the door. Moments later he reappeared in the driveway, walking briskly toward John.

"Oh shit!" John blurted. Had So-Long somehow seen him and recognized him as his friend's neighbor? Just as his panic reached a new height, So-Long turned the corner onto a side street.

John's exasperation became confusion. "Where the hell is he going?"

So-Long took a short street that dead-ended at the university campus.

Was he cutting through the campus to throw John off his trail?

John got out of the car and started walking after So-Long. So-Long seemed too preoccupied to pay attention to what was happening behind him. As they entered the campus, John prayed for more students. He could use them as cover to get closer to So-Long, but there were few around so early in the morning. He thought of his own college days. He had never registered for anything earlier than ten.

So-Long wove a path among the buildings. If John had been one step farther behind, he would have missed seeing So-Long go into an old building on the right. John ran to the entrance, fearing he might lose So-Long —and he was right. By the time he opened the door, there was no trace of So-Long in the long hallway.

He looked for stairs, but they were too far down the hall. So-Long could not have reached them before John entered the building.

"He is somewhere on the first floor," he assured himself.

John didn't know what to do. All the doors were closed, some with and some without names. Down the hall, beyond the stairs, on a plaque he could make out the words "School of Humanities and Social Sciences—Dean's Office." He thought of going there, but what would he say? Where is the hairy guy whose first name sounds like "so long"?

He was walking toward the stairs, wondering what to do, when a door opened behind him. He turned and saw So-Long coming out and the words "Men's Restroom" on the open door.

He turned instinctively to the bulletin board on the wall and perused the study-abroad announcements as So-Long passed by and started up the stairs. John raced after him and slowed down only at the top, when he had So-Long in sight. Three doors down, So-Long stopped, opened a door, walked in, and closed it behind him. John approached the door cautiously and read "Solon Gyftapolous, Professor of Philosophy."

"Solon, not *so long*, you dummy!" he chided, as if someone else were to blame.

This was not what he had expected.

Solon's workplace should be subversive and sinister.

He walked down to the dean's office and asked the secretary if she could give him a list of the courses Professor Gyftapolous would teach next semester.

"Are you a student?"

"Not yet, but I'm thinking of taking a few courses. I just retired."

"Normally, the admissions office is the best place for you to start, but let me print out Dr. Gyftapolous's schedule."

She hit a few keys, and a printer behind her whined. Moments later, John had his list of courses: two sections of Introduction to Philosophy and one of Philosophical Postmodernism. John did not know what to do next. He knew nothing about philosophy and was afraid that if he talked to him, Solon might ask where he lived. He knew a pyramid of lies would eventually backfire.

What would be the point of talking to him? he asked himself.

He smiled as a roguish thought crossed his mind. He could trap the professor in a heap of trouble, and he knew just the person to do it.

John left the building, crossed the campus to his car, and drove south toward the poorest, most crime-ridden part of town. After an hour he pulled up in front of what seemed to be a dilapidated saloon. In a crescent-shaped window a red neon sign blinked the name of a beer, and through the small, dirty glass on the front door one could barely read the sign: "Open."

He pushed the door open and stepped into the darkness.

His eyes needed a few seconds to adjust to the dim light in the room filled with a scattering of small tables. At the far end was the bar, where a tall, bald man was cleaning glasses with a towel that might once have been white. Near the entrance a man sat with his arms and head on the table, sound asleep. At the edge of the bar, a burly man on a stool drank from a cup.

No one paid him any attention, so John walked up to the bartender.

The bartender initially glanced at him with the normal indifference of "What'll it be?" But then his eyes flashed a mix of shock and hate.

"What the fuck are you doing here, you piece of shit?" the man snarled as he slammed the counter, smashing the glass he had been cleaning.

"It's nice to see you too, Hank," John muttered.

Hank's voice and the sound of breaking glass changed the room's mood.

The big man at the end of the bar leaned over the counter and came up with a baseball bat. In the mirror behind the bar, John saw the sleeping man come to life, stand up, and flick open a big knife.

Hank leaned to his right, and John figured he was going after a shotgun beneath the bar. Before he could straighten up, John hit him on the jaw as hard as he could. The bartender smashed into the back wall and fell facedown, unconscious.

As the man with the knife wove his way through the tables, the big man with the baseball bat came after John.

John stood still, as if nothing was happening, and then when the batter was within a few feet, he stepped nimbly aside and landed a sidekick to the man's left knee. At the sound of cracking bone, the man screamed, let go of the bat, and reached for his shattered knee with both hands. He collapsed on a table that splintered under him.

John caught the bat in the air and turned around like a batter waiting for a fastball. Instead of a ball, he sought a knife in the air, located it, and swung hard. Another sound of breaking bones, another cry of agony.

"You broke my arm!" the man shrieked as he collapsed to the floor, clutching a badly twisted right hand with his left.

As if engaging in an exacting dance that demanded each step's perfect execution, John dropped the bat, turned, and reached over the counter for the dazed bartender, who was just trying to stand up. John grabbed him by the shoulders, pulled him over the counter, dragged him to the wall, and slammed him into it, nose first.

"I came to talk and ask for help," John hissed, "but if this is how you want it, I'll show up every day and break every bone in anyone I find here."

The threat sank in.

Hank had no police protection. He would never call the police, and even if he did, they wouldn't show up. He was an outlaw, and the news of his death and destruction would be music to any policeman's ears.

John and Hank knew each other from way back when Hank had been in a religious cult that loved to skirmish with the government and John had been in the task force that sought to put an end to the cult's activity.

Hank's cult had been involved in murder and armed robbery. One of the members had killed two US marshals who tried to arrest him for parole violations. Although John's task force had not been able to pin anything on Hank, it had collected enough evidence to arrest key cult members and destroy the organization's effectiveness.

Most of the surviving cultists had become separatists living in isolated paramilitary enclaves. A few like Hank had stayed true to their fanatical mission, but they operated from within the enemy territory.

Hank had bought a bar and now used it to recruit for the cult and its paramilitary operations. Occasionally, he and his buddies knocked over a bank to meet the cult's financial needs. They were never caught, and the stolen money was never traced to Hank and the bar. Though the FBI watched the bar off and on, this hadn't provided the evidence needed to close it down.

John strangled Hank a little to get his attention. "I need your help. I need one of your thinkers to visit someone and convince him of the truth of your mission."

"Go to hell!" Hank spat.

John kneed him in the groin, hard.

"Here's the deal," John said calmly. "You give me the guy I need, and I'll disappear and never come to see you again. Or I will come see you every day for the rest of my life. And remember, I'm no longer with the police. I'm a private citizen who can fuck you a million ways."

"What do you want?" Hank barked, his voice edged with pain.

"I want one of your younger guys, one who really knows your way of life, to pose as a student and visit a professor at the university. I want the professor converted to your cause."

"Why?"

"Well, I've thought long and hard about you and your cult. I have reached the conclusion that the only way to demonstrate the validity of your beliefs is to test it on a worthy opponent, a scholar."

"Fuck you!" Hank did not buy a single word. "You're fucking with me. You're trying to set up a sting in my backyard and catch some asshole in it. You may even trap me. No way! I'll never do it."

"Listen, you piece of shit"—John increased the torque on Hank's throat—"I gave you your choices. Help me, or I'll be here every morning and tear anybody I find to pieces, especially you. What'll it be?"

The reminder seemed to help.

Hank looked like he wanted to talk but could not. John loosened his grip.

"Do you swear not to screw me and my people?"

"I have nothing against you. All I want is your best brain to act as a student and convince the professor to join you. He's a revolutionary. It would be a piece of cake."

"Then what?" Hank croaked.

"Then you direct him to any paramilitary group you like and walk away. I know you're in the recruitment business. I'll follow him and, at the right moment, bring down the wrath of God and government on him."

An agreement seemed to be taking form. John let go of Hank's throat and took a step back.

"You said he's a revolutionary. Which group?"

"None you know. He has his own. He's the Antichrist type, not one of your friends. In fact, I'll owe you a big one if you drag in a few of the professor's buddies."

"I'll see what I can do."

"When?" He took a step forward and stared into Hank's eyes.

"I'll start the ball rolling tomorrow. By next week I'll have a surprise student visiting your professor."

"Talk to you later."

John walked out, oblivious to the two men with broken limbs squirming on the floor in pain.

6

Something Exceptional

I smiled on how time could focus thought.

A week had passed.

What an eerie sense of comfort with a radical model of prehistory! Was it because a few others knew? They'd had to reflect on what they knew before putting me on the spot, though at comfort's right hand sat a world of antagonism. Having thought about the matter, would they see me as the one who had gotten them into trouble?

When they arrived, I saw signs of work. Each had a book or two and was rearing to dig into me, support me, or tear me apart. George was the exception. He carried a bloated briefcase. What a change! Last week no one had carried books.

Who would challenge me first? Would anyone look me in the eye and accuse me of cooking up a fictional story, perhaps for personal gain? It was logical. A claim of radical research into prehistory would seem like a cock-and-bull story to anyone but a friend. But they were friends, and for a transitory moment friendship could defy logic.

When we settled into our chairs in the basement, Solon smiled broadly and said, "Aren't we all bright-eyed and bushy-tailed today!"

"What are you saying?" Arjuna frowned, unable to hide his dislike of Solon's slang, of which he understood little.

Solon just grinned.

George came to Arjuna's rescue. "He says we are eager and energetic."

Arjuna scowled at Solon. "Why don't you say so? What is this flashy-eye and fluffy-tail language you are so addicted to?" He turned to me and said, "I think it's time to tell us your full story. The more we know, the better we can advise you."

I said, "I've given some thought to how to tell my story. First, a brief comet story. Then, a visit to the sacred texts and myths to look for footprints of an exceptional cometary phenomenon."

"That would be good," said Khufu. "We can support or challenge you with our sacred texts and what we know about myths."

George spoke next. "I have a suggestion. Why not let me give you a comet tutorial? Then everyone will know typical comet features. It will make everyone's presentations easier."

"Let me start with what I know," I said. Glancing at George, I muttered, "You can cut in whenever you want."

"Fair enough. Go on."

"To start, a little of what I know about comets. George, please help out when you can. Most of us, at some time in our lives, have seen a comet in the sky. Those that haven't, do see pictures or read accounts of those who have."

Solon interrupted gleefully. "I hate to rain on your damned parade and screw up your train of thought, but remember, you're trying to turn your radical theory into a rational statement. As a friend, you have my sympathy, but regardless of what you tell me about the comets, I will tell you up front: they have nothing to do with the prehistoric origin of myths and religions. A comet is nothing but a long streak of light in the sky. Even at its closest approach to Earth, it is still an ephemeral streak of light. So know this now. An antagonistic prick is going to push your button every time."

"You know I'll support you all the way on comet details," George said, "but I am with Solon. As a scientist, I know a lot about comets. The harder I think about a linkage to prehistory, especially as an origin of myths and religious thought, the less I find any. So expect me to kick your ass as often as Solon does."

The others wanted to continue to joke around, but Arjuna raised his voice and said, "Let the man talk. He is on the verge of quitting and telling us to find someone else to … bolt … heh … to screw."

Everyone laughed.

Comet basics were the first stop on my guided tour of the origin of religions and myths. I promised them many surprises. "As you listen to my story, there will come a time when you'll be amazed at its relevance to formation of myths and even religious thought in prehistory."

From the pile of books and folders in front of me, I took and held up a simple, hand-drawn picture of a comet and said, "A comet has a number of parts. There's a nucleus, which has most of the comet's bulk, a—"

George cut me short. "The best way to imagine a comet is to picture it as a dirty snowball, kilometers in diameter. Except for its size, it's just a mix of ice, dirt, and stone. If the ancients actually saw a gigantic snowball, they couldn't help but imagine God throwing it."

I continued, "So using George's model, the comet nucleus is like a dirty snowball, lots of ice with pieces of dirt and rock. A gaseous cloud called the coma forms around the nucleus."

George explained, "The coma is like hot gas and steam. It especially expands and becomes visible near the sun, when sunlight heats the snowball. It extends into a long tail of dust and ions. As you see in the diagram, the nucleus, the coma, and the tail combine to make up the comet. They give it the appearance of a long-haired star."

Not all parts of a comet were there all the time. Along most of its path, the comet was nothing but a large ball of ice and rock traveling the open spaces of the universe. The coma and tail manifested only when the dirty snowball got captured in an orbit around a star. The trapped comet would then behave like a snowy planet. During parts of its orbit, it would get close to the sun, where solar radiation would heat the icy surface, vaporize it, and release its material to form the coma and the tail.

I picked up another chart and said, "When a comet is captured in the solar system, it goes back and forth between being a dirty snowball and a long-tailed star. The long-tailed image we are familiar with is just one part of the comet's life, when the nucleus, coma, and tail combine to produce a dazzling show of light and motion."

Solon pointed at my chart. "Pardon my French, but I see nothing of prehistory in any part of your comet."

"Keep quiet!" Arjuna commanded. "Let him talk."

In Arjuna's objection I sensed no disagreement with Solon. He only wanted me, and no one else, to conclude that the prehistory had little to do with a comet.

They now knew about typical comets, but the comet that had mesmerized the ancients, the one with godlike features, had not been typical. As Solon and George had pointed out, a typical comet could put together only a short-lived streak of light.

"You're right about the typical comet," I said. "Nothing exceptional. But comets come in different sizes. Typically, they're small, just a few kilometers in diameter. However, some could be quite large."

"So your view of prehistory comes with a big comet," Khufu said. "I assume a *very* big comet."

"Yes."

"How large?" Solon asked curtly.

"I don't know," I said. "Any ideas, George?"

"A few scientists have looked at the cratering pattern on Mars. They estimate that a comet-like object with a diameter between 600 and 950 kilometers caused them."[1]

"What would that be? A supercomet?"

"You can call it that, a supercomet," said George. "In another example, others have looked at the dust and debris in meteorite showers as the leftovers of, let's say, a giant comet. They calculated such a comet's size at 50 to 300 kilometers."[2]

"So such supercomets, giant comets—they *do* exist?"

"We don't know," George said. "Not like we have seen any. All we have are the footprints—potential footprints. Would the shoe fit a supercomet or a giant comet? We're not sure. Some scientists would say yes; others would say no."

More than one voice asked, "What does that mean?"

George shrugged and said, "I don't know. It's a very tough question. If evidence in myths and sacred texts resembles the Martian impact craters or meteorite showers, it'll be hard, if not impossible, to work backward, to show they are the footprints of a supercomet."

"If the supercomets and giant comets are huge," Khufu insisted, "what is the size of a typical comet? Did I hear a few kilometers?"

George said, "Let me entertain you."

He picked up one of my charts and started to draw on its back. He first put a small dot on the paper and said, "See this dot? It's the size of a typical but large comet, a few kilometers in diameter. It's like the Shoemaker-Levy 9 seen in 1993. In 1994 it hit Jupiter. The snowball of the Shoemaker-Levy was about two kilometers in diameter."

George then drew a circle about an inch in diameter and said it was about the size of a giant comet. Its diameter would be about twenty times that of Shoemaker-Levy. He then drew a larger circle four to five inches in diameter and said it would be the size of a supercomet.

"What I've drawn is a simple size comparison of a supercomet, a giant comet, and an ordinary large comet. This comparison, however, misses the volumetric comparison. Hundreds of thousands to millions of typical comets would fit into a giant comet or a supercomet. The spectacle of a supercomet would have to be seen to be believed. Never would it be comparable to anything we've seen in a typical comet."

"I don't want to sound negative," said Solon, "so bear with me. Let's say a typical comet passes near the earth. We see a streaking light in the sky, visible for a week or two, and then it's gone. Depending on its orbit, it may visit us a few more times before it fizzles out and disappears. Now, after the typical comet comes and goes, a 100 percent supercomet enters the solar system. We see a streak of light much longer and much more intense than with a typical comet. For a few weeks it competes with the sun. But still it is a comet. It will move on, repeat the cycle as it fizzles out, and finally disappear like any comet."

He tilted his head to the side with a half-smile and asked, "Have I missed anything?"

George shook his head vigorously. "The comparison isn't that simple."

"What have I missed?"

"You're missing the fact that the supercomet would not remain intact. The sun's gravitational force would break it apart. You wouldn't have just one supercomet but a long string of giant comets and then, with further breakups, a much longer string of thousands of ordinary comets."

"How does gravity do that?" Solon asked.

"The force of gravity elongates the snowball in the direction of pull. I'll give you an earthly example, something you've definitely seen. Under gravitational pull, Earth's oceans elongate toward the moon or sun. We observe the effect as tides. The same type of tidal forces would act on the comet. And remember, the comet isn't hard. It's a fluffy snowball, so it readily elongates. When it does, it breaks apart. For a supercomet, each initial fragment would be as large as a giant comet."

"Okay," said Solon. "Under the tidal forces the supercomet would break into hundreds of fragments, or thousands of fragments. But still, each one would behave no differently from the damned typical comet. Right? *Right*?"

"Eh, right," George agreed reluctantly.

Solon put his hands over his head, annoyed at George's backpedaling, and said, "So what's the difference? Instead of one typical comet we'd have hundreds or thousands of typical comets. Granted, it'd be one spectacular sight, the sky studded with comets. But all of them would behave like a typical comet. They would shine for a while and then move away and disappear."

"That's where we run into differences of opinion," George said, "differences of imagination. Someone like you would look at a supercomet's fragments and see only a collection of a thousand comets. Someone else in prehistory might look at the same thing and see—"

"A giant dragon," I said, cutting in boldly.

"There you have it—a dragon, a celestial serpent. Some would even go a step further and imagine it as God. Such imagination would have had a profound effect on the formation of prehistory."

Confusion prevailed.

Some had caught a glimpse of the awesome sight a supercomet created, not a sight easily forgotten. Every orbit repeated the dazzling show. Could it do the same for tens of thousands of years? How long before a supercomet lost its mass and size to solar heating and fragmentation? Would people see the supercomet as another celestial light similar to the stars? Would a dazzling celestial show become the universal model for religions and myths?

Almost everyone doubted it.

It might have created the image of a giant dragon or serpent. Some might have even worshipped it as God. But surely it could not account for all the myths and religious thought in prehistory. Impossible.

I said, "I sense the end. I hear you saying the idea is too shaky, and we'd better pull the plug. Are we done? Or do you want some more?"

"More," most voices muttered, though the body language signaled otherwise.

If this had been a business meeting, I would have recognized the impossibility of a sale, called it quits, and taken them out for a drink. They stayed because they would not reject a friend. They had no intention of abandoning me, even when they already knew the final answer.

Solon asked George, "How quickly does a comet break into fragments? How many fragments are typical? What is the life of a fragment?"

"Scientifically, we've seen many breakups," George said. "Presently, the most spectacular was the Shoemaker-Levy comet: twenty-one fragments, mostly between one and two kilometers in diameter. Here! Let me show you its string of pearls."[3] George reached into his briefcase, pulled out a few articles, and leafed through them. "Here! Here, have a look. It's magnificent." He waved a picture in front of us and said. "Have a look at this one. A different distance from earth."

The pictures were compellingly impressive.

George rummaged through the briefcase and found more, including some that showed a string of cometary fragments approaching Jupiter.

"I *love* these pictures," Solon muttered. "If they were a million times more and bigger, they'd be *awesome*. To some it might be gods riding on chariots, but not all—not everyone."

"Let's not jump to conclusions," I said. "We've only seen one example. Can we assume that a supercomet's train is roughly the same as that of an ordinary comet? Perhaps with a supercomet there wouldn't be a train of fragments. It'd be more like a cylindrical swarm—a long, fragment-filled cylinder rather than a string of pearls."

"So long as you only *imagine* a cylindrical swarm, okay. But remember, science has yet to study a supercomet fragmentation. It may be a train or a swarm or something else."

Enoch laughed cynically. "Swarm, shwarm, who cares?"

I decided to take it one step further. "In fact, how do we know that people saw anything comet-like at all?"

"Don't keep anything on the back burner now," Solon hissed.

I smiled at Solon and then turned to George and asked, "What happens if a comet gets too close to Earth?"

He studied me carefully. Then his face brightened, and he said, "Hold it a minute. You're talking about a supercomet hitting the earth. Hey, that won't work. Nothing would survive it."

Arjuna looked at George. "You said a comet is like a snowball, not a rock."

"True," George said, "but the snowball's core is stone. A supercomet would have a large rocky core, many kilometers in diameter. *No one would remain alive on Earth to imagine any gods or shape prehistory.*"

"What if the supercomet did not hit the earth?" I asked.

"Then, hot shot, we'd be back to streaks of light in the sky," said Solon. "Heads up, folks—he's got another bright idea!"

I ignored Solon. "What if the supercomet did not hit the earth? What if Earth passed through its swarm?"

George sat motionless. "What an incredible scenario! Did you find it in the sacred texts?"

"Yes. Our planet did pass through the swarm. No head-on collision. No dinosaur-like extinction experience."

"That's *incredible*. I never thought of the possibility."

Solon shouted, "Wait one minute! What difference does that make?"

"The difference is immense." George giggled. "Earth goes in at one side of the swarm, emerges from the other. No head-on collision with any big chunk. It could even capture some small fragments around it in orbit. Wow! Earth could have a canopy in that scenario."

"A what?"

"A canopy, a shell. A covering, a cometary clothing, covering Earth on all sides."

Khufu asked, "How would it stay there?"

"That's the easy part: like a satellite. The captured fragments would stay up there and orbit the earth like a satellite. Any big fragment would act like a moon. Yes, every large captured piece would orbit the earth like a small moon."

George's excitement was contagious, and the caustic mood changed. Everyone was trying to imagine a canopied Earth.

We remained excited and loud for some time, until Enoch asked, "But with a canopy draping the earth, how could anyone see the comet passing by in the sky? And one more thing: if a canopy is so plausible, why didn't science know it already?"

"You see," George replied, "science has declared the planetary capture of an individual comet impossible. It either whizzes by or has a head-on collision. But with a swarm—a supercomet's swarm of fragments—well, that would change everything. No need to capture the whole comet. No need for a head-on collision. Earth could enter the swarm from one side and for a short time become part of the swarm. This might last just a few hours, but in that short time there would be many opportunities to capture small fragments. Earth would do even better if it met the swarm at near its own speed, or best if the swarm overtook Earth."

Arjuna suggested, "Why don't we continue with the story, this time more carefully?"

"How long could the swarm get?" Khufu asked.

George answered, "I don't know, not for a swarm, but I can give you a feel. The train of Shoemaker-Levy had twenty-one fragments and was about 160,000 miles long when it was first seen in March 1993. Gravitational forces constantly elongated it, and after nine months, the length had increased to about 600,000 kilometers. Before it hit Jupiter in July 1994, it was about five million kilometers long."

"Five million kilometers!"

"Yes, five million kilometers, but no cylinder, no swarm. The fragments lined up one after another—a string, definitely a string. That wouldn't have happened if there were a million fragments. If we were to imagine a swarm, it would probably be hundreds of thousands of kilometers wide, hundreds of millions long."

Khufu looked at George and asked, "What about the comet tails? How would they look? So many of them ..."

"It would be a spectacular sight, wouldn't it?" George mused. "Each fragment of Shoemaker-Levy had a coma and tail, but the tails were short. There isn't much solar heating near Jupiter. But a swarm! So many fragments, each dozens of kilometers across and larger. Near Earth, each would have a tail perhaps millions of miles long. I can imagine it, a many-armed, many-legged celestial monster moving toward Earth."

"Ah, a dragon."

"Yep."

"Perhaps even a god."

"Wait a minute," Solon moaned. "Didn't we just say none of this spectacle would be visible? Hello? Are you a few bricks shy of a full load? Didn't the fragments and the debris leave a canopy around Earth?"

"Not until Earth moves through the swarm," George replied. "Until then, it would be visible. The first sighting would be the approach of the many-legged celestial giant. Then people would see their planet being engulfed. Then darkness."

"How dark?" someone asked.

"Nothing serious, I assume. About like the worst of thunderstorms or a dust storm. It all would depend on how the canopy formed. If Earth went through the thin parts of the swarm, it would be a thin, dusty canopy. The dust would clear with time. Sunlight would get through. People would see the swarm again on its next orbit. But if Earth moved through the denser parts, a thick canopy would be inevitable, like a shield. It would block any sunlight. It would be dark for a long time."

"You're saying it might not be a one-time encounter," Enoch said.

"Right. The event would repeat each time the swarm orbited. Earth would go through it many times, capturing new fragments each time. The canopy formation would stop only when the swarm dissipated."

Arjuna observed, "If Earth went through the swarm repeatedly and did so for thousands of years, we should see today, at least, see some remnants of a canopy. George, didn't you say the captured fragments would be like a small moon or an artificial satellite? Most should be in orbit now."

"That's a good point. But I can't be definite. I don't know how the canopy actually formed or how stable it was."

"At the least," Solon said, "it should have left some rings like the rings of Saturn."

George added, "Or like the moons of Mars. The rings of Saturn and the moons of Mars come from captured fragments. Some fragments would break apart to form rings, like Saturn's. Others would not break apart and might even become larger, like the moons of Mars. Science would expect things like that in the aftermath of a canopied earth."

"But we see none," Arjuna pointed out. "The skies are as clear as can be."

George thought for a long time before answering. "What you say is true, but remember: if rings and moons are to last, they have to be stable. If not, they collapse, often without leaving a trace. In their absence, we can only search for footprints. Are there any footprints in myths and sacred texts? Are there any in science?"

"So even in its heyday, the canopy would have been like a couple of rings or some tiny moons? Is that it?"

George tried to smile but could not. "Yes … no … maybe."

"What do you mean—yes, no, maybe? What else *is* there?"

"I am certain about some things," George said nervously. "About others, I am not. In the center of the canopy, the rings should form. We see them vividly around Saturn, and Saturn isn't the only one. There are fainter rings around Jupiter and other planets. But I'm not sure about the moons. If there were only a few fragments, there would be a good chance for accretion. They would move closer, come together, and form a tiny moon we'd see. But around the earth, a canopy could place all sorts of pieces in chaotic orbits. Instead of accretion, everything could stay diffusely together, forming something like a shell, a solid-looking shell. Maybe outside of the shell some isolated fragments would form a couple of tiny moons. I can't say. God! So many ways to model a canopied earth."

Solon was not convinced. "Okay. A couple of rings and a handful of moons. I'll even throw in a shell. Is *this* the structure every bubblehead would see? If—"

"Wait! Why didn't I think of it sooner?" George interrupted.

"What?"

"I have thought of a better test. If Earth traveled through the swarm, then everyone should have seen one distinct effect: the Van Allen belts."

In exasperation Solon put both hands on his head and groaned. "The Van Allen *what*?"

George explained. He knew a lot about the Van Allen belts. "Earth's magnetic field exerts a force on every moving electrical charge," he said. "The magnetic field is particularly strong in two doughnut-shaped regions, where it traps a high concentration of charged particles. These two magnetic doughnuts are the Van Allen radiation belts. If Earth traveled through the swarm, the Van Allen belts would have trapped a great deal of dust and been the first dust-laden areas in the skies to become visible."

George concluded, "If Earth encountered the swarm, and if the experience was recorded in myths and sacred texts, one of the first references must be to the Van Allen belts. If there's nothing about the belts, then no swarm. I am sure of it. The shell would not obscure them. The shell would probably be *beyond* the Van Allen belts."

Arjuna asked, "How far out are the belts? Why don't we see them today?"

"We don't see the belts because today there is little dust in them to reflect sunlight. The distance … I don't know exactly. I can look it up. I think the inner belt is about a quarter of Earth's diameter away. The outer belt has a radius about three to four times Earth's."

"How big is that?"

"I don't remember the exact Earth diameter. Say about seven thousand kilometers. That puts the inner belt about 1,500 kilometers from Earth's surface, the outer belt about seven to ten thousand kilometers. The canopy would be outside the Van Allen belts. Otherwise, it'd be too close and quite unstable. So roughly, the canopy shell would be somewhere between fifteen and twenty-five thousand kilometers from Earth."

Arjuna said, "But that's too far. Would it be visible at such distances?"

"Yes. Very much so." George nodded vigorously.

Solon sought to wrap up the day. "So that's all she wrote. We finally have a picture of what the prehistoric world might have looked like—a triple-layered canopy, right, George?"

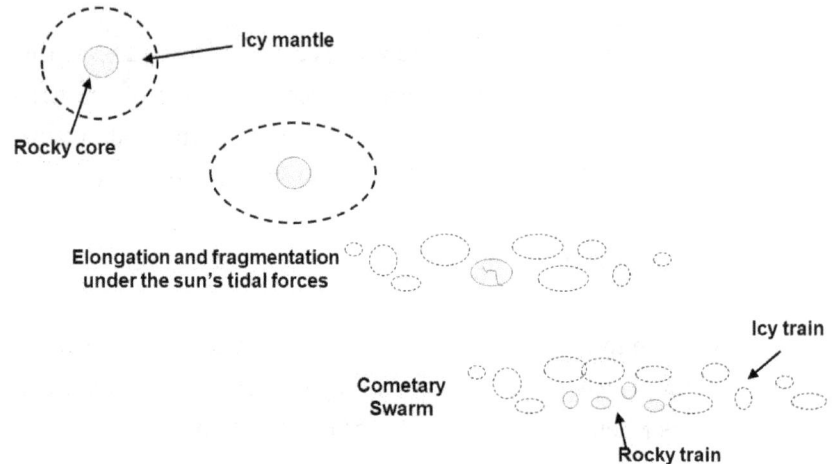

Icy mantle

Rocky core

Elongation and fragmentation
under the sun's tidal forces

Cometary
Swarm

Icy train

Rocky train

A large comet captured in orbit around the sun would break into a
long cylinder of rocky, icy fragments. With each orbit around the sun,
more fragments would break apart and collide with each other, causing
further breakage into smaller pieces.

—George

"Triple-layered?" George seemed perplexed for a moment. "Oh, you're counting the two Van Allen belts and the shell. I assume you're right. Yep. So long as you remember, the first two would be dust belts. Can't hold any large fragments. All the larger ice and rock fragments would be in the shell."

Solon said, "That's all right. So we have arrived at a three-layered structure, one mostly dirty ice and two mostly dust and debris."

"That is correct."

"And of course," continued Solon, "we have agreed to supplement the triple canopies with a few Saturn-like rings and perhaps some teensy-weensy moons."

"Yes ... I guess."

Solon turned to face me and said, "Are you telling me that in myths and sacred texts you're going to find a *triple*-layered, *many*-ringed, *few*-mooned *canopy*?"

I said, "Yes, mostly."

Solon frowned in disbelief and murmured, "A barefaced lie."

The others seemed to feel the same way, displaying varying degrees of indignation.

Arjuna sought a middle ground. "As incredible as it sounds, we've already learned something novel. A comet—a large comet—could do more than just light up the sky. More importantly, a friend is asking us to resolve a prehistoric dilemma. So let's work together. Either he can show convincing evidence, or he will fail. If he fails, he'll be most relieved and most grateful to us for, as Solon would say, saving his you-know-what."

A few chuckled.

My friends had come back to the circle. None were going to let me down.

I returned to the comet's pattern of regularly visiting the earth. In each orbit our planet would pass through the swarm. For a very long time the regular repetition of Earth–swarm encounters would dominate Earth's prehistoric life.

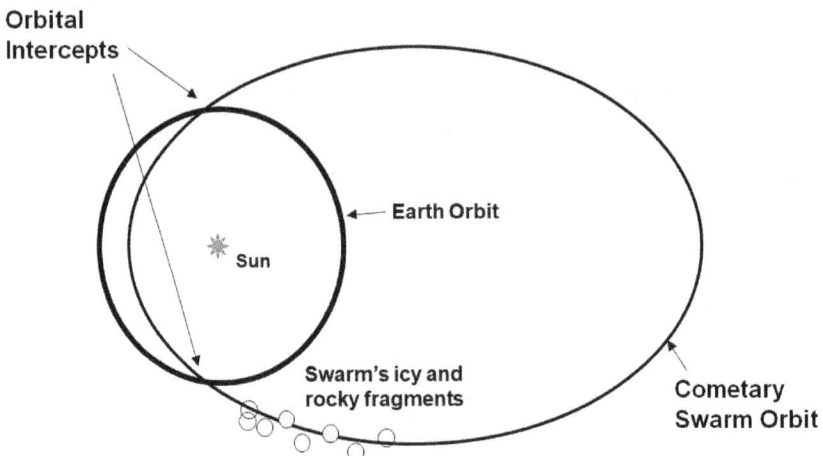

Orbital Intercepts

Earth Orbit

Sun

Swarm's icy and rocky fragments

Cometary Swarm Orbit

A supercomet enters the solar system and is captured in orbit around the sun. The tidal forces of the sun and the planets break it apart. A long train of ice and rock fragments forms. Any head-on collision with the swarm is fatal to planetary life. Some planetary orbits intercept the long, wide cometary swarm, enter on one side, and exit the other. At every interception, a canopy of ice and rock forms around the planet.

—George

Solon seemed ready to challenge, but George came to the rescue and said, "It is true. It is the way of a comet. Once Earth's orbit intersects the swarm's, the two have no choice but to meet regularly."

"Like seasonal dust storms in the Sahara," Khufu mumbled. "They come, cover you with a layer of dust, and leave to come again."

Enoch broke in. "I'm not familiar with Earth's dust belts. I can't imagine how they would look emerging from the swarm. But I can relate to snow and rain. When we get wet in rain or when snowflakes land on our coats, in effect a canopy or shell of water and snow is formed. Nothing penetrates very deep, so I wouldn't expect the swarm to leave any deep scars on Earth. No footprints on the surface."

George nodded in approval. "There you go! Good."

Enoch went on. "Moreover, none of the water or snow is permanent. After the storm, they disappear. We dry out after rain or snow, so perhaps the canopy wouldn't last long."

George leaned back and said, "Although I'd be careful with analogies, this one seems to work. Physically, the swarm should behave like a snowstorm, rain shower, or dust storm. If Earth were to intercept the swarm at its periphery, there would be only a light sprinkling of dust and ice. If it intercepted near the center, it would capture some large fragments. In some cases, direct impact of a few fragments would be possible—and dangerous. The encounters would cycle like earthly storms. Each orbit would bring new configurations. Each would leave its own version of a canopy."

"No different from rain, snow, or dust storms."

"But be careful of the scale," George observed. "They differ vastly. One is earthly, the other cosmic."

Arjuna said, "They also differ in another way. You said the swarm constantly loses material to Earth's canopy, into space, and to solar heating. So the swarm would eventually fizzle out."

George nodded and said, "You're right. With each orbit, the swarm's fragments break into smaller pieces. Some stray into space, lost forever. Near the sun, more of the comet evaporates into space from solar heating.

At each planetary encounter, part of the comet is lost to Earth's canopy. It finally exhausts the comet's snowball."

"So the size and intensity of the swarm and the canopies it creates would vary with the swarm's age. In other words, every feature would depend on the comet's age and the number of orbits it makes around the sun. Damn! I should have known this."

"You're catching on," George said. "The older the swarm, the more matter it loses. At the end, when it's old and decrepit, all that's left is a meteorite shower. Finally, not even meteoric fireworks. It dies."

Arjuna yawned. The old ones were tired.

There would be another weekend.

I gazed out the small window at a cloud in the distance, beyond the silhouette of the neighbor's house. There could be rain. I smiled as I wondered how I would feel walking in the rain, naked. Would I turn into a canopied human?

Then, peering through the basement's small window, for one fleeting moment I thought I saw light reflected from a pair of binoculars. ... Nah.

7

The Challenge of Learning

Solon was settling down to spend a few hours on canopy research when he heard an unexpected knock on the door. He was strict with students about office hours. He saw them only at designated hours. He had no appointment with a colleague. He hesitated a moment, hoping the person would go away, but the knock came again, insistent.

"Yes?" Solon said as he opened the door.

"Good morning, Professor." A neatly dressed young man smiled at Solon. His dark blue eyes suited his short blond hair. "My name is Joshua. Can I take a few minutes of your time?" he asked in a polite voice that Solon could not ignore.

"Please, come in."

The young man briefly described his background. He was a junior at another university across town and wanted to transfer so that he could learn more about the philosophy of the religious radical movements.

"I may not be the right person," Solon said, "and I don't know who in the department would be. My understanding of the religious radical movements is that they are based on paranoid theories about government conspiracies, jumbled up with the Bible to justify violence."

"That is the popular view the establishment promotes to mask the true nature of radical groups," Joshua said apologetically. "The truth is, they are preparing for an inevitable battle—namely, Armageddon. We can view that prospect in either religious or secular terms. It could be the Second Coming to establish God's law on Earth, or it could be world powers facing each other in a nuclear holocaust. Either way, human societies have to respond to the challenge of managing the world in the aftermath of a global confrontation."

Solon did not know what to say. On one hand, he wanted to throw Joshua out and work on the canopy. On the other, he liked a student who wanted to learn more than just enough to get a passing grade.

"My understanding," Solon said, "is that they often organize along racist and supremacist strands that pretend to trace the roots of Europe to the lost tribes of Israel. It declares white Europeans the chosen people instead of the Jews. Any such illogical linkage is at best a mythical reimagination of the lost tribes of Israel and at worst anti-Semitic theory propagated by a small group of extremists."

"That is one way of looking at it: Jewish conspiracy theory promoted by small groups hidden in armed camps. But the way I look at it, the movement is about the assertion of individual rights against federal encroachment. I know for a fact, and I'm sure you feel much the same, that the lure of tyrannical control of the masses fuels the government's tendency to limit citizens' rights—for example, to own and carry guns. The key question for me is whether society should move to empower the individual or empower the government that rules the individual."

Solon felt quite at home with federal encroachment logic. He always advocated the philosophical view that placed the individual at the top of the social structure. At the same time, he saw Joshua defending fringe groups that had little impact on society's treatment of the individual.

"Though I find your argument somewhat persuasive," Solon said, "I have to say that many groups, including the survivalists, the Klan, the Nazis, the skinheads, and the militias, use the same logic to espouse racist and supremacist views. Just the argument that a dominant government becomes corrupt and repressive does not justify those groups' radical behavior."

"That's where I would like to learn more," Joshua responded. "I have listened to the far-right biblical literalists who believe in millennialist cycles and are convinced that the Bible supersedes any secular government. I understand their position but do not find it necessarily appealing because it trades the yoke of one master for that of another. At the same time, I believe in inevitability of a final confrontation, religious or secular, that will radically change the world as we know it."

"Would you like to be a survivalist?"

"It is one strategy to adopt to deal with the apocalypse. For many radical groups it is the strategy of choice. In fact, after 9/11 most of the population behaves like survivalists, hoarding food, water, medicine, and other necessities in case of social disruptions. The only difference is the time horizon. Though most people have a short-term view, the committed survivalist believes in concepts such as the Antichrist that symbolize the last powerful government to rule the earth before Armageddon wipes everything out."

"You seek a new world order?"

"No, not me personally, but I'd like to be prepared to manage the new world order once it arrives. That is why I am interested in learning the philosophies that shed light on human behavior under such conditions."

The conversation had moved to the logic of defining who was fit to manage the world order. Could small radical groups organize and direct a new world?

Solon took the position that marginal groups could hardly manage their own enclaves, much less a global breakdown of the social structure. Joshua agreed that the fringe groups were marginal but took the position that white Europeans, not fringe groups, would save the day. He argued that white Europeans were responsible for most of the world's progress and wealth.

"We're back to racist, supremacist models," Solon objected.

"Not so," Joshua rejoined. "There is a strong element of truth in the mythical theories about the white Europeans. For example, one recent myth, which you pointed out, is that white Europeans are the lost tribes of Israel, that they're the descendants of the Old Testament Israelites who migrated from the Middle East to Europe thousands of years ago."

"But that's absolute nonsense."

"From the scholarly, historical point of view, yes, you're right. But from the mythical point of view, no, you're wrong. From the mythical point of view, white Europeans are the divine warriors that brought Christianity to the world and created the most powerful governments on the earth and raised the individual to prominence. The myth simply reflects the historical reality of the role white people played in setting the modern world's direction. The marginal groups defend that view vociferously."

They argued back and forth, one a seasoned veteran, the other a young man in search of knowledge, and both found the exercise exhilarating.

They similarly understood the strengths and weaknesses of radical fringe groups. Strong antigovernment sentiment could benefit individual rights and freedoms, but the hatred in portraying Jews as children of the devil instead of the descendants of the ancient Israelites undermined the rights of minorities and individuals both.

"The paramilitary militia movement," Solon continued, "is mostly a product of the 1990s. They came to life with the Waco disaster and the Ruby Ridge standoff that pitted a small religious group and a family against superior government forces."

"I expected the militia to be older," Joshua mumbled.

"The history of the United States is marked by acts of disobedience," Solon lectured. "The country came into existence by armed disobedience to the British government. More recently, the civil rights movement modeled nonviolent disobedience. And most recently, the emergence of small paramilitary groups demonstrates the same kind of disobedience that created the country in the first place—namely, armed disobedience."

"I hadn't thought of them as practicing civil disobedience," Joshua interjected.

"And even though the impact is not large, they do affect the behavior of larger organizations, like the NRA, or powerful individuals like Pat Robertson or Rush Limbaugh. And they motivate some people to engage in get-even actions, such as the Oklahoma City bombing. Civil disobedience has both symbolic and violent aspects. The civil rights movement was mostly nonviolent, as are the paramilitaries, but both are sometimes involved in violence. Someone like Jerry Falwell, who should spread the love of Christ, instead sows the seeds of violence by saying that the Antichrist has arrived—and he is a Jew."

"I don't want to disagree," Joshua demurred, "but the seeds of violence litter the Bible, not so much in the Gospels perhaps, but definitely in the Old Testament. The God of the Old Testament has no problem killing slews of women and children because somebody broke a rule."

"Do you know how the Bible came into existence?" Solon asked.

"It is the word of God delivered to humans."

"Not so."

"What do you mean?"

"No doubt the Bible contains some message from God, but that message, entering the human mind, passes into human words and preferences. The Bible—whether the Gospels or the Old Testament—is a collection of human writings and includes not only a divine message here and there but also things that the writers wished God said or that they thought would benefit the priesthood business."

"I can't believe that. The Bible is God's word, every word of it."

"You just pointed out that God does not sound like God when he orders innocent women and children killed, but rather he sounds quite human."

"Perhaps God had a purpose we don't understand for including such information or taking such action."

Solon paused and gathered his thoughts. "Who actually wrote the Bible down, the words—God or men?"

Joshua did not want to answer but finally mumbled, "Men."

"What kind of men?"

"What do you mean, what kind?"

"What I mean is, the men who wrote down God's words, in both the Gospels and the Old Testament, were Jews."

Joshua didn't know what to say.

"You know that Jesus was a Jew. You know that Paul, who claimed to represent Jesus, was a Jew."

Joshua gazed at the floor.

"Do you know that Paul's letters, today included with the Gospels, were corporate letters? They were letters written by the corporation president—namely, Paul—to the franchise churches owned and operated by his religion business."

Joshua remained silent as if he had not heard a word. But the beads of sweat forming on his face and occasionally running down in streams told a different story.

Solon realized he was not helping Joshua learn. He patted the boy's shoulder and went to the bookshelf across from his desk. He looked for a specific book, found it, and gave it to Joshua.

"I want you to read this at your own pace," Solon said, "and there's no rush to return it. It is the history of how the Bible, as we have it today, was put together. It is based on the records of the Christian church. It tells you which books were let in and which books were kicked out. Among the books that didn't make the cut, you learn which were close contenders and which ones were declared junk. It tells you that five of the fourteen letters ascribed to Paul are not Paul's but were added later because the church fathers thought adding them was a good idea. It tells you that the packaging of the Bible and the process of declaring it the word of God took place over centuries at church conferences such as the Council of Nicaea and the Council of Ephesus … Okay?"

"Okay."

"I have enjoyed our conversation," Solon said, and he meant it. "Whenever you're ready, we can sit down and talk some more about your plans."

Joshua got up and headed for the door. As he opened the door, he turned and said, "Next week is spring break. I am going to visit some friends and relatives at Almighty City. Would you like to come with me as my guest?"

Solon knew of Almighty City, one of the most notorious armed militia enclaves. He had always considered the possibility, but Joshua's offer caught him off guard. "Let me think about it."

"I'll call you tomorrow if it's okay."

"Fine. Nice meeting you."

Joshua walked out, and Solon returned to his desk and university routine.

"Shit," he moaned. He had totally forgotten a class that would meet in less than half an hour. He had not prepared his lecture. He wondered if he could lecture on millennialists, fringe groups, and lost tribe philosophies.

8

Seeing Sex in the Skies

Another week passed, every moment amplifying the sense of adventure. When the time for our next session finally came and we got together, lunch turned into elated jubilation. We ate, joked, laughed, and did everything hilariously but in a hurry. We all wanted to get to the basement quickly.

My wife threw me a "What's wrong?" look.

I smiled and shrugged my shoulders. Her stare sternly demanded a more detailed explanation later. I disagreed. No need for her to know the cause of excitement.

That day, nothing seemed to have gone well for my wife. When Solon had come in, in addition to books, he had carried a package resembling a gift-wrapped book.

My wife smiled at him and said, "For me?"

Solon turned red and muttered, "No. I'm sorry. It's Arjuna's." He gave the package to Arjuna and said, "Here."

Arjuna was genuinely surprised. He tore through the wrapping, and his eyes opened wide. "A slang dictionary! Great! Thanks." He shook his head in disbelief and murmured, "I did not know they made slang dictionaries. I thought slang was just the language of the streets. Thank you. Thank you."

Many of us had known each other for years as friends, yet knowing one another was not the same as removing barriers and letting our hair down on deeper beliefs. Friendship often implied a predefined distance: come any closer, and you may find nothing but strangers. Despite this, remarkably, we had arrived at an intriguing conclusion: that a comet might be more than just a light in the sky. It could also be a planetary canopy-builder that brought exotic phenomena to life.

There was one key thing we did not know, not yet: which canopy feature in prehistory resembled a god?

We were poorly prepared to identify godlike canopy features in myths, sacred texts, or science. Cherishing the thrill of a treasure hunt would not generate a road map. Yet we had willingly embarked on a journey into the depths of human history to discover a canopied earth. Had it ever existed? If it had, what had it looked like? How would it look to someone like us? How did the ancients see it?

In the prehistoric mindset, they had seen gods. Would we see one?

We rushed to the basement like children let loose in a playground.

Arjuna was eager to begin. "I don't know about you, but I have spent a lot of time thinking. I am a novice about comets and things circling the earth. That puts me on the same level as the ancients. They didn't know anything about comets, less about things circling the earth. I can sense their feelings as my own. I think, in their own terms, they were quite capable of describing what they saw. I am sure that in their models of the event, they would have captured the main features of whatever they saw."

Khufu thought a moment and then said, "As old as I am, my mind is exactly like those that came before me. If I see a comet fragment in the sky, and to me it resembles a tiny moon or a wandering star, those before me also would have thought it was a moon or a bright star. So, George, if you can tell me what I would see in a canopied earth, I can search in books like the Pyramid Texts for correspondences. Arjuna can do the same with the *Rig-veda*. Enoch can comb through the Torah, and Solon …" He paused, as though not knowing what to say, and then asked, "What sacred texts do Greeks have?"

Everyone but Solon laughed.

Half-angry, half-mocking, Solon said, "I may no longer have a Greek sacred text, but I do have what remains of a religion that transforms into a myth." He raised a thin book. "This is Hesiod's *Theogony*. It will be your Greek source. There is a lot about gods in *Theogony*—nothing as original as in *Rig-veda* or the Pyramid Texts, not as well-organized, but it offers the Greek perspective of gods in Earth's skies."

I interrupted and asked, "Can we do it a bit differently?"

"Ay, we forgot," Arjuna said. "It is *your* model of prehistory. Tell us how you would like to proceed."

I said, "I would like for us talk about the canopy, what it does after it forms as a chaotic shell of cometary material. I know this much: first, the canopy would be like an eggshell covering the earth on all sides, but after its initial formation, it couldn't possibly hold its shape at the poles. Maybe the polar material didn't have enough room for circular motion to stay up there. I don't know. Whatever the cause, the material at the poles regularly falls down. It creates an opening in the polar skies."

"That makes sense," George admitted. "Captured fragments need the right velocity and a reasonable orbit. The closer to the poles, the faster they have to move to stay in orbit. If they ever lose speed, they spiral downward. Come to think of it, the polar downflow would be the most plausible way for the canopy to lose matter. It would be gradual, not a sudden collapse, but ultimately would exhaust the canopy."

"Would cometary matter's polar downflow be the only change after the initial canopy formation?" I asked.

"No. It would also start to form bands," George said. "The chaotic motion would give way to ordered motion resembling vortical bands. In fact, I would not be surprised if the prehistoric scholars modeled it as fingers of God wrapping around Earth. In effect, that is what you see on Jupiter—it is almost a universal planetary feature, not something limited to Jupiter. Those general features have relevance to the canopied earth. Something similar would have existed on the canopy shell."

According to science, Jupiter was not the only planet with a banded upper atmosphere. There was similar banding in other planets' atmospheres, a reflection of the fundamentals that governed formation and maintenance of a stable, banded canopy. Jupiter, Saturn, Uranus, and Neptune exhibited a remarkably similar banded appearance.[4]

"Are you telling me science has evidence that chaotic motion transforms into a banded structure?" Solon asked skeptically.

George nodded his agreement and said, "Scientifically, two features of the canopy shell are quite simple. First, as cometary material circles the earth, it loses speed and falls at the pole—the downflow. The process thins out the material at the polar circle and may even totally clear it from dust and debris. If so, the downflow will end or become very small, and the sunlight will penetrate through the polar opening. Second, as soon as the canopy's chaotic energy decreases, it will transform from a smooth egg-like shell into a Jupiter-like banded shell."

We had become comfortable with the spherical image of a canopy shell around the earth. We could see the cometary material falling down at the poles. We could see the chaotic, structureless canopy transform into a banded, Jupiter-like arrangement.

But that was us, now. What about those living in the prehistory? Would they also have looked at one another and said, "Oh, that is just a polar downflow, and yes, the canopy just transformed from the chaotic to banded state"?

When I posed this thought, George chuckled and said, "That's interesting. How would we have modeled the phenomenon of polar downflow in a chaotic canopy if we were a group of humans living in prehistory?"

"Exactly," I replied.

Enoch had been silent for some time. While everyone else seemed occupied with thoughts of prehistoric modeling of canopy events, he frowned and said, "I'm not clear about one thing. If in its initial formation the canopy surrounded the earth, it would immerse everything in darkness. Then how could people see the polar downflow? How could anyone see anything?"

Solon added, "Yeah, if no sunlight came in through the canopy, no one could see it; no one would see shit."

Khufu said, "They could. In fact … they would see the polar downflow colored red."

"How the heck do you know that?"

Khufu replied, "I know because the sacred text says so. Or even better, putting it in our host's preferred language, I learned the color from a *model* that the ancients put together for the phenomenon."

This was the first time someone in the group had offered ancient evidence to support the canopy idea. Khufu turned to his left awkwardly, reaching for something. George saw his intent and helped him. He picked up a pile of books behind Khufu's chair and handed them to him.

Khufu held one up and said, "This is an edition of the Pyramid Texts. I can also find the same thing in the Coffin Texts, which I also have." He opened the book and looked through the index. "Here, Utterance 313. It says, 'The phallus of Babi is drawn.'"[5]

Khufu looked expectantly at us, as if asking, *Why are you not applauding in appreciation?*

"So what?" Solon shouted. "Who is Babi?"

"Babi is an ancient Egyptian god. He has the form of a monkey. He squats on the earth with an erect penis."

Solon murmured, "No way!"

George motioned Solon to be quiet and asked, "A monkey's butt is roundish and reddish, isn't it?"

"Yes, it is."

"And a monkey's erect penis—is that also reddish?" George asked.

Khufu blushed and said, "Since I am the only one here who's seen a monkey up close, you'll have to take my word. Yes, it is red."

"There you have it," George said, "an ancient model."

"What model?" Solon exclaimed. "Why are we wasting our time on monkey crap?"

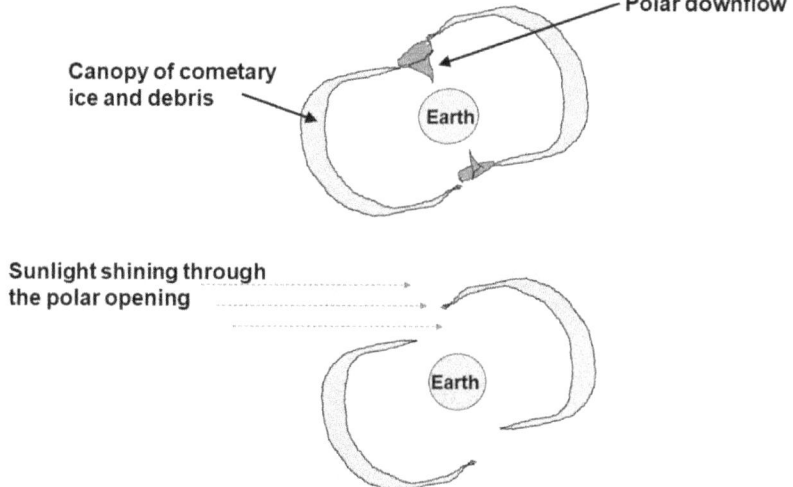

Polar downflow

Canopy of cometary ice and debris

Earth

Sunlight shining through the polar opening

Earth

Illustrative representations of the canopy model with the closed and open polar areas, demonstrating the polar downflow in the chaotic canopy and the open polar circle in the ordered canopy.

—George

George ignored Solon and said, "That's how Khufu got the color right. He looked at a prehistoric model of the canopied world. Fascinating— just a few components used to set up an ancient yet vivid canopy model. You see, the polar opening is the monkey's butt. The downflow is its erect penis. The ..." He stopped and asked, "The monkey's body ... is it dark?"

Khufu nodded corroboration.

Solon seemed quite carried away. "That doesn't make any sense. The sunlight either gets in or doesn't get in. The wretched canopy either surrounds Earth or doesn't. If sunlight gets in, there's light, and we see things. If light doesn't get in, no one sees shit. Now where does this reddish light come from?"

George whispered, "I'll show you."

The spotlight was on George. He tried to draw us a mental picture of the way the canopy would have formed.

In the aftermath of the swarm crossing, alongside the canopy's chaotic motion, there would have been ionically charged particles that gave the canopy a magnetic field. The chaotic motions and the opposition between the earth and canopy magnetic fields would have trapped most of the captured cometary matter around the earth and would not have allowed it to fall earthward. When chaotic motion decreased, and more ionic charges combined, weakening the canopy's magnetic field, gravity would have taken over and cometary matter would have started to fall down at the poles.

Still, nothing would have been visible on Earth. However, as cometary matter was lost to downflow, the polar circle would have grown wider and thinner. Although over most of the planet very little sunlight would have gotten through, at the pole sunrays would have begun to pierce the thinning cloud of ice and dust particles. Sunlight would have scattered through the dust and ice to reach the earth. The light that reached the earth would have been reddish because of scattering from cometary matter.

"It would have been the same red we often see in a sunset. People could see two canopy features: the polar circle's reddish glow and a reddish phallic downflow."

Solon was not satisfied. "Back up a minute. How does the sunlight get into the polar circle? Sunlight travels in a straight line—that I know. It's like firing bullets at a garbage can. The bullets will only hit the side. They can't drop in, even if the top is open. So no sunlight in, no redness, no matter how big the canopy opening."

George grinned and asked, "What if the garbage can is tilted? Can bullets get into the top of a tilted can without being blocked by the side?"

Solon grumbled, but George continued. "Earth is tilted twenty-three degrees relative to incoming sunlight. That's why we have seasons."

Slowly, Solon endorsed the seemingly obvious. "You say a tilted garbage can. The sunlight hits the polar opening directly. The shell can't block it … Adorable!"

George resumed his account. The canopy had the same tilt toward the sun as did Earth. When Earth's Northern Hemisphere tilted toward the sun, so did the canopy. The polar circle acted like a window set at a twenty-three-degree angle to sun.

When the Southern Hemisphere tilted toward the sun, the northern polar circle was in darkness. Sunlight would shine through the southern polar circle. In six months, the situation would reverse.

"It sounds like seasonal polar lighting," Arjuna said, "the basic stuff of Earth's orbit. The canopy would change none of that."

"What about the damned color?" hissed Solon. "You said something about scattering from the pieces of ice and rock. How does scattering cause the red color?"

"The canopy lighting is no different from a sunset today," said George. "Sunlight is a combination of colors from red to blue. Blue is more prone to scatter, red more likely to travel straight. During the sunset, the light penetrates through the atmosphere's molecules and dust particles. More red rays last, and the sunlight turns reddish. The same thing happens in the canopy."

"The body parts of the monkey god Babi," Khufu said.

George nodded his agreement.

Solon remained in his rebel mood. He saw the simplicity and conciseness of the prehistoric model but still persisted with the idea that we might be misunderstanding the phenomenon. "If this canopy feature is a dead ringer for a giant penis, then by extension that implies something long and cylindrical moving in and out of the canopy opening."

George listened attentively but impatiently waved the mental images aside and said, "I am troubled by the notion of in-and-out movement. The more I imagine, the less I think such motion is physically possible."

I looked at George and said, "Initially, the polar downflow would be somewhat pointed, true, but the tip becomes round when it enters the atmosphere. Why? Because there it explodes in the shape of an inverted mushroom cap. Was it the force of explosion that pushed it up and created the illusion of up-and-down motion before the next atmospheric entry?"

"No, of course not!" George muttered. "First, consider the atmospheric explosion. When the downflow is outside the atmosphere, it would be like a waterfall, but once it enters the atmosphere, its tip would explode upward and outward. The waterfall and explosion combination would make the downflow look like a huge penis, twenty to thirty thousand kilometers long. But that does not create an in-and-out motion through the polar opening. It would be a continuous explosion in the atmosphere. There you go. There you have it."

I objected, "It is not just a fixed feature. I am taking Solon's side. From my research, I know it didn't just fall down. It moved in and out of the canopy. I don't know how, but it did."

"You've gotta be out of your damned tree!" Solon said, switching sides.

George was not paying attention to either of us. He was talking to himself. "Moved back and forth. Hmmm. Moved back and forth. Moved … back … and … forth."

Solon snarled, "You don't know Shinola, but I'll help you. Maybe it wasn't a physical movement. Maybe the people who saw it imagined an upward movement, even though everything was actually flowing down."

George jumped out of his chair and shouted at the top of his lungs, "Of *course!*" Waving his coffee mug from side to side, he said, "Fundamentally, it's so simple even a child should understand. Yes! The canopy downflow did move in and out of the opening."

"Tell us!" Solon bellowed. "Or are you going to write a paper and mail it to us?"

George recounted a simple and fascinating story. He did not have all the pieces, but he knew enough to draw a picture of the downflow moving back and forth through the sexual orifice of the polar opening.

To understand what was happening, he explained, we first had to look at the side of the canopy facing the sun. Half the canopy's surface would have faced the sun; the other half would not. Solar radiation constantly heated one half and melted its surface. The resulting fluid spiraled poleward and fell down through the polar opening. The flow, however, would not have been constant. The fluid would have accumulated at the canopy's top and then fallen down. Each cycle of accumulating and falling down would have looked like a long cylinder moving back and forth through the opening.

George asked, "Have you seen water dripping from a faucet?"

"I'm sure we all have," Khufu said, "but what does that have to do with the downflow from the canopy?"

George pointed out that the leaking water reached the faucet continuously, but it did not—could not—fall continuously. It fell as drops. The flow had to accumulate to a certain size before it could tear itself off the faucet and fall.

George was not throwing us a curve. We had all seen it. There was nothing unexpected or unpredictable about a leaky faucet.

When George said that the surface tension of water was the cause, most of us took this as a fact. I conceived of surface tension as some sort of net that water held around itself. It had to be. We had all seen water drops take shape, grow and grow, reach a certain size, and then fall.

George said, "Surface tension is a property of every fluid." Cometary fluid was no different. When it reached the canopy top, it would not fall at once. It had to attain a certain mass and overcome the forces that held it before falling. While the fluid accumulated at the top, nothing fell. The downflow still in the chute would thin out, which would have made it look as if it were moving up toward the pole. Then the accumulated fluid would fall down, and what looked like a retreat would once more look like a thrusting movement.

Solon said, "So that's it? Surface tension? Hey, it's in the bag! The theory is solid. Who hasn't seen drops form and fall?"

George replied, "There's a scale problem."

"What scale?"

"Surface tension works for something the size of a faucet, but not for something kilometers across."

A dreadful silence fell. A winning model had shattered. Size did count!

Arjuna asked, "This isn't water falling. It has rocks in it, ice. Would that make a difference?"

"No," George replied.

Arjuna persisted. "What about those things, those charged things you said get trapped in the dust belts, those Van Allen belts?"

"I love you, old man," George burbled. "You just made my day."

"What difference does that make?" Solon asked.

"The cometary fluid is full of charged particles," George said. "As a moving, charged fluid, it has a magnetic field. To fall, it must counter Earth's magnetic field. It can do that only if it reaches a certain size. *Magnetic forces*, not surface tension, make the downflow move in and out."

"So screw the dripping faucet?"

"No, the dripping faucet is a small-scale version of what happens. It is not the best model, but in a pinch, it will do."

Solon was glad. "I'm sold. Where do we go next?"

"The charged particles and magnetic fields are not the whole story," George continued. "There's also the matter of the canopy's vortical energy."

Arjuna cupped his ear. "Vertical energy? What's that?"

"No, not vertical. *Vortical*, like the motion of a vortex."

"Aha. Like a whirlpool."

George nodded. "In this scenario, everything on the canopy rotates around the earth in a vortex. Close to the canopy top, the vortices become smaller in diameter and move faster. The vortical energy at the top keeps the material from falling, and the downflow has to overcome both vortical energy and magnetic forces."

Solon said, "There's not much mileage left in this idea, just a balancing act. When you dig into it, there's nothing spectacular about the back-and-forth motion."

George warned, "Our view is imaginative and original but simplistic, no different from the prehistoric Babi model. Whatever we say will have to stand up to scientific articulation before it can pose as the final view of the canopy structure that affected the design of the prehistoric social structure."

"Finally, sex would rescue us all," Solon said with a grin.

Arjuna was not pleased with the conversation. "I find the excessive, crude, and improper use of sexual symbolism unacceptable. I often don't understand Solon because of the vulgarities that so routinely permeate his speech. I know I am old-fashioned, but please! Can we describe the canopy some other way?"

George turned to Arjuna and said, "Simple, robust models have a premium. A sexual model simply and effectively depicts the structure and dynamics of an event. Even after tens of thousands of years, the sexual features cannot be mistaken. Just look at the monkey god model. Something long, cylindrical, and mushroom-headed moves in and out of an orifice in a place colored red, bounded by darkness. It's readily understood after tens of thousands of years. There's little chance for distortion or misinterpretation. It is a good scientific model given to us by the prehistoric scholars."

Though to a degree I sympathized with Arjuna, I agreed with George. "Solon's vocabulary is foul, but George is right. Being subtle and indirect doesn't work, and being abstractly concise works even less. Looking through the sacred texts and myths, I often come across a name as a descriptive word for a canopy feature, but today no one knows what that name means. The meaning is irretrievably lost. I am sure they knew it once. Whoever chose it probably thought, *This is a good word to describe that feature.* But over tens of thousands of years, the meaning failed to transfer from one generation to the next. Or I look at the Egyptian model, the god Babi. Instead of giving a certain feature a name, they described what they saw as a monkey god. Even after millennia, seeing or imagining the red bottom of a squatting monkey delivers the originally intended meaning. Not so for veiled names or abstract descriptions."

Enoch agreed. "That's absolutely right. One obscure word suffices to shroud the meaning of many. It is difficult to maintain meaning, to make it travel across millennia when the meaning is attached to an ambiguous name." He sighed and muttered, "We no longer know what Yahweh means, and he's supposed to be my God."

"I hear you," Arjuna rejoined. "I am not blind. I see the simplicity, the effectiveness of the monkey god. But I strongly object to genital-laden language. There are better words." Then he asked me directly, "What else are you going to tell us? More of the same X-rated stuff?"

I smiled as cheerfully as I could and said, "Enough of phallic downflow and monkey butts. Here is another canopy feature, though I warn you—it's been modeled sexually." I wanted to talk about vortical motion. On that subject, George would be but an ally.

At its formation, the canopy would have been chaotic. Every piece of rock and ice moved individually. Collisions were frequent. Fragmentation was intense. Collisions and fragmentation drained the energy that kept everything chaotically independent, and the discrete pieces slowed down and ordered themselves in relation to each other. The canopy gradually changed from total chaos to a diffusely chaotic shell and then to a more ordered, banded structure.

"On gaseous planets like Jupiter, banding is inevitable," said George.

"But Earth is not a gaseous planet," Solon pointed out. "Remember! It is solid. The canopy shell is also solid. So where did the Jupiter-like bands come from?"

George prepared to contradict Solon. "The canopy is similar to Jupiter's outer layer. In other words, Jupiter's outer layer is no different from a canopy around Earth. They would behave the same. Both are affected by vortical energy. As soon as the vortical energy diminishes and cannot sustain chaotic motion, the canopy would assume a banded structure. Today's science readily supports and models such chaos-to-order transformation."

Solon acceded and asked, "Okay, what's the big deal about canopy banding?"

"Just another canopy feature," I said, "a visible one, readily observed from Earth and easily described. The banding was recorded and passed down in myths and sacred texts."

"You said the bands are modeled sexually," Khufu muttered. "How would it be possible?"

"This much I know through Egyptian myths. The whole banded canopy was called Osiris. The canopy's top band was Isis. The two were seen as brother and sister because they appeared at the same time. They were also seen as husband and wife because the top band circled the phallic downflow and formed the vagina through which the downflow moved."

Before I finished, Khufu had begun to page through the Pyramid Texts. He then straightened up and said, "Here it is, an example of what you are referring to, Utterance 600. I've always found it quite disgusting as an act of God. Listen. Listen carefully. The utterance describes the god Osiris as 'mummy fucker.'"[6]

Arjuna was visibly upset. "Who would do such a dreadful thing to a mummy?"

Any person engaged in such an act would be mentally sick. But how sick would a god have to be to do it?

"Get off your moralistic perch," Khufu said, smiling. "It is a model—a prehistoric model. Moreover, it is not about God; it is about majestic canopy features presumed to be God by prehistoric societies that lived in the canopied earth. The mummified body is a model of the canopy bands. The phallic downflow belongs to Osiris and moves in and out of the bands, in and out of the mummified—banded—canopy. When one looks from the point of view of a prehistoric but nonetheless scholarly model, what a fascinating combination of canopy downflow and banding!"

How did I miss that in my research? I wondered. Khufu seemed to have known it intuitively.

The "mummy fucker" was not a god having sex with mummies. It was the "celestial penis" of polar downflow moving in and out of the banded canopy.

George concurred. "What a beautiful model! Only two words, fucker and mummy. Universal descriptors. The meaning will last forever."

Enoch asked, "Does this mean Egyptian mummification imitated the banded canopy?"

"Definitely!" Solon roared. "Every human would want to be like God, and if the god Osiris appeared in front of you and looked like a collection of bands going round and round, why not resemble him when you're dead? Entering the next world dressed like a god would be cool."

Khufu agreed. "I don't know how it got started in Egypt, but I can imagine the entrepreneur who offered it to the public. Anyone who could afford it would be wrapped and preserved like Osiris."

We tried to imagine how a banded canopy would have looked. If I had been alive on a canopied day, how would I have seen the bands? The Egyptians had modeled the banded canopy as a mummy, and the model then had been further refined. Each band was perceived as a distinct, separate god. The top band was Isis, the sister of Osiris. Isis was also wife of Osiris because the phallic downflow went through her.

"Let me read a spell from the Coffin Texts," Khufu suggested.

"What is a spell?"

"A literary unit, like a paragraph. In the Pyramid Texts it is called an utterance."

Solon nodded in appreciation.

Khufu smiled at him and said, "Spell 148, a not-too-sexual model of banded canopy, a model of Osiris and top band Isis: 'The lightning flash strikes, the gods are afraid, / Isis wakes up pregnant with the seed of her brother Osiris.'"[7]

"This spell is not just a sexual model," George said. "It says more than that. It points to the effect of canopy instabilities. Its shape changes. Remember that Earth, in its orbit, passes through the swarm regularly. Each time it passes through, major instabilities follow."

"I don't understand. What is an instability?" Khufu asked.

George thought a moment and then said, "When the canopy goes through the swarm, it is like a car going through a storm. Have you ever felt the force of strong wind on your car? How it almost forces your car off the road? That is one kind of instability. In this view, the swarm pushes the canopy bands around, making them irregular and distorted."

George stopped momentarily again, thinking, and then said, "Also, every time the planet meets the swarm, new cometary matter adheres to the canopy, an extra load the bands must carry. The bands feel the strain of added material and move irregularly or chaotically to reflect the added pressure. Does that answer your question?"

"Yes," said Khufu. "When I was young, I used to overload the donkeys as I'd jump up and sit on top of the load. They staggered under the load. Now I know. They were suffering from instabilities."

We laughed, and George continued.

"Then there is the charged particle density—with lots of electrical discharges between the canopy and the earth and on parts of the canopy itself. Anywhere a blast of electrical discharge hit, the force would distort

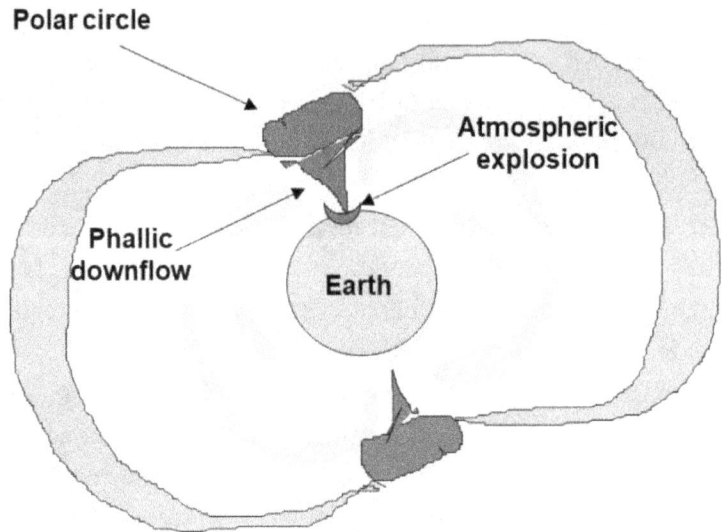

The phallic downflow was one of the most noticeable features while Earth was under the chaotic canopy. In the dim reddish light of the polar sun, the pulsating motion of the polar downflow and the explosion of its tip upon entry into the atmosphere could be best modeled as a celestial penis thousands of kilometers long.

—Solon

the canopy. I believe the Egyptians perceived and modeled the distortions as 'being afraid,' the way a human would distort his face in fear. The Egyptians expressed the distortions and instabilities as an expression of fear by canopy gods."

Solon laughed and asked, "But what about being pregnant? How does the top band get pregnant?"

"It's all there, in the model," George said. "At each swarm encounter, the canopy captures new material, which breaks apart and flows poleward. One obvious effect would be an increase in the size and bulk of each band, especially the top one. It could get big enough to almost close the polar opening."

"Wow! By enlarging, the top band *does* become pregnant," Solon murmured.

"Beautifully simple model," George said. "I bet the overloaded top band looked like a pregnant belly, pregnant with the seeds of Osiris. I bet the seeds were the ejecta of the downflow's atmospheric explosions. The explosions splashed a lot of things upward toward the top band, splashing on Isis—thus the model of making her pregnant with the seeds."

Arjuna's body language continued to signal displeasure with the sexual models being discussed.

Khufu, seemingly muttering to himself, said, "Let's get away from instabilities … the ejecta." He leafed through the Pyramid Texts, ready to come up with another discovery. Then he mumbled somewhat sarcastically, "I apologize, Arjuna, for sexual models."

Arjuna did not like Khufu's tone and said wearily, "It is *sick*."

"It is *sick* only if you do not see it as a prehistoric model," Khufu rejoined. "Such models capture and preserve significant information. More importantly, they show the extent of the tools the prehistoric scholars had at their disposal to capture their experiences. If only we could see it—the top canopy band appearing to sit on the phallic downflow and being splashed by exploding ejecta. I know I would be hard pressed to come up with a better model."

"You are missing the point," Arjuna insisted. "In every human action, in every model, in anything a human does, there is an inherent question of right and wrong. If we deem it wrong for a human to have sex with his sister or mother, should we develop models that use morally unacceptable concepts?"

Enoch had a suggestion. "There is another possibility," he said. "The Egyptians may have wanted only to highlight the difference between humans and gods. A model doesn't have to be an affirmation. It could just as well be an attempt to capture a fact about gods while highlighting a radical contrast with humans."

Arjuna could only wave a hand of dismissal.

At that moment I could not feel sorry for Arjuna and his position. I only felt it was time to switch from Egyptian to Indian sacred texts. We had spent enough time on the Egyptians. We needed the Indian view of the canopy.

I asked, "Have you had enough of Egyptian models?"

Arjuna raised a thumb skyward and said, "I am sure the Indians observed the canopy but never considered the filth of sexual modeling. You'll find no such thing in the *Rig-veda*."

I said, "But you can."

"You show me *one*—anything, anything vaguely resembling what Osiris is doing to Isis—and I owe you a lunch." He was firm. He knew his *Rig-veda*.

"I may not find an explicit sexual model," I said, "but what does 'his sister's lover' tell you? It is in the *Rig-veda*."

"You're just joking."

"And what about this? 'His mother's suitor.'"

"Where? Where are you getting these?"

"From *Rig-veda*, Book 6, Hymn 55, Verse 5."

Arjuna grabbed the book and fumbled through the pages. Squinting, he muttered, "Book 6, Hymn 55, Verse … Ay-ay-ay! The damned Yama."

Khufu raised his hairless eyebrows. "So! You also have sexual canopy models, you dirty old Indian!"

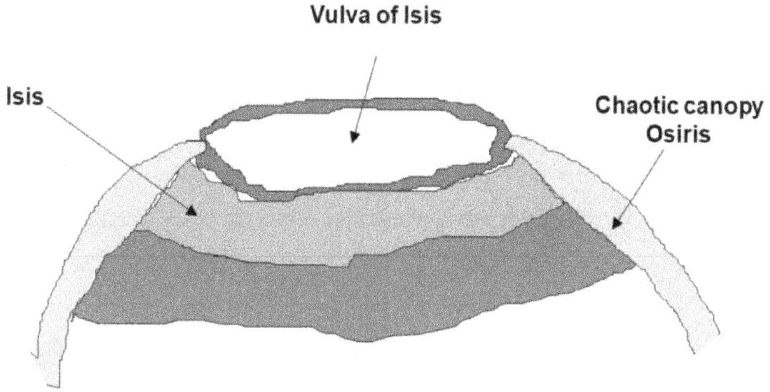

Vulva of Isis

Isis

Chaotic canopy Osiris

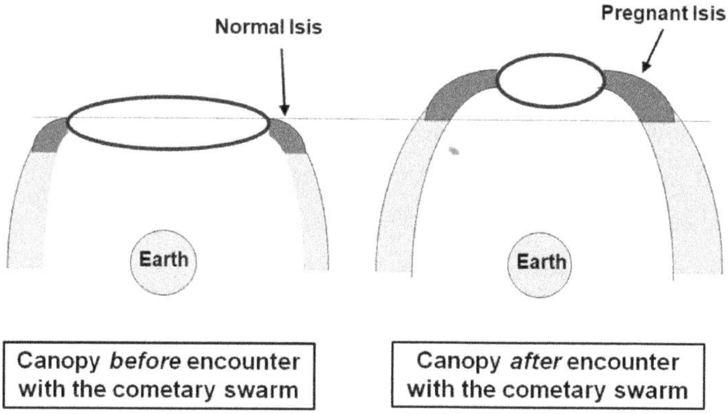

Normal Isis

Pregnant Isis

Earth

Earth

Canopy *before* encounter
with the cometary swarm

Canopy *after* encounter
with the cometary swarm

Each encounter with the swarm added material to the canopy shell. The bands swelled with new material and expanded poleward. The polar circle narrowed. The Egyptians noted the "lifting up" of the bands. More specifically, along with the lifting up, the wider top band and its higher arch reminded them of pregnancy.

—Khufu

"In *Rig-veda*, Yama is an insignificant god. He is one of the earliest gods. We consider him primitive. Usually, we ignore him."

"Let's see if I get it right," Khufu said. "Your god Yama had sex with his sister, which I assume is the top canopy band. He had sex with his mother, which I assume refers to the banded canopy, just like Osiris. But you claim you have a higher sense of morality because your text used the words 'lover' and 'suitor' instead of 'phallus' and 'vagina'? Or because you *ignored* such verses?" He paused and then said, "Your ancestors observed the downflow, and instead of Osiris, they named it Yama. What did they choose for Isis?"

"Yami," whispered Arjuna in a barely audible voice.

Khufu continued with gentle irony. "So we Egyptians had Osiris and Isis having sex with each other. You had Yama and Yami *loving* each other. Therefore, you are more moral than I am?"

An intense argument followed.

Arjuna insisted that he had not meant Indians were more moral because they used the word "love" and Egyptians less moral because they used more explicit words but had meant that societies differ in the degree of social pressure to repress references to genitals.

I raised the key question of where to draw the line. "Why is 'Yama loving Yami' a proper expression of an undesirable relationship and 'Osiris having sex with Isis' not? Or at what point should we cease saying anything about Yama and Yami or Osiris and Isis altogether?"

"You're aligning with those who think it's 'moral' to burn books because they don't like the ideas in them," George said. "People have always tried to destroy ideas and lives by erecting moral barriers. Look at it this way. Penises and vaginas are ordinary body parts. There's nothing moral or immoral about them. If an incomprehensible natural occurrence can best be likened to a penis, it should be so. Discarding the penis-based model or replacing it with a 'love model' only blurs or destroys valuable structural and dynamic information about human history."

Arjuna thought a while and said, "Let me show you an example of the *Rig-veda*. You tell me if you see anything wrong.

"*Rig-veda* has a creation hymn. Many believe it refers to the creation of the universe. I believe now it probably refers to the formation of the canopied world. Here is a verse that may correspond to a first sighting of the polar downflow. It is in Book 10, Hymn 129, Verse 4: 'Thereafter rose Desire in the beginning, / Desire, the primal seed and germ of Spirit.'[8]

"What a beautiful expression," Arjuna said, emphasizing his point. "It summarizes the downflow in a single word: 'desire.' As concise as any Egyptian model, but without a single vulgar word or improper relationship."

"To be honest, it stinks," George rejoined sarcastically. "You say 'desire' would transmit the message across thousands of years. I receive it, look at it … and do I get any sense that something long and cylindrical is moving rhythmically back and forth through a circular opening? Do I see any form of banding resembling the human fingers gripping the in-and-out motion? No. Your sexual inhibitions sterilize the information. None of the canopy's structure and dynamics gets through. I haven't read *Rig-veda*, but I bet whatever it says about Yama and Yami is a moral pronouncement, not a description of what they are doing."

Before Arjuna could say a word, I cut in. "You guessed right, George." I started to read from *Rig-veda*, Book 10, Hymn 10, Verse 9: "In heaven and earth the kindred pair commingle / On Yami be the unbrotherly act of Yama." A few lines later, Verse 13 said, "Alas! Thou art indeed a weakling, Yama."

George had heard enough. "Exactly my point. The main information is moralizing about 'unbrotherly love' or being a moral 'weakling' for doing it."

"I see your point!" Arjuna exclaimed. "As you have already noticed, I rarely pay attention to Yama hymns. My ancestors found it difficult to describe events that seemed like phallic acts of a god. I still think they were right."

Enoch offered his understanding. "So the Indians were reluctant to describe the downflow in terms of genitalia. They shied away from gods having sex with each other. What's wrong with that? We do that every day. We're not explicit about lots of things. Instead of an explicit word, we're given a model of 'birth of desire.' There's nothing wrong with that. Instead of graphic language, it's poetic and beautiful—another way of observing life. People have many ways of expressing their experience of life."

George concurred. "I didn't say it didn't have value or beauty. I really wanted to emphasize how different we are, how differently we perceive and articulate things."

With that Solon got up and declared this the end of the meeting.

That was unexpected.

He seemed preoccupied with something else, something important.

"Are you okay?" Enoch asked.

"Yeah … sure," Solon mumbled. "Too much work and a trip I don't know how to fit into my schedule."

"A conference?"

"Something like that."

9

The Ghost of a Trip

Joshua's Jeep pulled up at Solon's house at six in the morning, and the young man didn't have to wait long. Solon appeared in the driveway in battle fatigues, carrying a backpack. Joshua could not help laughing out loud.

"What?" Solon looked at him in confusion.

"The way you look, no one would believe you're anything but a militia leader."

Solon smiled and joined Joshua in the Jeep. Their destination was Almighty City, and despite Solon's insistence that they take a plane to a city near there and then drive, Joshua had insisted on taking the car. Solon had finally agreed, figuring that Joshua either did not have the money for a plane ticket or was carrying things that would not be allowed on a plane, such as guns.

They were to arrive late in the evening. Solon hated the long drive. On the positive side, he would have an opportunity to talk to Joshua and learn more about the militia groups—and to teach him some things he did not know.

They drove almost an hour without talking, glancing at each other occasionally and smiling.

Joshua broke the silence. "I was surprised to read that the Christian creed that declares Jesus divine was determined by four ecumenical councils spread over four hundred years."

"Even then, they didn't stop with theological and scholarly arguments. A bloody war followed, fragmenting the church, and the breakup continues even today."

"Why aren't we told about that?"

"People love settled, stable things, not only in religion but in everything else. Business and government are the same. We rarely want to go back and see how things started, whether right decisions were made." Solon paused and then added, "One person made a lot of choices about Christianity on behalf of everybody."

"You mean Paul."

"He recast Jesus as the savior god of Greek and Roman mystery religions that were quite popular at the time. Paul chose to follow the day's popular trend."

"The book said nothing about mystery religions."

"Remind me when we get back. I'll give you a book on mystery religions. You'll be amazed at the comparison."

Christ lived at a time of intense spiritual awakening, Solon explained. Not only were the Jews awaiting a messiah king, but the Greeks and Romans were also searching hard for savior gods. There were competing movements in philosophy, the occult, and astrology, among other fields.

Solon summarized the mystery religions' key and common features. The gods named Dionysus, Mithras, Osiris, and Bacchus were all the same. All were "sons of God" incarnate meant to save humans, children of a father God and a human virgin mother. All were born on December 25 in a cave or a barn. They all offered their followers rebirth through baptism. They all turned water into wine and rode into some town on a donkey. They all died at Easter as a sacrifice to rid the world of sin. After death, they spent three days in hell and then rose from the dead and ascended to heaven. Each one's death and resurrection was celebrated by a ritual meal of bread and wine, and the followers awaited the return of the son of God for ultimate judgment.

"You're pulling my leg," Joshua complained. "What you said is Christianity, not Greek mystery religions."

Solon laughed. "That was a problem for early church thinkers like Tertullian and Justin Martyr. How to account for the similarities between Jesus and gods like Osiris, who predated Jesus by thousands of years? How do you think they resolved it?"

"They didn't tell anyone."

"You *are* bright. So long as Christians did not know about the mystery religion parallels, Christianity and its claims were safe. In fact, the church has used that strategy for almost two thousand years. But notwithstanding the good operational strategy, the church had to come up with some theories for its own internal documents. The first theory accused the devil of plagiarism."

"That's cool."

"The church said the devil copied the story of Jesus and disseminated it as stories of mystery religion gods."

"But that's absurd. That would make the devil more powerful than God because he was able to read God's mind long before God decided to act."

"Good observation," Solon said, "but at the time, that was the best they could put together to explain the undeniable similarities. Perhaps that is why the later church thinkers dropped the devil and claimed instead that the mystery religions were 'prophecies' of the coming of Jesus."

"That is also pure bull. It is like saying people could read God's mind and knew what God would do. It makes God's behavior deterministic, machinelike."

"But it sounds much better than saying the devil did it."

Solon decided to tell Joshua about an aspect of Christianity that was as foreign as Joshua's radical beliefs. "In our conversation last week, you said you distrust government and its encroachment on individual rights."

"I meant every word," Joshua said. "Every government act is a form of tyranny imposed on the individual."

"With that view you're going to face a paradox because Christianity was not adopted freely by the masses. The government forced it on them."

"Where did you get that idea?"

"In the fourth century, Emperor Constantine declared Christianity the imperial religion. The story goes that he wanted to make a mystery religion the official religion and had his eye on the cult of Mithras, which was very popular with the Roman armies. But some around him convinced him that except for the name, Mithras was the same as Jesus and that Jesus was a better choice because he came with some established books."

"I didn't know," Joshua admitted.

"The rest is the ordinary history of a conqueror. Empowered with that declaration, the church started using the government machinery to destroy the opposition. They declared all other religions and sacred texts heresies, and some, like the Gnostics, were hunted down and their books burned. Eusebius, a confidant of the emperor, took on the task of writing the history of the early Christian church and combined his imagination with all sorts of fabrications and legends to produce the only document that survived as the early church's history. Your fear of a tyrannical government came true in the Roman Empire. Anyone who refused to assent to the new religion's demands was punished or executed. Those who worshipped mystery gods like Dionysus, Osiris, Mithras, and Bacchus were told the new religion was the same. Only the God name was different. All they had to do was change one name for another. That accelerated the forced propagation of Christianity across the Roman Empire."

Joshua listened intently but without any comment.

To lighten the mood Solon said, "Emperor Constantine was a strange character. The notion of one religion and a single god appealed to him because it laid the foundation for one emperor for one empire.

He was good at putting to the sword anyone who opposed Rome or the emperor's interests. He killed his own wife and son. But most perfidious, he postponed his own baptism until he was at death's door so that he could sin as much as he liked, then get last-minute forgiveness and a guaranteed place in heaven."

Joshua reacted with a rueful smile.

Solon thought about changing the conversation's direction. He debated whether he could share with Joshua something that he had intended to keep a secret. He finally succumbed to what he perceived as Joshua's need to know.

"What would you do if I told you that many religious beliefs emanate not from an experience of God but rather from the experience of an exceptional physical phenomenon that took place in the earth's skies thousands of years ago?"

"I would ask for documented proof."

"Assume I provide the documents and you find the claim to be true. Then what?"

"You said the event happened thousands of years ago," Joshua said. "Then it wouldn't apply to Christianity, which appeared only a couple thousand years ago."

"Let me ask you this. If *you* experienced something exceptional, how would you express it? In Chinese?"

"Obviously not," Joshua countered. "I would describe it in English. That's the language I know."

"Assume the phenomenon has to do with natural plant life. What use of English language would you emphasize?"

"Plant biology, of course."

"So if tens of thousands of years ago, the language that described gods was around the experience of a single physical phenomenon, and it was used and fused in sacred texts like the Old Testament, what language do you think would be used to describe the New Testament's god?"

"Are you telling me Jesus is not real?"

"That is a different story. Assume Jesus was an exceptional human who looked godlike to his contemporaries. How would they describe the divine Jesus?"

Joshua paused and then said, "In the language already developed for describing gods."

"Then you see, the physical phenomenon that served as the origin of the oldest religions determines the language for expressing godlike figures in newer religions."

"Getting back to something you said earlier," Joshua said, "is there any evidence that Jesus was not real?"

"Personally, I believe Jesus was an exceptional human, and his exceptional character got him into the Gospels. But many have studied the Gospels and have concluded that the Jesus described there is more a concocted imagery than the real person. Assume for a moment that you know nothing about Christianity and by accident find the Gospels of Mark, Matthew, and Luke in a jar buried underground."

"Like the Gnostic Gospels everyone thought the church had burned to the last copy but were found fifty years ago in a jar buried in Egypt?"

"Yes, like that," Solon said. "Now you read these ancient books about a virgin maid who has sex with God, gets pregnant, and bears a child who walks on water and returns from the dead. How much of that would you believe?"

"Doesn't sound believable, but that's why we call it faith."

"Remember, you are seeing the Gospels for the first time. There is no place whatsoever for faith, which is simply blind acceptance of something because our forefathers accepted it blindly. So put yourself in the position of the first person to find and read the Gospels. Would you believe them? Or would you say they are myths?"

Joshua frowned. "Under such hypothetical circumstances, the story would be seen as a myth. But the Bible is not the only source of information about Jesus. What about the Jewish historian Josephus? He talks about Jesus the same way the Gospels do."

"Josephus would be a good example," Solon smiled. "He was Paul's contemporary, and it seems logical he would know and write about Jesus.

But consider this. From Paul to the early church fathers, there is not a single mention of Josephus connected to the Jesus story. Then in the fourth century, Eusebius produces a version of Josephus that contains a paragraph mentioning Jesus, in the style of the Gospels, for the first time. What do you think is happening?"

Joshua thought about the alternatives for a moment and said, "Either Eusebius doctored Josephus, or he was the first to find it?"

"Which do you think is more plausible?"

"What about the other writers of the period? I'm sure Josephus was not the only Jewish writer, and I bet there were a whole host of Greek and Roman writers. What about them?"

"Exactly. What about them?"

"Are you telling me none wrote anything about Jesus?"

"None. Philo, a Jew who wrote about fifty books, does not mention Jesus. Roman writers of the time of Jesus, like Seneca, Pliny the Elder, Plutarch, Ptolemy, and many others, say nothing about Jesus. In fact, Josephus is quite negative about Jewish messiah figures. Worse, even the Gospels say little about Jesus, and when they do, they are full of contradictions."

"What do you mean?"

"Tell me, what is Jesus' family lineage?"

Joshua shook his head. "I don't remember exactly, but it starts at Joseph and ends at David, doesn't it?"

"The Gospels of Matthew and Luke start with Jesus, then Joseph, and that is where the commonality ends. From there on, back to David, the names on the two genealogies are different and have no resemblance to each other. Matthew stops at David, but Luke goes all the way to Adam. What basic problem do you see in both genealogies?"

"None," Joshua said. "Starting with Joseph and ending with David is all you need. Nobody knew much about the ones in the middle, so the gospel writers could have gotten mixed up."

"Fascinating," Solon said with a smile. "Even someone as bright as you cannot catch the fallacy of the Gospels' genealogies."

Joshua shook his head as if to say he saw nothing wrong.

Solon recognized the challenge. "Do I need to tell you that Joseph was not the father of Jesus? Jesus's mother was a virgin impregnated by God, and therefore *God* is the father. If you agree to that, the only genealogy Jesus has is linked in one step to God, not through Joseph to other mortal men like David."

"Come to think of it," Joshua said, "Mark's gospel says nothing about the virgin birth or Jesus's family tree. Shit! So you think Jesus was not real?"

"No, to the contrary. I believe Jesus was real and exceptional, but the description of his life fell into the hands of people more interested in setting themselves up in business than in getting Jesus's words out. Paul tops the list of people who regularly distorted Jesus's view. He wanted a franchise business, and … I have to admit, he created one of the best in the world. Just look at the number of churches Paul's franchise business is operating today all over the world, and you'll recognize him as a master at creating and running a business to serve customer needs. The customers wanted a mystery religion, and in response to that market demand, Paul changed Jesus into a mystery god instead of delivering Jesus's message about the kingdom of heaven. The message became secondary and later was totally ignored. We have evidence that Jesus knew about the kingdom of heaven and had shared it with everyone, most vividly in the Sermon on the Mount."

Joshua recited, "I tell you truly, that there are some of those standing right here who will never taste death before they see the kingdom of God."

"Exactly," Solon affirmed. "It is sad. So little has remained about who Jesus really was and what he wanted to say to us."

Joshua sighed, and Solon sighed back.

They remained silent for a long time.

They had taken turns driving for almost eight hours, and it was Joshua's turn. Solon was tired and closed his eyes for a few minutes. He sensed the car slowing down for an exit. At an earlier exit, just a while ago, they had stopped to use the restroom and eat. He didn't understand the need for another exit.

"Do you need to stop?"

Joshua seemed not to hear him, so Solon repeated the question.

"Just a quick one. No big deal."

For the first time, Solon felt threatened. Joshua's face and demeanor did not match his words. Something was wrong.

Was Almighty City really the destination?

Was Joshua taking him somewhere else he did not want to reveal?

The last thing Solon wanted was to be bound, blindfolded, and taken to a secret destination from which he might never return.

As Joshua drove, Solon took comfort from the well-traveled road and the signs directing traffic to an airport. "Are we going to the airport?" Solon asked as Joshua took the airport exit.

Joshua didn't answer. Minutes later, he pulled into the row of randomly parked cars in front of the departure terminal. "Get out," he commanded.

"Are we going to fly from here to Almighty City?"

"Get out!"

Solon got out of the car. Joshua closed the door, rolled down the window, and said, "Take the next plane and go home."

Solon was flabbergasted. "What the hell is going on?"

Before he could say another word, Joshua turned the car into the road and was soon out of sight.

Solon didn't know what to say or do. Something had happened, but he had no idea what. One moment he had been heading for an armed militia enclave, and the next he was being dumped at the curb like an uninvited guest. He wanted to do something violent, like hijack a plane to Almighty City, but instead he sighed and headed for the ticket counter.

10

Gigantic Eyes .... Looking Down ... Staring at Humans

The days passed slowly. My friends seemed so distant. At any rate, I had to wait until the weekend, and I did, though each day tested my endurance.

As retired people, Arjuna and Khufu always had the time but not the energy. Not so for the rest of us. The workplace ruled our time and energy. Almost everyone had work to do—unending, repetitious, often meaningless, draining work. The hook that brought everyone back each day was wages, the next day's nourishment. After work, only a few evening hours remained. Most just rested to get ready for the next day's labors. Few used the short hours to perceive and comprehend life independently, free from perturbation.

In spite of the boredom and lassitude I sometimes felt, I tried to keep up appearances, tried to seem energetic and satisfied. But my charade always seemed to fail with one special person—my wife. Why was I so transparent to her?

She could sense my despair miles away. She smiled mysteriously, and on my behalf, she appealed to the gods. She burned incense in an ancient ritual to channel natural and supernatural forces in my favor.

Her prayers seemed to make no difference at the workplace, but they made me feel better.

Finally, the weekend came. At lunch everyone seemed tense but not nervous. They all wanted to be there, but they wished they could be someplace else too. Perhaps they suffered from the burden of the books proliferating so profusely. Everyone had the Pyramid Texts. They had all bought a copy. Everyone wanted to read it firsthand, develop his own understanding.

After lunch, we ambled down to the basement. The tea, coffee, and cookies were in place. Each settled into his favorite chair.

Arjuna opened the discussion. "I hope we are done with canopy sex. My mind cannot imagine another thirty-thousand-mile anything."

Solon rejoined that at our age once a week was one time too many, and we all laughed.

The time was ripe for a new canopy feature. Who would accept it? Who would want to debunk it? Somewhat apprehensively, I began to draw a picture of the holes and openings in the canopy shell. To the ancients who had seen them, they resembled "the eyes of God" looking down on the earth.

Khufu responded first. "Interesting subject. You know, the Egyptian sacred texts say that fear—or should I rather say 'real fear'?—came to exist when the eye of God looked down upon humans."

Enoch asked, "What could those eyes be? I can imagine a hole in the canopy, but how could it resemble an eye?"

"Hmm," George said. He seemed to be going off on a mental scientific journey of his own.

Since I already knew more about the canopy eyes, I decided not to wait and went on. "One feature of the eye is color. Listen. This is from *The Book of the Dead*, chapter 177: 'There came to thee Horus with blue eyes, do thou guard Horus with red eyes in his sickness and in his wrath.'"[9]

What feature of the canopy could look like a blue or red eye? I continued, asking them to listen to another piece from the Pyramid

Texts, Utterance 43: "Take the two eyes of Horus, the black and the white."[10] I challenged, "What do you think? What's happening?"

Solon tried to apply strict logic and said, "Color always means light. Anything like red, blue, or white means light. Black means no light. As far as we know, the sun would be the only source of light for the canopy. It would come through the polar circle or through holes in the shell. Hey, George, could light shine through holes in the canopy?"

"Hmmm? Holes? No. Yes."

"Just *one* answer, please."

"Sorry. I wasn't listening," George said. "I was thinking … the sun has to shine through the hole to make it look colored."

"Solon just said that," Khufu pointed out.

"He did?" George sounded embarrassed.

"Okay," Solon said. "Here's something to keep you awake. Let's add a little bit of your vortical energy, some sunshine, some dirt and ice, and of course one gigantic cometary ring, mix it all around, and voila— we've got a damned red eye on the canopy shell." He looked around and grinned.

George frowned and then cried, "That's it, cyclonic vortices!"

Solon looked surprised. "I was just joking."

"Cyclonic vortices. Yes!" George was ecstatic.

The canopy team was on the move.

To understand the "eyes" that had formed on the canopy, we had to start with Earth's atmosphere, itself a thin, gaseous shell. Some of its features resembled the canopy. The most familiar atmospheric feature was weather. Atmospheric chaos and disturbances created weather. We knew the intense disturbances as storms.

"What is the largest and most dangerous storm?" George asked.

"The tornado," Solon answered confidently.

"No."

"The hurricane?" Enoch volunteered.

"Yes," George said. "The biggest and most dangerous atmospheric storm is a hurricane. What's unique about a hurricane?"

Enoch answered at once. "The eye. Hurricane winds whirl around a central eye. The eye is free of clouds, but the strongest winds circulate immediately around it. The eyewall destroys anything in its path."

"And if we know about cyclonic eyes in the atmosphere," George said, "what can we say about the canopy?"

"If you are trying to tell us that hurricanes can exist on the canopy, just tell us," Arjuna said. "Enough question-and-answer."

"Okay, but I'd rather call them cyclonic vortices than hurricanes. They are cyclones. The canopy's vortical energy would create them. Nonetheless, on the canopy they would have the same shape, structure, and function as atmospheric hurricanes."

"I see them differently," Khufu ventured. "On Earth we can never see the whole hurricane. We can't see the eye at its center. But if there were a cyclonic vortex on the canopy, we could see it all. It would be like being in a spaceship and looking down on the atmosphere."

George liked what he heard and went on. For a human standing on Earth, there would be a big difference between hurricanes in the atmosphere and cyclones on the canopy. On the canopy, a person could see not only the whole cyclone but also a shaft of light penetrating through the canopy to the interior.

Enoch frowned. "Even if sunlight were to shine through the openings, shouldn't it be golden … white … or, well, the color of sunlight?"

"Yeah, that's right. Where do the red and blue come from?"

"I know where the red comes from," George said, "and the black, but I have to think about the white and blue. Black is the easiest. The sun would shine on only one half of the canopy. The rest would be in darkness. On the dark side, a cyclonic vortex would not be lit. Its eye would look black."

Arjuna narrowed his eyes. "I can't visualize it."

George explained, "It's like a small window in a house. Do you remember the bathroom in my house? I think you have all seen it."

"The one with the stained glass window?"

"Very pretty when sunlight shines through it."

"Right," George said, "but at night, it's dark, no color—dark as the night. During the day, a colored beam of light shines through."

"That's a ten-four," Solon concurred. "You have it just right. The canopy would be like a wall with round windows. What a mind-boggling thought! At one time, everyone on the planet lived in a humongous celestial house. It must have been killer seeing the canopy eyes as the earth rotated." He whispered to himself, "Could that be heaven?"

"What about Earth's rotation? What do you mean?" Khufu asked.

"As Earth rotated inside the canopy, for twelve hours the surface would face the side of the canopy where the sun shined through the cyclonic holes. That would be the canopy's night side. The eyes would be like very bright stars. Then for twelve hours humans would be on the side with no shaft of light coming through the eyes. That would be the day side. There, the reddish polar sun would shine."

Solon's eyes widened. "Get this! Imagine the canopy as it received the polar sun's reddish light. That's the side with the black-eyed cyclones. Imagine! A world of reddish light and black eyes in the sky. Then imagine the opposite, the part of the canopy that got no polar light and was in darkness. Into the darkness shined glorious beams of cyclonic light, red and blue and other colors, wandering about like searchlights. Boy, what a mind-blowing show of celestial oppositions!"

"This is so confusing," Enoch moaned. "Didn't you say the canopy itself would rotate? You called it vortical energy. So both the canopy and Earth were rotating? If Earth rotates once every twenty-four hours, how often would the canopy rotate? Instead of day and night as we know them, would the canopied Earth switch from a day of reddish light to a night of spotlights?"

George opened his mouth to answer, but Enoch went on. "I have another question. The shaft of light through your stained glass window moves. It changes direction. I assume Earth's rotation is the cause. Would the shaft of light penetrating through the cyclonic eye do the same—move and change direction with Earth's rotation? And also do the same with the canopy's rotation? What is the combined effect?"

"I didn't think of that," George admitted. "You're right. The light shining through the bathroom window does move, but it moves primarily because Earth rotates. The shaft of light through the cyclone would also move because the canopy rotates. Wow! Imagine the combined effect of both rotations! Each cyclonic eye would resemble a randomly moving searchlight. The canopy day would be a day of diffuse, reddish light. The canopy night would be a dark night with searchlights moving around at random."

Arjuna was suddenly excited. "Hmmm. Oh boy! Give me a minute to look. Gods … Varuna … Mitra … eyes like searchlights …" He picked up a book and murmured, "Very strange … though they *are* the ones looking for wrongdoers."

Arjuna finally found what he wanted and said, "Here. This is from the *Rig-veda*, Book 6, Hymn 51, Verse 1: 'With the same eye of thine wherewith thou lookest, brilliant Varuna, / Upon the busy race of men, Traversing sky and wide mid-air, thou metest with thy beams our days.'"[11]

He then flipped to another page. "Here is another one in Book 5, Hymn 66, Verse 6: 'Mitra, ye Gods with wandering eyes.'[12] I know there is more. The gods Varuna and Mitra provide grounds for the cyclonic eyes. The 'eyes' are their key attribute. Those who saw Varuna and Mitra certainly saw searching lights with no fixed course, wandering in the skies. Wouldn't they naturally model the random shafts of light as gods looking for wrongdoers? *That* exact verse I can't find. Let me keep looking."

For a while we were lost in our own thoughts.

I thought mostly about the Indian code of morality.

Who would not devise a strict code if God's flashlight shined through the corner window all the time?

George broke the silence with a smile. "I think I know where the colors come from." He paused and added, "But first let me ask a trick question. What would be the color of the sky when the earth is canopied?"

"Blue, of course," Solon replied.

We can look at a tree's leaves and discern the shape of an animal or a human face. Clouds can seem to be all sorts of things, from animals to faces. Such is the power of human imagination. A picture of Jupiter shows a gaseous planet's surface, nothing but gas whirling about at various velocities and densities in different directions. Yet from this picture of Jupiter, I can sense the Egyptian fear of the cyclonic eye, menacingly staring back at anyone who dares to look. I can imagine looking at the sky and seeing God's eye gazing upon the human. Would my imagination violently jolt me into the *real fear* the ancient Egyptians felt?

—Rafi

George wagged a warning finger. "No. It would not be blue. We see blue because the sunlight scatters directly through the air, but under the canopy no sunlight would fall directly onto the earth. So no blue sky."

"Sorry. Forgot. We already talked about the reddish light shining through the dust and debris at the pole. So the sky would be reddish."

"You're half-right. The sky would be reddish where the polar sun shines. On other side, the night side, it would be colorless, just like it will be tonight."

"Wait a damn minute. What do you mean, colorless? When a shaft of light shines through the eye, it creates a patch of light in the atmosphere. Yes! It creates a blue patch. Isn't that how the cyclonic eye gets its blue color?"

George looked at him with admiration. "Brilliant, absolutely brilliant!"

Enoch, with a wave of his hand, brushed the mutual admiration aside and said, "The cyclonic eye is on the canopy. The patch of blue is in the atmosphere, tens of thousands of miles away. On the canopy, the cyclonic eye itself couldn't be blue." He scratched his head. "But then the human line of sight could superimpose the two. We would see them combined like a blue cyclonic eye. Sorry. Sometimes I am really slow."

George beamed at him. "You're not only slow; you're brilliant! You just solved my problem with the white eye."

"I did?"

"Yes. If a person's line of sight includes both the cyclonic eye and the patch of blue atmospheric light, he will see a blue eye. But if the two are not lined up, he may see a faint white light at the eye. That's the scattered light that reaches the surface unobstructed. But then I could be wrong. Enoch ... sorry. I don't know what makes the cyclonic eye seem white. Perhaps ..."

Solon interrupted. "Okay, Mr. Scientist, tell me—how do you turn a blue eye into a red eye?"

"That's easy. A sprinkling of dust, debris, and ice crystals in the light's path. Then it would be as red as your face."

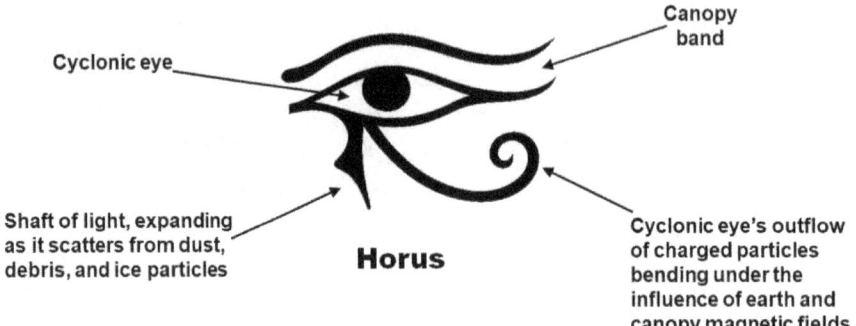

Cyclonic eye

Canopy band

Shaft of light, expanding as it scatters from dust, debris, and ice particles

Horus

Cyclonic eye's outflow of charged particles bending under the influence of earth and canopy magnetic fields

The ancient Egyptians described and modeled their canopy experience in words and pictures. They drew symbolic designs of what they saw. The cyclonic vortex was the god Horus, drawn as an eye with both spiral and straight extensions. The cyclonic opening was the eye itself. The shaft of light piercing the eye was the straight extension. Highly charged cometary material spewed earthward through the cyclonic eye and spiraled under the influence of Earth's and the canopy's magnetic fields. The Egyptians modeled the material flowing from the cyclonic vortex as the spiraling extension of the eye. The eyebrow and the contours of the eye symbolically defined a canopy band within which the cyclonic vortex moved.

—Khufu

"And the canopy would be accommodatingly full of dust, debris, and ice crystals."

"You know it."

"In that case," Solon concluded, "most eyes would be red, blue eyes rare."

George nodded in agreement. "That's how I see it. It would be rare that the light would reach the atmosphere directly with no dust or ice in its path."

We then changed our focus away from colors. George asked us to imagine more than just one cyclonic vortex on the canopy.

Very likely, a number of cyclonic vortices would exist simultaneously. Sunlight would shine through the cyclonic eyes in different colors, mostly red, some blue, some white, some other colors. As the shafts of light randomly moved through the canopy, they would form an array of multicolored celestial searchlights.

"Without being able to see them, it is really hard to give a true description."

"We have just begun," Arjuna said comfortingly. "Have patience, my friend. There is much to be learned, and at every step we will learn more. Two weeks ago, we never thought a comet could create a scene that might be mistaken for God. Today we are dissatisfied because we cannot see the faces of the canopy gods clearly. Have patience. We will come close to seeing it all."

The day was coming to an end. I needed to share one more piece of information—another physical model of the cyclonic vortices.

I picked up my copy of the *Rig-veda*, opened a marked page, and read from Book 10, Hymn 67, Verse 10: "Men praised Brhaspati the Mighty, bringing the light / within their mouths from sundry places."[13]

Arjuna reacted strongly. He recognized a popular practice of Brhaspati's worshippers. They held lit candles in their mouths and danced.

Before I could say anything, George jumped into the conversation, more excited than ever. "Absolutely brilliant," he said.

How ingenious the prehistoric model was! How had the ancients come to think of it?

Solon hesitated in obvious confusion and then asked, "What is brilliant about holding a candle in your mouth and prancing around like a moron?"

"Don't you see?" George rejoined. "We're talking about a shaft of light. The ancients saw it firsthand. They thought the vortex and its spirals looked like a mouth. The eye of the vortex looked like the lips circling a candle. The body of the candle was the shaft of light coming through the cyclone's eye. The flame was the patch of light where the shaft of light entered the atmosphere. As a physical model it is absolutely astounding."

"I take it back. It *is* brilliant."

Arjuna saw the model taking shape but asked, "Tell me, why does the shaft of light become most visible only in atmosphere?"

George started to deliver a lecture. "Light moves along a straight line, invisible unless it hits the human eye directly. When the human eye is not along the cyclonic light's path, only the contour of the shaft of light is visible. The contour is defined by the light scattered in all directions from dust, debris, or air molecules. Part of that scattered light is directed toward the human eye and defines the celestial candle's body."

Any sight was the result of sunlight reflecting from objects.

Arjuna now realized that the cyclonic shaft of light was scattered by the thinly distributed cometary matter inside the canopy. Where the matter was thin, the scattered light would not be intense, and only the faint outline of the shaft of light would be visible. The Indians saw the thinly scattered light and identified it with the candle body. When the shaft of light reached the atmosphere, it scattered heavily in the dense air, with a lot of light getting directed along myriad paths, including the one meeting the eye of the Indian observer.

The Indians, looking at the faint cyclonic shaft of light, saw more intensely scattered light in the atmosphere and identified it with the candle flame.

> # Men praised Brhaspati the Mighty, bringing the light within their mouths from sundry places
> ### (Rig-veda X.67.10)

The Indians developed a physical model that captured the geometry and illumination pattern of a cyclonic vortex. They incorporated it into a worship ritual that enhanced the transmission of knowledge of the vortices. It is a simple but complete prehistoric model. A man holds the end of a lit candle in his mouth. The mouth and lips are the cyclonic vortex and its spirals. The candle is the shaft of light coming from the cyclonic eye. The cyclonic eye is the opening created by the lips tightly holding the candle. The body of the candle is the shaft of light, barely visible through the dust and debris. The flame of the candle is the visible light created in the atmosphere because of intense scattering by air molecules. Even after thousands of years, the knowledge that the Indian model transmits cannot be lost or misunderstood.

—Arjuna

George concluded his lecture by saying, "I am dazzled by the simplicity and completeness of this model."

Enoch asked, "Is this the same phenomenon, today, that means the higher one moves in the atmosphere, the darker it gets? When we are out of the atmosphere and surrounded by the darkness of space, the sun is just a point of light. To see it, you have to look directly at it."

"Yeah, the same thing. Outside the atmosphere, there is no scattered light. The sun looks like a point of light embedded in a background of black velvet. As sunlight penetrates the atmosphere, it gets scattered by air molecules, and by the time it reaches the surface of the earth, it has scattered in so many directions, its diffuse light bathes everything. That's why everything is so visible. Whatever we look at, that object reflects some measure of diffuse sunlight toward us."

Khufu put down his empty cup. "That is confusing. I always thought sunlight reached the earth directly."

"No," George replied. "Only scattered sunlight reaches us, and the Indians were brilliant enough to recognize it. The candle model correctly shows the lighting pattern of a cyclonic vortex."

Arjuna got up, his bones creaking, and without looking at anyone, he slowly walked to the window. "The sun is about to set," he said.

It was the end of another day.

I imagined the cyclonic vortices wandering on the canopy face as men with candles in their mouths danced and honored the magical show in the skies. How astonishing that such a simple ritual, captured in two lines of a verse, could transfer knowledge from one generation to another across thousands of years.

I shook my head in amazement. Then I smiled at my new sense of things.

The sun was not setting.

Earth was just rotating away from the sun, away from the scattered light.

Where had we gotten the illusion of a setting and rising sun?

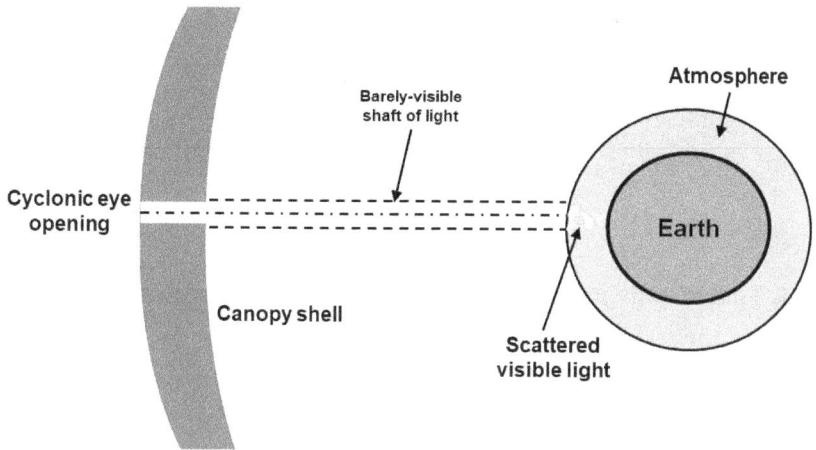

From science we know the cyclonic eye's light beam would become visible only when it scattered from the dust and ice crystals inside the canopy. With scattering being small, only the outline of the beam would have been faintly highlighted. The Indians used the body of a candle as a physical representation of the outline of the beam of light. The most intense scattering and thus the greatest visibility came when the light beam reached the atmosphere and scattered from the air molecules. The candle's flame ingeniously modeled this key feature of the canopy.

—George

11

Competition

This time his patience didn't last ten minutes. No matter what he did to position the dish, he got gibberish from the basement. As he pondered what to do next, he remembered Hank the bartender. He had not heard a word from him about the sting.

"It's about time to pay that piece of shit a personal visit," John muttered. He strapped on his shoulder holster and checked the gun before putting on his jacket. If Hank had chosen to be nonresponsive, John might need to do more than break a few bones to get his cooperation. Things could get ugly, and John wanted to be ready to leave a lasting impression.

Outside the bar he noticed more cars in the street and expected to see a few more customers than before at the bar. He stepped through the door, and the first person he saw was a man sitting at a table with his right arm slung in a cast.

"Hey, what's up?" John said.

"Fuck you!"

At the end of the bar, the burly man from last time was eating lunch, forced into an awkward position by the cast and brace on his left leg.

Hank saw John enter the bar and was watching with a calm that John found threatening. Before he could figure out what might have been set up in anticipation of his arrival, he heard movement behind him. He turned and saw the barrels of four guns pointed at him.

"I hope you like the reception committee," Hank giggled.

Another man approached cautiously, frisked him, found the gun, took it, and put it on the counter in front of Hank. Then he reached into a shoulder bag and pulled out a device that John immediately recognized as a Zap-Checker. The man ran it over John's body a couple of times.

"He's not wired," the man whispered. Then he rushed off, as if late for an appointment.

John remained silent. He had miscalculated and was badly outgunned. He had to figure out what Hank's intentions were, and Hank seemed to be in no hurry.

A few minutes later, the man who had searched him returned, breathing heavily. "I checked around the bar and talked to guards to make sure. There are no support or backup cars."

"So you've come alone," said Hank.

"I'm here to check on our agreement," John said, as if nothing out of the ordinary were happening. "What's the latest on your plant?"

Hank responded by yelling at the top of his lungs. With angry red eyes and a voice that cut like a knife, he said, "I lost my best boy to your fucking sting. Instead of him getting the professor, the professor got him."

John couldn't believe his ears. Guys like Hank were eternally committed to the cause. There was no way of convincing them otherwise. How Solon had changed the plant's mind, John did not know.

Hank took a deep breath, leaned over the counter, and said, "His name is Joshua, my youngest brother. He is now studying philosophy and wants nothing to do with the militia—or me. It breaks my heart to see such a beautiful boy wasted."

John did not know what to say or do. He thought of jumping over the counter and taking Hank hostage behind the bar, but four guns were trained on him, and Hank had his gun.

"Do you know why you're still alive?" Hank asked.

John did not answer.

"You're alive because Joshua asked me for two favors: not to harm the professor and not to harm you. I understood why he didn't want the professor killed. But you? He said something about forgiving the enemy. The kid must have gone loco, but I promised to do what he asked. So turn around and walk out. But hear this: if I see you again, one or both of us will die."

John took a slow step forward and carefully took his gun from Hank's hand and holstered it. Then he turned around and walked leisurely to the door.

At the door, upon passing the man with the arm in the sling, he could not resist slapping him on the arm in a friendly gesture. The cry of agony momentarily brightened what had been a dismal afternoon.

He came home disappointed. He had lost another round.

The basement meeting was still in full swing. He tried one more time to listen and then threw the headphones down in disgust. A light drizzle was making reception even worse than usual.

He decided to take a long walk. He took off the holster strap and gun, put on his cap, and went out. Though it had started to rain in earnest, he did not take an umbrella. He had to think, and he did his best thinking when walking.

First among his viable options was to break into Roughie's house to hide a microphone in the basement, but this went against all his training and principles. He couldn't act like a thief.

A few blocks down the street, he turned and walked past Jenny's Gardens, the neighborhood park and playground. There he noticed something peculiar. Besides street parking, Jenny's Gardens had a few parking spots inside the park. With the rain, he did not expect to see anyone in the park or playground, and indeed there was no one—except a man behind the wheel of a lone car parked in one of the spots. It looked like a surveillance car.

John played it cool but crossed the street to get closer to the car. The driver seemed to watch his every move in the rearview mirror. To confirm that perception, John raised his hand and waved and got a curt, hesitant response from the driver. He walked on nonchalantly, but the man slumped lower in the seat, as if to avoid another encounter.

As he continued walking, John could not forget the man in the car. What was he doing? Who could be under surveillance in this neighborhood? He thought of the basement group but rejected the idea. For surveillance, the car was too far away from the house.

On the way back, he avoided Jenny's Gardens. He didn't want to alarm the man. He planned to check on him a few hours later. If this was a matter of surveillance, John would find another car with a different driver at the same spot. Surveillance was round-the-clock and required different people in shifts.

He returned to the house and put on the headphones but could distinguish little other than the occasional "can OP" he had come to hate. After a few minutes he returned to the comfort of watching football. The rational game kept him centered and sane. "Darn it," he cried at the last play of the game. The pass fell incomplete in the end zone, and his favorite team lost.

He got his binoculars, went to the window, and scanned the house across the street. He could see nothing in the basement, but the sight of the women rushing around led him to guess the party was over. His mind drifted back to the car at the playground. He decided to take another look.

As he turned the corner to Jenny's Gardens, his heart pounded. "I'll be damned," he muttered. Another car was parked at the same spot. Initially, he thought there was no one in it, but as he approached, John saw the top of the driver's head, his body slumped in the seat. He made up his mind to stop and strike up a casual conversation.

As he approached, the man slid even lower.

"Good evening," John said, putting on his best smile and speaking softly.

The man looked at him with an air of concern, straightened up, lowered the window, and said, "Good evening. Can I help you?"

John froze at the sound of the man's accent. To John it was a replica of Roughie's. He maintained his composure and said, "I live around here and thought maybe you were looking for someone or something. Just wanted to see if I could help."

"Oh no, I'm just waiting for a friend."

"A friend?"

"Yes. He and I play catch all the time—to stay in shape, you know. And the weather doesn't bother us."

"Funny you say that," John said nostalgically. "I did the same with my friends in college. We played football, rain or snow."

"Yes." The man sounded disinterested.

"Well, okay. Have fun."

John waved and walked away, wearing a smile of discovery. The man had electronic equipment in the front seat. The blanket thrown over the equipment for cover had not hidden the rectangular contour of the objects underneath. Further, John had seen the imprint of an earphone on the driver's left ear.

John was sure. It was a twenty-four-hour surveillance, and it was neither the police nor the FBI. He knew their standard response if someone questioned them. The behavior and the Middle Eastern accent were dead giveaways of something nefarious and illegal. He wondered if he had accidentally discovered the true terrorist ring.

If he had stayed home, listening to the nonsensical basement chatter, he might never have walked out in the rain and seen the car. If the day had been sunny, the car would have been indistinguishable among others at the park and playground.

As soon as he got home, he set the alarm for two in the morning and went to bed. He wanted to talk to whoever had the graveyard shift.

When the alarm went off, John needed a few seconds to find his bearings. Then he rose and dressed in all black. He retrieved his handgun, checked it, and put it in the holster strapped to his left shoulder. He slung a small black bag across his chest and put on a black wool hat. He left the house and moved stealthily to his car. He drove at normal speed past Jenny's Gardens and saw another car parked at the same spot as before—but with no one visible in it. He drove to the other side of the park and parked at a secluded spot out of the surveillance car's line of sight and least visible to the houses surrounding the park.

He turned off the engine and lights and sat motionless for ten minutes to make sure neither the man in the car nor the neighbors had noticed anything. He took a roll of duct tape from the bag and taped over the interior lights so that his opening the door would not light the interior. He got out cautiously, even though he figured everyone in the neighborhood was deep asleep.

Hunched like an animal, he cut his way through the trees and the bushes toward the surveillance car. He then dropped to his belly and crawled the last twenty feet like a snake. Panting, he cursed himself for being out of shape.

Close to the car, he rested a minute to catch his breath and then moved to the driver's side, took his gun out, and squatted by the rear door. With the gun barrel he lightly tapped the driver's door once.

A head appeared in the window, straining to find the sound source, and then the door opened. That was all John needed. He grabbed the man's arm, pulled him out, and brought the butt of his gun down hard on the man's head. The man fell motionless to the ground. He was wearing an earphone. With catlike speed John slipped into the car and smashed the interior lights with blows from his gun. He looked around to make sure no one had seen him.

He hauled the man to the nearest tree, where he took duct tape and rope out of his bag, bound the man's hands and feet, and taped his mouth. Then he pulled him by the ankles across the park to a corner where dense trees provided good cover.

He returned to the car, found the fuse box, and removed all fuses so that neither the brake lights nor any other light worked. Then he checked the car. Underneath the blanket he found top-of-the-line eavesdropping equipment, the kind that required microphones installed at the location under surveillance.

"What if …?" His heart skipped a beat. What if these guys were doing exactly the same thing he was—eavesdropping on the house? He wanted to catch the basement group red-handed. Was it possible these guys wanted to recruit them?

He went over the car inch by inch, especially the trunk, but found nothing that shed light on the surveillance target. The batteries that operated the surveillance equipment filled most of the trunk. The surveillance equipment had three active channels. He put on the earphone and listened as he switched from one channel to the next. He couldn't detect anything. "Even crooks have to sleep," he grumbled.

He pulled down the hat to turn it into a ski mask and went back to the bound and gagged man, careful to move from tree to tree so as not to give anyone a chance to detect him. The man had regained consciousness and was groaning in pain.

John caught him by the neck, pulled him up, peeled the tape off his mouth, and slammed him hard to the ground. "What are you doing here?"

"I am a servant of Allah," he coughed. "I will die before I tell you anything."

John pressed the barrel of his gun into the man's mouth and hissed, "You want to die? Just say the word."

In the fury of his own adrenaline rush, the man's calm shocked

John. He really was ready to die. He took the gun out of the man's mouth and looked at him in surprised disgust as the man muttered incomprehensible prayer-like words that John guessed were in Arabic. For a moment John lost control, and he slugged the man in the head with the gun. He barely kept himself from hitting the unconscious man a second time.

He took a deep breath, walked a quick circle to regain emotional balance, and then started going through the man's pockets. He found a wallet and some coins. Then he searched him for anything strapped around the waist, arms, or legs.

Just as he was about to accept that there was nothing else, against the background of the man's short, dark growth of beard a white cotton string caught his eye. He pulled it and brought up a medallion with a design he had not seen before. He put the wallet and the medallion in his bag, turned the ski mask back into a hat, and returned to his own car. He drove his car back and parked it next to the man's vehicle. After looking around to be sure nobody was watching, he transferred the surveillance equipment to his car and drove home.

John could not sleep for the rest of the night. He had set up the new surveillance equipment and impatiently switched from channel to channel. At one point he heard the sound of footsteps going away and then, from a distance, the sound of a toilet flushing and a shower running. Then the footsteps returned, and moments later John heard someone praying in Arabic. He almost wept for joy.

It was Roughie's voice.

12

A Breathing Shell

Our group's esoteric knowledge of life had grown.

Within the span of a few weeks, we had become avid readers of obscure books such as the *Rig-veda* and the Pyramid Texts. As our minds dwelled under the canopy, the sacred texts and myths spoke little about God but much about the human attempt to discern God.

Revealing the cometary swarm's true face had required a high level of discovery and achievement. But the discovery was not complete. We had arrived at the base of the mountain, but reaching the top demanded more time and resources. We were eager to get there and see more of the profound unknown, to see more of the canopy. But still, we had so little time for the journey to the summit. How to find time to spend on what we wanted most?

The demands of our personal lives consumed much of our time. The workplace was worse. There, no one understood the need to study the ancient texts for weeks or months. Yet the restrictions were not without merit. With constraints, there could be no rush to conclusions. We had to meet regularly and briefly, think methodically, assess, and reconsider what we had learned.

A bad omen almost cancelled the next basement meeting. Arjuna was ill for a couple of days. We feared for his life; he was so fragile!

Almost in the same days, business travels swamped Enoch. We had to wait until the last moment to be sure everyone could attend. My wife worried about Arjuna constantly and sought to help with new and different arrangements for the meeting.

Then, as suddenly as they had begun, the uncertainties ended. We were together again.

Arjuna looked pale, and everyone saw to his needs. We made sure not to let him carry his books and helped him down the stairs. He appreciated the extra attention, though at every step he adamantly reminded us that he was back to normal and needed no help.

Once we had moved to the basement, my wife brought coffee, tea, and cookies. Under her arm she carried a blanket for Arjuna. "Put it on your legs. Keeps you warm."

Arjuna took her hand in his shaking hand and tenderly kissed it. She left swiftly, trying to hide her misty eyes.

Arjuna smiled at being the center of attention and said weakly, "These past few days, I have thought about life and death and the canopied earth. I thought, if I died, I would miss you miserably and miss our canopy discoveries. I also thought, God forbid, if something happened to us all—like if an earthquake brought this roof down and took our lives—who would tell the story of what we have found?"

Solon said, "You're letting your fu … your … your imagination get the better of you, my dear old friend."

"No! I am serious," Arjuna rejoined. "My illness has brought me to see how fragile knowledge is, how little society is prepared to receive exceptional knowledge. There is no Ministry of the Preservation of Knowledge, not anywhere. There is no Department of Exceptional Discoveries at a place like the Department of Education. There is no one that we could go to and say, 'Sir, we have found this. We are working on it. Store it in something more lasting as we add to it.'"

George said, "Perhaps for discoveries like ours, you're right, but agencies like the patent office *do* preserve exceptional ideas about things humans make and use."

Enoch joined the discussion. "I am concerned not with knowledge loss but with something more serious."

Curiosity brightened every eye.

"For the past week I've been troubled by a different thought. What if the sacred texts are not from God, not even inspired by God … just … just human imaginings of God? And if so, then where is God?"

Khufu nodded and said, "I have the same exact concern. Aren't we destroying every god men have known for thousands of years? What are we offering in their place? I see nothing but unconditional destruction of the past. We will expose humankind to a vacuum. No new view, no replacement view of what God could be, no recipe to relate to Him. I find this categorically wrong."

"Screw you!" Solon said, his eyes as cold as steel. "There's nothing wrong about it. To the contrary, it is wrong to look at a cometary canopy and presume it to be God. If our theory about the canopied earth is true, then men have been far from God for thousands of years. Do you want to stick to religion and prolong the frigging separation by thousands of years more?"

Arjuna said, "There is no other way. It is entirely wrong to continue with chants and prayers to cure an illness if we know there are doctors and medicine to cure it sooner and better. That our ancestors relied on chants and prayers does not make the switch to medicine and physicians wrong."

"*That* is exactly my point," Enoch said. "We are making everyone stop the chants and prayers without offering any physician or medicine in place of those traditions."

"We don't have to offer anything in return. If we know and can show that prayer and chants do nothing to cure illness, then we must say so."

George cut in with conviction. "Knowledge is the only way to discover God. Otherwise, humanity will be stuck in the mistaken assumption that the sacred texts have already discovered God."

"Sacred text, my ass!" said Solon. "*Now* we know. The diddly the ancients saw and characterized as God was not God. They just made it up. They imagined it."

Arjuna tried to calm us. Canopy logic and blind faith were incompatible. Seeking to reconcile them would inevitably make someone's blood boil. "Your argument is nothing new. It is already vividly and wisely addressed in *Rig-veda*. It is part of the creation hymn: Book 10, Hymn 124, Verse 6."

Like schoolchildren, each of us picked up his own *Rig-veda* and found the creation hymn as Arjuna read it aloud.

> Who verily knows and who can here declare it, whence
> it was born and whence comes this creation?
> The Gods are later than this world's production. Who
> knows then whence it first came into being?[14]

Arjuna read the words musically. I was mesmerized as much by the tone of his voice as by the words' meaning. He paused and looked around. Did we see what he saw in those verses?

The Indians had looked at the canopy at great length and in detail. They had subserviently bowed before its features and called each a god. Yet at the same time, they had dealt with facts realistically to avoid a complete distortion by personal feelings. They admitted they did not know where the display they saw in the heavens had come from. Within the realm of their own sensible experiences, they properly confessed that only later was the dimension of divinity attached to what they saw.

Arjuna read one line again: "The Gods are later than this world's production."

Solon was not impressed. "That warning didn't make any difference. Your ancestors went on to see gods in every canopy feature."

Arjuna accepted the logic. "Perhaps it is the human condition to look at the face of the unknown and call it God. Look at the Indian experience. For most, when the celestial event came, the timing mattered. They knew that only later was the God label put on the celestial event. Would they have done that if they had known the origin of their beliefs rested at a celestial event caused by a comet?"

Enoch showed no signs of conceding. "This brings us to what I said earlier. There is no canopy around Earth. Whatever it was, it's long gone. Over thousands of years, much has been added to the sacred texts based on God, not the canopy. We cannot treat the sacred texts solely as canopy records. They also contain much about the true God, just like the verses Arjuna read."

"You are wrong!" George said, looking at Enoch contemptuously. "The sacred texts may be a mix of God and canopy, but they are nevertheless deeply tainted with human ignorance and misconception. I don't see any problem in calling the sacred texts canopy records. The main problem, in my opinion, is with people who would readily seek a new unknown and declare *it* God. How do you stop *that*? What remedy do you have to counter *that*? I can easily imagine that plenty of people, mostly opportunistic charlatans, would offer their own artifacts as God to replace the gods we have found to be reflections of canopy features."

Enoch was more sad than provoked. "The new unknown, the one they may turn to, will be the one you forced on them. When are we going to offer an alternative not based on ignorance? If ignorance of God is all we have to offer, then what already exists is supremely better. Why do we want to destroy it and return humanity to the Stone Age?"

The argument touched Solon. "You forget, my friend—religion has always been in the Stone Age. Never came out of it. Our ancestors looked at the canopy and declared it God, and we've been stuck in that shit ever since. We have been worshipping ignorance forever. Once we show the sacred texts to be canopy records, we will have two choices. We can go on and worship ignorance in a new way, or for the first time we can seriously look around to see where God is. It would be a profound moment of transformation in the human view of life. But I must admit, I am stupidly optimistic. Who says the emotional and psychological gridlock of religious ideas and rituals can be broken? What has existed for thousands of years could go on for thousands more. Every baby born will be conditioned to serve the gods of some religion before he has any chance of learning better. It will be tens of thousands of years before what we're learning about the canopy will become common knowledge. Until then, the damned canopy will go nowhere fast."

George narrowed his eyes, faced Solon, and said, "I know science will be the first to search for God once people know of the canopy."

"Is that so?" Solon retorted. "I wouldn't be too frigging sure. Science's attitude toward God is worse than religion's. Instead of looking, science has just said God doesn't exist. That's a bigger hill of beans than looking at a canopy and calling it God. When it comes to religious ideas, science doesn't have a pot to piss in."

I tried to defuse the argument by reminding my friends that even the most overpowering doubts in any of us should not put a damper on our desire to discover the canopy's secrets. I pointed to the need to return to the beginning to develop a better sense of perspective. Our odyssey had all started with my radical views of prehistory. I had asked others, my friends, to help resolve my dilemma: what to do with the radical model? We did not have much to go on, but somehow we had excelled at playing it by ear.

After only a few weeks we had cautiously come to see the faintest light of merit in my prehistoric model. We were like children peering through a crack at a taboo adult world. We were well aware of the possible consequences, even though all we had looked at were just a few scattered pieces in the sacred texts. We were as far from declaring the past a "cometary past" as the ancients had been from God when they saw gods in the canopy. It was too early to talk seriously about destroying ancestral gods, much less to ask, what next? We still had plenty to discover beyond the distant horizon that we could see but had not yet reached.

Solon clung to the idea. "The canopy is a bitch—very impressive, difficult, complicated, and a real ballbuster in terms of what it does to religion. But here is the catch: when we get around to declaring the whole religious enchilada as having a comet up its you-know-what, we may find out that no one at all cares, let alone the ordinary Joe. We can't even be sure where *we* would stand. For all we know, people—including even us—may go on worshipping the gods made out of the canopy features forever. Don't forget, God is always a human choice. We've never had any other kind yet. So as for the notion that we may be destroying God, it's utterly naive. At best we're just putting a new spin on the gods of the past."

Khufu added, "People could even choose to see the cometary swarm as sent by God to image divine features in earthly terms. If so, they will worship it all the same. Nothing would change. Our worries are meaningless."

In my view the discussion was back where it had started. The concern for destroying God remained unresolved. The concern about revealing the sacred texts as canopy records remained. How could I break this cycle of thought and bring everyone back to the sacred texts and the canopied earth?

With a loud voice I tried my best. "Before the polar sun was born, in total darkness, another canopy feature occupied men. They noticed it immediately. What was it?"

They seemed momentarily confused by the subject change.

"An occasional falling piece," George said disinterestedly. "They would see flashes and streaks of light, like meteorites burning in the atmosphere."

"No," Solon countered. "The total darkness means a highly chaotic canopy. Any flash or streak would be shielded by the dust and debris, unless you were very close to it. Then some light might be visible. But too close—nobody would survive a close encounter to report what they saw."

George conceded that. "You may be right. Early on, the dust and debris would block out light from the exploding pieces." He stopped to think and then suddenly shouted, "Hey!"

We knew he had found something new.

"It is the *sound*. People could not see the light, but they could hear the falling pieces explode."

Solon seemed in a lousier mood than usual and wanted to fight a little longer. "But even that kind of sound would be heard best near the point of impact. Ten miles away, you'd probably hear diddly-squat. If you were too near it, the shock wave would blow you away."

George was taken aback and had to admit that the dusty atmosphere would also muffle sound. Moreover, the number of explosions would decrease in time as the canopy took form. He shook his head and whispered, "Immersed in total darkness. What else could it be?"

Arjuna, who had dozed off, opened his eyes and said almost inaudibly, "In the absence of sunlight, wouldn't everyone notice the cold?"

Solon froze wide-eyed and said, "That's it, you magnificent old fart. People would freeze their asses with no solar heating. That … is … it!"

George murmured, "True, it would get a bit cold, but how cold? That's the question."

"It would get *quite* cold, extremely cold. Freezing cold. Sheets of ice covering not just the poles but everywhere."

George shook his head. "I'm not sure. You see, the canopy would let no sunlight reach the earth, but at the same time it wouldn't let any heat escape either. It would shield the earth from the cold of the space. So off the top of my head, I would expect the climate at lower latitudes to cool down a bit. But the poles would get warmer."

"Get warmer?" Solon squinted.

"Yes. Under the canopy, Earth's surface temperature would become homogeneous. Today's temperature differences are caused by differences in solar radiation. Under a canopy, there would be no such differences. So with the canopy's arrival, the warmer tropics would get colder, and the poles would get warmer. There would be some chill but no sheets of ice. Definitely."

Arjuna looked at me and asked, "What was your point when you first challenged us? Was it the cold? The explosions? Or the faint light of the explosions?"

"It was the sound," I said. "You came up with that and more—though the sound I was looking for was heard regularly and all over the world."

George narrowed his eyes and said, "I hate to say impossible, but what you say is nearly impossible. We've already concluded that the sound of the explosions would be muffled, and the explosions would be random. They wouldn't be regular."

"I did not mean the sound of explosions. I mean the sound of God breathing."

George stared at me, annoyed. "You're pulling my leg! There can be no such thing."

I explained that when the canopy enveloped the planet, people could hear a certain regular sound. The only explanation the prehistoric people could come up with was the sound of God breathing. The sound had started from the first moment the canopy formed.

No one said anything, but their faces conveyed a clear message: "You're mistaken." There could be no source of gentle, rhythmic sound in the canopy, not with the regularity of breathing.

"What about the polar downflow?" Solon suggested.

"No, that wouldn't do," George said. "The downflow would hit the atmosphere with a sudden explosion. Breathing has two similar but gentle sounds: inhaling and exhaling. Just listen to your own breathing. The sound of inhaling is softer, and exhaling is noisier, but neither is explosive. Maybe it has something to do with the magnetic fields. Maybe … I don't know. My best bet is this is a mistaken idea."

Arjuna adjusted the blanket covering him and said, "I bet I know where you got the idea of the breathing god."

"I bet you do," I said.

"From *Rig-veda*, the creation hymn."

"Yes," I said. "Book 10, Hymn 129, second verse. It describes the canopy's earliest stages. The first part of the verse focuses on the absence of day and night: 'Death was not then, nor was there aught immortal: / no sign was there, the day's and night's divider.'"[15]

Enoch protested mildly. "I see the reference to the absence of day and night, but why an absence of death and immortality?"

Arjuna wanted to respond, but before he could, George said, "I can answer that in terms of chaos theory. In a situation of total chaos, no pattern of movement dies, and at the same time nothing seems permanent. Everything constantly changes. Nothing seems to last or totally disappear. I would probably model the canopy chaos the way the Indians did—an absence of death and immortality."

"But they couldn't have *seen* what was going on. They couldn't have seen any of the chaotic motions. It was all darkness." Enoch seemed tormented.

"True," George said, "but remember, they didn't write the creation hymn in the darkness, when Earth first went into the swarm. They lived through things falling and exploding. They saw more of the same in the dim reddish light shining through the polar circle. *Then* they saw that the normal day and night no longer existed. Then they wrote about it and passed it on."

"That makes sense," Enoch admitted.

I resumed my initial train of thought. "After the darkness and chaos, the second part of the verse describes God's breathing: 'That One Thing, breathless, breathed by his own nature: / apart from it was nothing whatsoever.'"[16]

Solon pouted and asked, "How can it breathe and yet be breathless?"

"Not a paradox," Enoch muttered. "The canopy is tens of thousands of miles from the surface of the planet. They heard a rhythmic sound like breathing but felt no wind—no breath. Therefore, it seemed breathless."

George said approvingly, "Brilliant. Er ..." He seemed to want to say something else but changed his mind and said nothing.

Enoch paused and then went on. "Breathing has both a blowing aspect and a sound. The Indians heard the sound, so God was breathing. But no movement of air came with the sound—thus breathless."

George narrowed his eyes and said, "I think you are right. Any sound has to come from vibrations in the atmosphere. In the first, highly chaotic canopy, all sorts of dust and debris would have fallen into the atmosphere. It would have been like a huge dust storm rubbing against the atmosphere. Now I see it. It *could* make a lot of sound without making any wind."

"I understood the sound, but I still don't get it—why no frigging wind?" Solon asked.

"Wind is born from atmospheric temperature differentials. Inside the canopy there would be none. The movement of dust and debris at the top of the atmosphere would be diffuse and across constant temperatures. So I wouldn't expect it to create any air motion, at least nothing that would be felt at the surface. So there would be sound but no wind."

In a poetic voice, Arjuna added, "Thus a breathless god that breathed."

Silence seemed to signal a tentative conclusion. The sound of breathing was the friction of dust and debris against the atmosphere. People had heard the sound of God breathing. I could not help but remind myself that the analysis had yet to account for a *rhythmic* sound. How could the flow of dust and debris alternate regularly?

I asked, "So? That's it?"

Heads nodded until George said, "Not so fast. Dust and debris create sound. That's all—sound, not rhythmic sound, nothing like breathing."

How did it become rhythmic? How did it sound like breathing?

Solon's face lit up with mischief. "Remember the recipe. Just add some vortical energy, a touch of tidal forces …"

"The moon!" George shouted.

"What about the moon?" Khufu shouted back.

After we all calmed down, George explained that the tidal forces would be the cause of the rhythmic sound. "Earth is not alone in space. Other bodies influence it. If Earth were alone, the canopy would be spherical, like the earth. But add the sun, the other planets, and the moon, and the canopy would not be able to stay spherical. Other bodies would apply gravity and change it into an ellipsoid."

Khufu cleared his throat and asked, "An ellipsoid?"

George smiled. "Egg-shaped."

"Then it's like the moon pulling on Earth's oceans?" Enoch asked.

"Exactly," George replied. "The oceans are like a watery canopy. The sun and moon define the oceans' shape. They bulge toward the sun and the moon, especially the moon because of its proximity. When the sun and moon line up, the bulge in the oceans is largest. The canopy is no different. The 'breathing' is like the movement of the ocean tides."

"I don't get any of it," said Arjuna.

"How does the bulge give it an egg shape? Even with an egg shape, how does it create the breathing sound?"

According to the picture that George drew in our minds, the canopy resembled an ocean of dust, debris, and ice particles, exposed to the gravitational forces of the moon and the sun, which defined its shape. It often bulged moonward and became ovoid.

The secret of the canopy's "breathing" lay in the way its surface withdrew from Earth and then returned. Within the canopy, the planet rotated once every twenty-four hours, and as it rotated, relative to a given point on Earth, the canopy surface moved in and out. The canopy surface rose and fell relative to any given point on Earth.

At first, in total darkness, no one could see the in-and-out motion, but they could hear the difference in the sound, the sound of cometary dust and debris rubbing against the atmosphere.

George said, "Think of a place on Earth under the canopy—a city, for example. As Earth rotated, there would be a regular change of distance between that city and the canopy. As the density of dust and debris hitting the atmosphere over that city changes, the sound the city heard also would change—louder when there was more dust closer to canopy, softer when there was less, farther from canopy."

"Am I imagining it right or what?" Solon asked. "It'd be like six hours of inhaling, six hours of exhaling—a god that breathed twice a day."

George said, "That's right. The canopy's tidal cycle would be no different from the ocean tides. It would rise and fall twice a day."

Khufu murmured, "Six hours? Wouldn't that be difficult to distinguish?"

George opened his mouth to answer, but Arjuna motioned him to remain silent. "Why would it be difficult?" Arjuna asked. "Buried in darkness, scared to death, we would be listening attentively to every sound for clues. If we had been on the canopied earth, I am certain that within a few days we would have picked up the pattern and quickly determined that whatever had stretched over the skies was breathing slowly, like a giant."

Khufu grumbled, "Then your ancestors should have said God breathed twice a day. Wouldn't they? Did they?"

Arjuna shrugged his shoulders. George said, "Let's think about this one. Apparently, the creation myth talks only about breathing, not its frequency. Could there be some magnetic effects superimposed on tidal effects to make the breathing seem more frequent? I don't know. The only fact we know is that at any given point on Earth, there would have been a regular change in the distance between the canopy and the earth. It would create a regular, rhythmic sound."

"Does this mean the breathing was strong in the beginning, then died out when the canopy changed from chaotic to ordered?"

George replied, "Yes, I think so—though remember, there'd be more encounters with the swarm when the canopy would become chaotic again. The hard-breathing god would return every time Earth interacted with the swarm."

Solon blurted, "And later, when the light reached the interior, everyone would see that the shell was moving in and out just like a chest. Wow! That would be another way of breathless breathing."

As though he already had known what Solon had pointed out, George said, "No doubt, seeing the in-and-out movement would have reinforced the breathing model. With the polar sun, they could see the canopy's chest moving in and out. But still, I side with Khufu. Why didn't the Indians say God breathed twice a day? The movements were definitely twice a day."

Arjuna said, "I believe I have an answer. ... Consider breathing. How many times does a person breathe, say, in a minute?"

"It depends," Solon quickly replied. "He could be walking or running."

"*That* is the answer," Arjuna said, smiling. "God's breathing would also depend on His exertion. My ancestors couldn't say for sure that He breathed just twice a day. The next day, He might run and breathe harder. In fact, the sound of breathing did cease once the canopy became less chaotic. So the only certain thing they could say was that He breathed. And *that*, they said."

"It is true," Khufu mumbled. "They lacked precedent. They could not be sure of how often God would normally breathe in a day."

It was not late, but in the dim basement light, Arjuna seemed even more pale. We worried about his health. Everyone wanted to end the meeting so that he could go home and rest.

Khufu got up and stretched.

Enoch rose halfway from his chair but then sat back, frowning, and said, "Can we take a few more minutes?"

Khufu grumbled and sat down.

Enoch looked at the table a few seconds before he said, "I wasn't going to say anything more, at least not today, but I feel I am hiding something, and it's not fair. It doesn't seem right."

We didn't know what to say. We waited for Enoch to explain.

"For the past few weeks I have constantly hoped that there would be no canopy in the Torah, that this holy text would be different from the *Rig-veda* and the Pyramid Texts. I truly wanted nothing ever to be found in the Torah, thus demonstrating—proving—that it came from a different source, that it came from God, not from an attempt to explain a canopied earth."

Arjuna said, "I have the same concern. Obviously, there are some things in the *Rig-veda* that look like the canopy features. But I hope the *Rig-veda* is not all canopy information. Alongside the canopy information, I expect a divine aspect independent of the canopy."

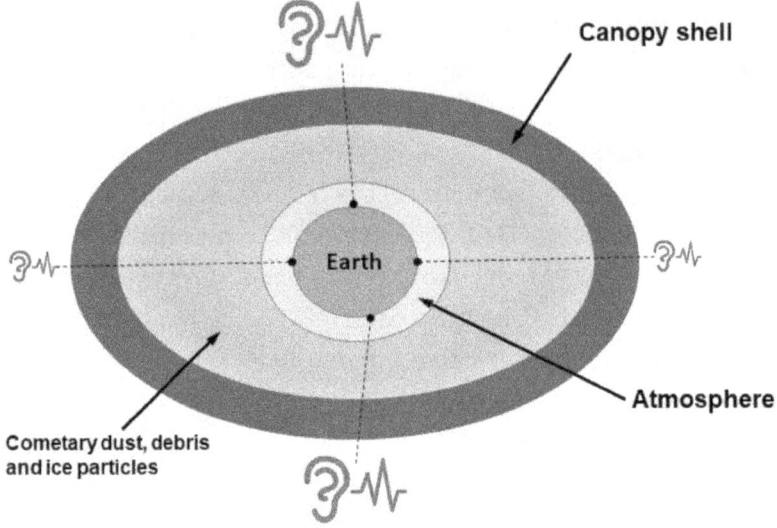

Canopy shell

Earth

Atmosphere

Cometary dust, debris and ice particles

In total darkness, a person would hear the canopy's breathing sound as Earth's rotation brought him closer to the canopy and then took him away in a cycle that repeated every six hours. Later, when a dim reddish light shined through the polar circle, he also could see the in-and-out motion of the canopy. The chest of God moved with the sound of breathing.

—Arjuna

Enoch swallowed hard and said, "Perhaps that's the best I can hope for. So here it is, the first piece of canopy information from the Torah."

Solon leaned toward him and said, "That's great!"

"Let me read a verse from the book of Genesis, chapter one, verse two: 'And the Spirit of God was hovering over the face of the waters.'"[17]

"We just learned that the Indians saw God breathing," Solon said. "Are you saying the Hebrews also saw the breathing and modeled it as the spirit of God?"

"No, I am not. The Hebrew word translated here as spirit is *ruah*. It also means breath."

"Breath?" George and Solon blurted simultaneously.

Enoch continued. "We already know the chaotic canopy brought a constant downpour into the atmosphere. Almost all the falling debris was ice. When it entered the atmosphere, it melted and created a constant downpour of water. My ancestors saw the breathing of God, but they also saw a heavy shower falling incessantly. So whatever was breathing was also watery. Whatever the breathing was, it happened on the face of lots of water."

"Another beautifully logical model!" George said. "If you looked at the canopy moving to and fro like a celestial tide, and from it a constant downpour soaked you to the bone, how would *you* describe it?"

"A celestial ocean, a celestial body of waters," Solon said, nodding earnestly.

"So logical," said George.

Enoch spoke with undisguised emotion. "My distant ancestors described the domain of breathing as 'waters.' Apparently, they didn't pay much attention to the breathing sound or assumed that once they said 'breath,' we'd know there would be an accompanying sound and an up-and-down motion. So the breath of God was moving back and forth on the watery canopy face. Anyhow, that's how I see it at this moment."

Solon shook his head and said, "I have read the first chapter of Genesis a thousand times. Not *once* did I think to ask what was meant by spirit or waters. That is *so* poor!"

"We've said enough about God's breathing," George said, "but not as much about the waters on which the breathing took place. I am of the opinion that the Hebrews meant more than just lots of water falling down. I bet they also saw the chaotic band's vortical motion—the tube-like, belt-like celestial rivers. Yes, those sights would have resembled rivers going round and round about the earth. The vortical tubes that made up the canopy shell would not yet be like ordered bands. *That* would happen later. But even initially, there would be a number of river-like vortical tubes, belts, whatever you want to call them. The movement would resemble rivers, visible in the first appearance of the reddish polar light.

"Just think of it! Combine the whirling vortical rivers and the incessant celestial downpour. You'd also reach the conclusion of 'waters' as a canopy model. The Hebrews didn't want to call them rivers, simply because the word 'river' does not imply a circular flow of water onto itself. So 'breath on the face of waters' was the best representation of what they saw. I'd say they were superb. They captured the facts without saying anything to confuse the reader with the earthly landscape."

Arjuna repositioned the book he was holding open on his chest and said, "I am looking at the Bible, chapter 1 of Genesis, first verse. It starts with the canopy's chaos and darkness. Let me read it: 'In the beginning God created the heavens and the earth. The earth was without form, and void; and darkness was on the face of the deep.'[18] Isn't this the same? Do you see the same chaos and darkness the Indians saw? Like my ancestors, the Hebrews talk about chaos and darkness before they mention the breath of God."

The comparison revived Solon. "It *is* the same, the same damned thing observed and reported by two groups of bananaheads. It's obvious. 'Heavens' is the Hebrew word for the canopy. Buried in darkness, with muddy water falling from the skies, who could see anything? You didn't have to be a Jew to know that at that moment the world was devoid of anything that gave shape and form to life."

Enoch murmured, "I hope that in the Torah, this is all there is about the canopy."

Our reserve of nervous energy had run out. Arjuna needed George's help to get out of his chair.

Both joy and despair showed on the faces of my friends. Most regretted that we might be destroying things held dear by others for thousands of years. Only Solon and George could laugh at such concerns.

I imagined Solon saying, "That's life. Change is the shit of life. It happens."

I agreed. Change was the embodiment of the flow of knowledge. Without it, life could not go on, for humans or any other being. Yet accommodating the new knowledge was unfathomably hard.

13

In Search of the Wise One

It was Monday morning, and John was in heaven. He now had microphones in the house's bedroom, guest room, and basement. He had heard his targets talk on all three channels. When Roughie's wife sent him to the basement to bring up the teacups and dishes from Sunday's party, John heard him complaining. It was music to his ears. He was going to hear every word in the next basement meeting.

John finally felt tired enough to go to bed, but his eyes were barely closed when a dreadful thought occurred to him. What if the guys—the terrorists—who had put in the microphones came and took them out?

"The sons of bitches know someone has the equipment!" he shouted as he got out of the bed and slumped into a chair, holding his head between his hands.

He took a shower to calm himself down and think clearly.

What would the terrorists do?

Breaking into Roughie's house in the daytime would be dangerous. The neighbors might see and call the police. At night the neighbors would be sleeping, but intruders would risk waking Roughie and his wife.

"When would *I* go in?" he asked himself, trying to put himself in their shoes.

The terrorists knew as much about Roughie's schedule as he did. The best time to break in would be Tuesday morning. Not only would Roughie be at work, but most Tuesdays his wife went shopping. If it were John, he would plant or take out the microphones then.

Grudgingly, he went to bed. He had no idea what he would do to stop them.

Tuesday morning came. John sat watching the flow of people and traffic. The men and some women in the neighborhood went to work, and about an hour later, Roughie's wife headed out to shop. About the time John thought most opportune for a stealth operation, a white van came down the street and turned into Roughie's driveway. Two men in white coveralls got out. One pulled a small ladder from the back of the vehicle, and both walked to the back of the house. John felt helpless. Calling the cops would not help. They probably had a work order that they'd claim was issued to the wrong address, and others would come right back until they got the microphones. Worse, if he reported it, they might find out who John was and where he lived. He could be their next target.

He put on the headphones and switched between channels to see what they were doing. All he heard was the shuffling of feet. Then as quickly as they had arrived, the men returned to the van and drove off. He could hear the van changing gears on all three channels. He was straining to hear any words they might speak when what sounded like a bomb suddenly went off in John's ears.

"You sons of bitches!" he yelled and threw off the headphones. One of the terrorists had smashed the microphones. Cursing in pain, he imagined the terrorists laughing out loud. They had gotten even.

An hour later, his ears still ringing, John was back to thinking through the situation methodically. He had to learn about the new group that had entered into his domain. Who were they, and what did they do? He remembered the man's wallet and the medallion. He had gone through the wallet multiple times, and he'd found nothing significant.

He picked up the medallion and wondered about its design, a circle with a symbolic eye inside it. Two lines came out of the eye, one straight, the other a spiral. The outer circle had the shape of a hillside leaning inward. "This could mean anything," he said, agonizing.

He put the medallion down and surveyed the wallet, again. He had looked and found nothing but a driver's license, an insurance card, and a few dollars. He felt the urge to tear it to pieces and obeyed the impulse. As he tore the third flap, a square piece of paper the size of a dime tumbled out and fell to the floor. He had not noticed it previously. It must have been hidden inside the corner of one of the pockets. He carefully tore the wallet into smaller and smaller pieces but found nothing more.

The square paper was neatly folded at each corner. John lifted the four corners and saw writing, tiny and indecipherable, like nothing he had ever seen before.

He picked up the phone and called a buddy who had joined the antiterrorism task force after 9/11.

"I need help," John said.

"Anything I can do," the friend said, "so long as I don't lose my job."

They both laughed.

"I'm looking for someone that most terrorists would think is smart … wise."

For a few seconds there was silence on the other end of the line. "Are you looking for mullahs we suspect of having links to terrorism?"

"Not really," John said. "I'm looking for an expert in Middle Eastern secret societies, someone who understands symbols, language, and theories."

"Why the sudden interest in that kind of shit? You were never the intellectual type."

"I'm writing a book," John lied. "I want to give it a little different angle from just cops and robbers."

"What about the library? They can show you all sorts of books about secret societies."

"I want to interview someone unique, not just copy what someone else wrote."

The silence returned.

"Are you there?" John asked sheepishly.

"I know this guy I met in strategic planning a year ago. He's an expert on the origin of fundamentalist groups in the Middle East. I'll see if he can find somebody. Now remember … the name I get might be for someone in the Middle East. Don't tell me you don't like it and want someone in town."

"I won't."

Two days later, the phone rang. John's antiterrorism friend had come through. The name Pasha Jamal did not sound impressive, but the friend said the man was one of the best—and the only expert in the US. He was a four-hour flight away.

John called Pasha Jamal, and the old man's cooperative spirit impressed him. He was more than willing to talk to John but would not make a specific appointment because of his poor health.

"I apologize for the inconvenience," Pasha said in a trembling voice, "but I have a kidney disease that periodically disorients me and sends me to the hospital. It's good you phoned now, while I feel well. Perhaps we can talk now?"

"I need to show you some symbols and writing."

They finally agreed that John would be there the next day, and if they could not meet, John would stay in town until Pasha's health improved.

John hung up the phone, wondering about human differences. An old man, perhaps on the verge of death, had apologized for his health. John could not understand such behavior.

That afternoon John was on a plane to Boston to be at the old man's house early Wednesday. When he arrived at the address the next day, a young man introduced himself as Pasha's grandson and led him to a room where the old man sat comfortably in a chair. John couldn't hide his happiness at finding the frail man well. He wanted to rush right to the medallion and the square paper, but Pasha wanted to know something about him before they talked business. John told him about his police days, his retirement, and his concern about terrorism.

"Very sad," Pasha mumbled. "So many people see the achievement of their goals in the destruction of others."

"Terrorism must be stopped," John asserted.

"But more than that," Pasha replied, "our constant preparation to wage war must come to an end."

"But we have to defend ourselves."

"That is also the terrorist's logic. So long as we see a need to destroy others to maintain our way of life, we hurt not only others but also ourselves. When two men or two societies point weapons at each other, neither is justified. They are both to blame."

Pasha coughed and turned a bit pale. John worried because he didn't have the luxury of talking about the human tendency for organized violence. He wanted to know what the medallion and the writing meant.

Pasha seemed to read his mind. "Tell me what brings you here."

John took the medallion from his pocket and carefully laid it in front of Pasha.

The old man's eyes widened in surprise. "Where did you get this?"

John did not reply but reached into his wallet and took out the small square paper and placed it next to the medallion.

"God help us all!" Pasha exclaimed in astonishment. "Do you know what you are putting in front of me?"

"No, I don't. That's why I'm here."

"Only the dead give up these treasures. You must have killed the owner."

"I did not. I suspected him of doing violence to others. I knocked him out and took these. I need to know which group he belongs to and their purpose."

Pasha didn't look good. He was growing more pale and excited at the same time. He began hyperventilating.

John ran to the door and called for the grandson. Almost instantly, a half dozen men and women swarmed around Pasha. One gave him a pill. Another gave him a cup of tea. Another massaged his shoulders.

"Should I leave?" John asked the grandson.

"Not yet."

Color returned to Pasha's face, and his first words were an apology. John was embarrassed.

Then Pasha sent everyone out, and they were alone again.

"What you have shown me," Pasha said, "is most rare. I have only heard of these things from my masters, who learned from theirs. None had seen these items with his own eyes. The medallion is from a secret society whose name we do not know, but we call them the Watchers. The writing on the paper is in humanity's first sacred language, older than Sanskrit or Hebrew. This tiny square paper is the password seal. It lets the owner into the inner circle of the most secret society on earth."

"Can you read it and tell me what it means?"

"No. I have seen and know a few words of the ancient sacred language, but only the Watchers can read the password. Not only is it primal; it's also coded."

"Do you know their secret?"

"It is said their secret is the knowledge of God. It is said they are the guardians who will choose the time to release knowledge of God, when men are ready to understand it."

None of this made sense to John. A secret society that held exceptional knowledge yet eavesdropped on a bunch of people with nothing divine about them?

"Do you suppose the person who had the medallion and the paper got them from someone else?" John asked.

"Perhaps, but that does not change their value and meaning. It matters little who has them. What matters is where they point."

"Can you tell me where to find this group or, better, where I can use the password to the inner circle?"

Pasha smiled, shook his head, and said, "My grandson tells me about something called a black hole. It is very powerful and pulls in anything near it, yet it cannot be seen. The only way you can sense it is to look at the pattern of spiraling matter around it being pulled into oblivion. The same is true of the Watchers. Every once in a while, either accidentally or on purpose, they release a bit of knowledge and create a new movement in human societies. People like Buddha, Mohammed, Moses, and Jesus either were members of the Watchers with an assignment or were individuals the Watchers chose to disseminate new knowledge."

"I don't buy any of that," John said. "Not for Jesus. He was the son of God and came to the earth to forgive our sins."

"You don't read your Bible well, do you?" Pasha challenged. "Read the Gospels. Nowhere will you see the phrase 'son of God.' Jesus constantly calls himself the son of man—a human being."

"I really don't need this."

Pasha paused, took a sip of tea, and said, "Let us not get sidetracked by what I said about Jesus. Let us return to the Watchers. More than releasing knowledge through religion, they release it to secret societies. Secret societies, more than anything else, point to the invisible Watchers."

"Where do I find the offshoots?"

"They are everywhere. Have you heard of the secret society that worshipped Baphomet?"

"No."

"But you have surely heard of the Knights Templar."

"I think so. Weren't they the Christian warriors that took Jerusalem back from the Arabs?"

"They did that and more. They also found some of the Watchers' knowledge repositories while digging tunnels under the Temple Mount, searching for treasure. The Watchers turned the Knights into the Baphomet secret society. The name was an encoded form of the name Sophia, which means wisdom and knowledge."

"So that is how the Templars became powerful."

"Never underestimate the power of knowledge."

"But the king of France destroyed the Templars years ago. There are no Templars to teach me about the Watchers."

"I did tell you the structure is like a black hole. You know of its existence only from the material that spirals around it. The Templars are one group. Then there are the Essenes. All we know of them is from the library one of their members left behind, fifty-two wonderful books that existed nowhere else on earth but at Nag Hammadi, buried in earth in a sealed jar."

"What about the Dead Sea Scrolls?"

"The personal library of a small group and not a Watcher repository."

"You're giving me long-dead secret societies," John objected.

"What about the Masons?"

John knew a little about Freemasonry and had a friend who was a Mason. He had once asked John to join, but John had declined. To him the Freemasons were the leftovers of the guilds that had set prices and controlled members, very much like today's labor unions.

"They are not a secret society," John said matter-of-factly. "I know a friend there and can become a member anytime I wish."

"Perhaps," the old man said, "but Freemasons are nevertheless one of the branches that emanated from the Watchers years ago. In prehistoric times they used their knowledge to build structures like the great pyramid of Giza. Without them the Egyptians could build only poorly designed pyramids. But the Masons were ready to receive the true knowledge of pyramid building—and the Watchers provided it. When men began to develop an understanding of science, a Freemason created examples of scientific institutions by starting the British Royal Society. Perhaps you do not know that a number of US presidents, including Washington, Jackson, Roosevelt, and Truman, were Masons. The art of leadership and the notion of democratic government are among the ideas the Watchers released when humanity was ready."

"You're telling me the Freemasons started as a secret society, an extension of the Watchers."

"The Lodges and Temples you can join are branches of a much thicker and more secret trunk, at whose roots are the invisible Watchers.

That is why the Watchers are known by another name: the Bloodline Keepers."

"Where do I find the Bloodline Keepers?"

"Wherever you find the Watchers. Both names imply a simple truth about the human societies. There is ancient—divine—knowledge available to men, and we are quite good at destroying it. Thus the need for Keepers and Watchers."

"They are like librarians then."

"Perhaps, but with universal responsibility over thousands of years."

Pasha told John about other secret societies that had emerged from the Watchers, including many John had not heard of and some he had but knew nothing about. They all hid the secret of their black-hole origin.

The two men talked for almost two hours, and John was just beginning to scratch the surface of knowledge-based secret societies when an old woman came into the room, apologized for the interruption, and told Pasha it was time for his nap.

John assessed the situation. He had taxed Pasha's frail body. The older man's mind was willing to talk for hours, but his body could not manage this.

John said goodbye as he gently shook Pasha's hand and thanked him for all the knowledge he had given him.

"See you tomorrow morning," Pasha said gently. "And oh, if you wonder where I stand, I am a Freemason."

John smiled. He had an insider who could tell him a lot about the Watchers.

At the hotel John reviewed the next day's agenda. He would keep the meeting short, no more than an hour, but would focus on documents he could read, especially anything Pasha could lend him. If he read and learned, he would be in a better position to acquire Pasha's deeper knowledge.

As he was beginning to think of sleep, the phone rang. It was Pasha's grandson.

"I am sorry to disturb you," the young man said, "but we had to take

Pasha to the hospital. We don't know when he will be home. I will call tomorrow and give you an update."

That was bad news but not unexpected. Pasha had told him very clearly that he cycled between home and hospital. John hoped the hospital stay would be short. He didn't want to go back home and listen to "can OP" gibberish. He wanted Pasha's knowledge.

The next day, he sat all morning next to the phone, waiting for the grandson's call. About two in the afternoon, he could not take the suspense of not knowing and called Pasha's house. The grandson answered, but before he said a word, John heard the wailing in the background. His knees buckled, and he couldn't stop himself from falling to the floor in a heap.

The grandson confirmed it. "I am sorry, but Pasha is dead."

John hung up the phone. Whom else could he find? He did not know.

"Oh hell," he said, trying to comfort himself, "I don't need to find the Watchers. All I need is to watch the basement, and the Watchers will come to me."

But despite the positive spin and though he had spoken with the man for only a couple of hours, he felt as if part of his heart had been cut out and thrown away. He missed the old man miserably.

14

The Challenge of Subtle Questions

A week passed without event, and the weekend arrived on schedule. Arjuna's cheeks showed some color, and his step, the tiniest bounce. Enoch seemed normal, which comforted me, since I planned to focus on the Torah. Would he see his ingenious ancestors recording canopy observations or only the loss of a god who had ruled undeniably supreme for millennia?

My wife stood beside me, smiling nobly. She had prepared an excellent meal, mainly for Arjuna. I wondered if, with a full belly, Enoch would be less concerned with the fate of the Torah and its god.

We moved to the basement. My wife brought the coffee, tea, and cookies. An extra dish of halvah and baklava meant special treatment. I smiled at her as she set the plate on the table. I wondered if she had sensed my premonition of trouble.

We basement dwellers, like the ancients before us, had stolen a glance at a canopied world in prehistory and were swamped by what we had found. We had yet to understand how they had seen the canopy, or whether they had understood it. Nonetheless, everything from them was before us, in the sacred texts and myths that quantified prehistory.

Some patterns were evident.

When the writers lacked full understanding, they had differed in expression. Some, like the Indians, relied on explicit questions to express their lack of understanding and challenged others to find a better model, a more profound meaning. Others, like the Egyptians, rarely raised questions. What they had was all they had. They could not have done more.

Then there were the Hebrews—no explicit questions like the Indians, but no lack of questions like the Egyptians. They had played the middle ground and arranged the records of their observations proficiently to force the reader to raise questions about prehistory. They knew human nature well: Let the reader decide. Does he need more from the text, or is he satisfied with what he has? They posed the facts to satisfy both needs. For those who wanted to dig deeper, understand better, questions would subtly emerge.

When I expressed these thoughts aloud, Enoch listened patiently, though he appeared to be fighting off a sense of threat.

"What do you mean?" Enoch said. "How does the Torah ask unspoken questions?" He saw the sacred book as an exposed target, himself its lone defender.

I sought to soften the blow and said, "Instead of asking direct questions, as the Indians did, or instead of giving everything as if facts like the Egyptians, the Hebrews related their canopy experience in a way that forced the hearer or reader to come up with questions."

"I still don't get it."

"What he means …"

I interrupted Solon and said, "Forget about what I mean. What about an example?"

"An example it is," Solon mumbled.

We started with canopy lighting. In general, sunlight could reach the interior only through the polar opening, which initially was covered by dust and debris. Only a scattered, reddish light reached the earth. Later, when the canopy had formed bands, the polar opening would become mostly free of dust and debris, and shafts of golden sunlight would reach the interior, reflected earthward from the canopy shell's interior.

Arjuna said, "I understand that. Light has to get through the polar opening. The body of the canopy doesn't let sunlight reach the earth directly. Everything gets reflected, and no direct sunlight, red or gold, hits the earth. So where is the hidden question? George?"

"Right!" George said. "Whether it's reddish from the dust or golden, the canopy shell blocks the sunlight. It can't shine directly on Earth. The polar sun shines on the canopy shell interior and then reflects earthward. Except! Except for shafts of light from the cyclonic vortices. They could hit Earth directly, but most light would come through the polar opening and reflect earthward."

I smiled nervously and said, "As the planet rotated, people would have moved from the canopy day to the darkness of the canopy night. They would have seen the polar sun rise and set."

"So?" Solon moaned.

"The polar sun"—my voice quivered—"would not rise and set the way we are accustomed to. Under the canopy, the sun would not rise in the east. It would rise in the west."

George thought deeply and then drew something in the air with his right hand, looked at it, and said, "Wait a second! Wait a *second*. Yes! It *does* rise in the west. The canopy switches directions."

"I can see that too!" Solon reacted, equally excited. "The light *does* arrive from the opposite direction."

I picked up a paper pad and drew a circle. I wrote "West" at the bottom of the circle and "East" at the top. I drew arrows toward the left of the circle and wrote "Sunlight" above the arrows. I said the circle was Earth. It was not fixed. It rotated clockwise.

"You mean counterclockwise," George rejoined.

"Okay. Counterclockwise." I gathered my thoughts and went on.

"Today, as Earth rotates, we are first brought into the path of sunlight from the east. East is defined by the first light we see. Under—"

George grabbed the pad impatiently and drew a larger circle around Earth. He labeled it "Canopy." At the top and bottom of the canopy, he drew two smaller circles tilted toward the sunlight, wrote "Polar circle" by the top circle, and then extended the line from the arrows to the larger circle and deflected the line earthward. With a self-satisfied grin, he said, "As you see, under the canopy, there is a radical departure from traditional lighting. The canopy changes the path of sunlight. Instead of shining in front of the planet, the reflected sunlight first reaches Earth at the back."

Solon noted, "Sunrise and sunset are reversed."

George held his drawing up and said, "Just look. As Earth rotates, the first light of sun is seen where west used to be when there was no canopy. With the canopy, people saw the polar sun rise and set opposite to what had happened before the canopy."

Khufu shook his head. "Let me see if I understand it. If I used to see the sun rise over the mountain range to the left of my house, under the canopy I would see the polar sun set behind that same mountain."

"Exactly." George smiled. "That is how you know for sure the sun's direction has reversed."

Arjuna said, "What you have told me so far makes sense. Fits the physical structure of a canopied earth. But I have yet to hear something from the Torah about how night and day reversed."

Enoch said, "I was going to raise the same question. I am obviously familiar with the Torah, but I don't recall any mention of day and night swapping places."

Like everyone else, the Hebrews had observed the sunrise and sunset reversal. Seeing the event was not the point. Everyone in prehistory had seen it. Everyone had recognized the drastic change. Surely many had recorded and reported it, but almost none of those records survived. The challenge had been how to record the prehistoric event permanently for future generations.

Those who had observed the event had no fixed point of reference. They had looked at a polar sun radically different from the sun disk. The canopy had undoubtedly taxed and often exhausted their ability to explain their surroundings. They could not have written, "On a canopied world, sunrise and sunset are reversed."

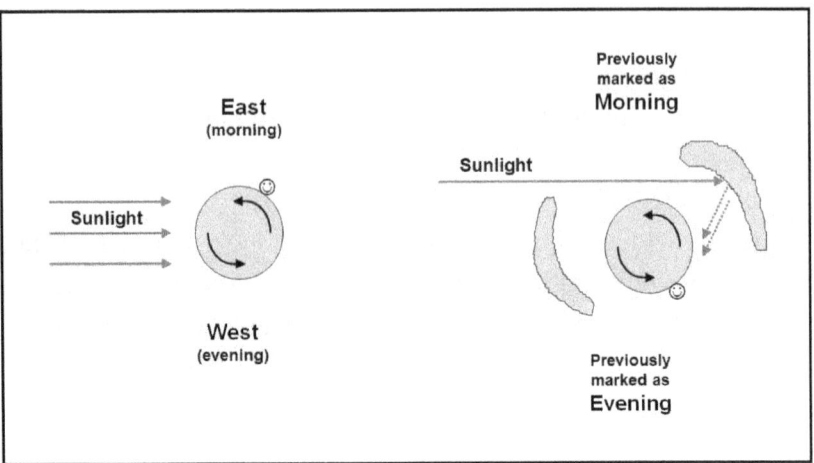

Without a canopy, the human (☺) would first see the sunlight in the direction designated as east. It might mark the left window of a house or a range of mountains on the right side, where the first rays of sunlight touched first. Such markers physically defined east. As Earth rotated, the human (☺) would see the sunlight fade in the direction designated as west.

The canopy allowed only the reflected sunlight to reach Earth. As Earth rotated, the first sunlight reached the human (☺) from the direction he had known as west. All the physical markers the human had associated with dawn, like a window of the house or a mountain range over which the sun used to rise, now witnessed the setting sun. The sunrise would have appeared from the opposite direction of where it used to appear in a world without a canopy. The polar sun would have set in the direction the human had known as east. The distinct east and west direction reversal is undeniable. The polar sun of the canopied earth rose and set opposite to the rising and setting of the sun in the blue-skied, canopy-free Earth.

—Rafi

At the time, the people would have had no concept of Earth inside a canopy. How could they tell the story of their canopy experience?

I decided to test Solon. "How does one report the obvious reversal of night and day? How would *you* do it?"

"I'd wet my pants first. I wouldn't initially think the sun had reversed. Given all the chaotic stuff, I might think the earth had tumbled over—that soon I would fall off and get creamed!"

We all laughed at his vivid imagination.

He then got serious. "What would have happened if as an ancient man I had recorded only the facts of the event? Say I faithfully recorded it: 'sun rises in the west and sets in the east.' What would happen next?"

George said, "I can relate to that. It would be seen as an initial theory. Science routinely looks at old records as the beginning of a theory and often replaces them with a better theory or experiment. Correcting a deficient understanding of reality is the norm of science. So today, thousands of years after you wrote, 'The sun rises in the west and sets in the east,' I would look at it and say, 'That's a mistake. Somebody either didn't understand directions or made the wrong entry in the record.' That's it. Your factual record would not survive. It would be rewritten, superseded."

"You're right," Solon sighed. "After the canopy disappeared, any moron would see that record as inaccurate—even if it were in a sacred text, a divine statement. Anyone coming across it would call it wrong. People would ultimately change the text and make it right, so that the sun rises in the east."

I nodded. "So factual recording would never make it. It would never remain intact to reach the future generations."

"Perhaps that is why I can't recall anything in the *Rig-veda* about direction reversal," Arjuna said. He then turned to Khufu and asked, "Have you seen anything in the Egyptian sources?"

"Nothing I can recall."

We were discussing the tendency to change what did not seem right. This was not something new. The ancient Hebrews had been well aware of the issue. They knew human behavior well. If they had reported precisely what they had seen while Earth was under the canopy, future generations would have readily assumed a mistake in the sacred text. To set the record right, anything "inaccurate" would have been changed. With that in mind, how could they have designed the text to keep the facts intact and convey the essence of their experience? The ancient Hebrews had done just that.

Enoch said, "I think I know where you're going. You'll soon say the Torah—Genesis, chapter one—says that 'evening came and morning came.' You'll claim it says so purposefully to capture the reversal of sunrise and sunset without exposing the record to corrections."

Without any pleasantries I said, "That's right."

"Wait one minute," said Solon excited. "Let me think. 'Evening came and morning came.' I see it! And I'll be damned if it doesn't beat the living daylights out of saying that east and west were reversed!"

Almost instantaneously, George joined in to acknowledge the ingenious articulation of the reversal of morning and evening. "Wow! It begins the day at evening." Then he turned to me and asked, "Is *this* one of the subtle questioning designs you were talking about?"

I nodded.

He whispered, "I feel it. I feel the urge to ask why the evening comes first and not morning."

It was not an explicit question, but anyone who read it should ask himself how it could be possible.

"*There.* There you have it, the subtle question embedded in the text," George rambled.

"I sense the emergence of the same question in my mind," Khufu said. "More interesting, I feel no urge to change it. If it said something like 'the sun rose in the west,' I would feel no question but would immediately sense the urge to change what I know is wrong."

Solon turned to Enoch and asked, "Why didn't the scholars recognize this earlier?"

"I am sure they looked at it," Enoch said. "I even remember the typical answer. Since darkness ruled the first day of creation and light appeared on the second day, the evening of the first day came ahead of the morning of the second day."

Arjuna said, "That sounds okay. The first day was essentially all evening, wasn't it? There was no morning."

Enoch murmured, "Yes, something like that. The standard line of reasoning, I suppose."

"That doesn't make any sense," Solon said, shaking his head. "Here in the Bible it clearly says the evening and morning of day one. Then it goes on to the evening and morning of day two, and so on. Where is there any mixing of the evening of the first day with the morning of the second? I see none."

Enoch did not want to duel with Solon. "I didn't say the biblical interpretation was correct," he said. "I only gave the usually offered explanation. Perhaps you are right. Why do I hesitate to give credit to my ancestors? Like you just said, saying things directly would have risked misunderstanding and misinterpretation. They were bright enough to anticipate it." He thought it over a minute and said, "Now I see. The writers of Genesis *repeated* the 'evening came and morning came' as a refrain. The force of the refrain nullifies the logic of the darkness of the first day coming before the light of the second."

Solon said insistently, "It wouldn't be reasonable even for the first day. Even on the first day itself, as the Torah explicitly says, there is both an evening and a morning. Do we just throw away the morning of the first day and say it was too dark to be morning?"

Arjuna waved Solon to be quiet and said, "A refrain? You said the statement that 'evening came and morning came' was used as a refrain? How interesting! The *Rig-veda* hymns regularly use refrains for emphasis."

Khufu added, "Even more so in the Egyptian texts. Repetition is the norm. It is often so excessive, it gets boring. Distracts from the main theme."

"There's little repetition in Genesis," Enoch said. "Limited use of refrains. The refrain 'evening came and morning came' is unique. So it has more significance as a divider of the days of creation. At the end of each day, we hear 'evening came and morning came.' There is definitely emphasis there. I think the force of the refrain seeks to balance any inherent vagueness. If the ancients had used anything vaguer, the meaning would have been lost. If they had been more explicit, it would have looked wrong and been corrected. The refrain itself amplifies the information in two ways. First, it demands attention. Second, it counters the temptation to correct."

Arjuna said, "I easily see what would happen if it was said once. It would be either ignored or changed. But said repeatedly, especially at important junctures, it leaves no doubt—not a mistake, not something to be changed. Structured so tightly, it begs for examination. The repetition amplifies the subtle question: why did the evening come first on every day of creation?"

"Anything as simple as sunrise and sunset would have been vulnerable to criticism," Solon observed. "If it contradicted what men knew post-canopy, it would have been changed or ignored. So the challenge was to make the record non-contradicting, self-sustaining, and—most important—question-raising. I am amazed by the ancient Hebrews. They achieved the seemingly impossible with only two words: evening and morning."

Even Enoch could not hide his unavoidable joy. An ingenious people had meticulously preserved an astonishing feature of the prehistoric canopy. No one else's record had survived. Nothing remained from the Indians, the Egyptians, or others about the way night and day had reversed.

We all shared Enoch's joy of renewed discovery. The Hebrews had held down-to-earth views of man and his nature. They knew themselves well. They knew they did not have all the answers.

Amazingly, they had searched for answers in the distant future. They had devised an ingenious scheme to convey a simple canopy fact: that the polar sun had risen in the west. A simple but discriminating use of *evening* and *morning* masked the sunrise and sunset and shaped the story to veil a subtle question. They had lowered the risk of the record's premature loss and preempted anyone who might call the ancient record wrong and ignorantly make it "right." The Hebrews had provided the best evidence that looking at the canopy might have seemed easy, but telling others about it never was.

Exhaustion ruled. The day had gone, along with our energy. We had talked much longer than anyone intended. Solon joked about the absence of baklava and halvah being a divine signal that he and the others should pack up their things and go home.

Nothing that day had changed my view of the human condition.

We were time travelers who were bringing truths to light through words, wisely or deceptively, for those who would come after us. The words of the Torah had traveled for thousands of years like a celestial missile seeking their target, the human being, one who would look at "evening came, and morning came" and ask why—and then take a step beyond just asking why. Undeniably, we had done that.

We were possibly the first not to dismiss the question raised by the Torah. No mere explaining away. No urge to change words to make it "right." Yet how could we take any credit? The difficult task had been to design and put together a time capsule that would travel intact across thousands of years, a durable questioning package with an ingeniously ambiguous message. The ancient Hebrews had done it.

Enoch finally sensed the human ingenuity and marveled, "The day they came up with the refrain, the biggest smiles must have adorned their faces!"

The rest of us could not have agreed more. They had successfully launched a time traveler, assured to last a very long time. They had prudently counted on the ingenuity of others to decipher and solve the celestial riddle they had posed. How did they know someone would eventually look at the question and perceive the sun rising and setting differently under the canopy?

They didn't. They knew the question only. They knew it well. If they posed the question, someone else might have the answer. They counted on that.

Our joy of discovery was mitigated by the realization that we were not as bright as our ancestors.

I suddenly realized I had been thinking for too long.

Solon hissed, "You're lost somewhere in the past, I bet."

"No, not the past." I smiled softly. "Just thinking about thousands of years from now."

He laughed. "Who cares? Thousands of years from now, we'll have thrown Earth away like that Mustang of yours. We'll be wearing shit-eating grins on a planet light-years from here."

Khufu overheard and asked, "What happened to the Mustang?"

"My daughter has it."

"Poor girl," George chortled. "If you paid more attention to the present, she'd do better than a Rustang."

I nodded and smiled. He was right. The Mustangs did rust like crazy.

"So you passed the Mustang on to your daughter," Arjuna said, rising gingerly. "Khufu could have given her a camel. More reliable."

"We gotta go," Solon blurted while laughing.

They all nodded in unison, and the pack broke up.

We would play again next week.

15

The Science of "What the Heck Is This?"

The holidays and travel could have wreaked havoc with our regular meetings but did not. Prudently, despite our interest in the canopy, we recognized and respected family time and the needs of others. For two weeks my wife, busy with other things, could not accommodate lunch, and thus we met in the afternoon without sharing lunch. Waiting was not easy for a mind restless to think about the canopy.

It was another afternoon, and we were going to talk about the canopy again. I felt a mystic air of power, the magical sensation of breaking through boundaries beyond which no one had ever gone before. And here was the beauty of it: we knew so little. When it came to scientific modeling, most of us didn't know straight up from sideways, yet that hadn't kept us from giving a powerful, blow-by-blow account of canopy-related events. Participating in such an exceptional thing seemed to bestow power. The feeling grew enormously when we were together, deep underground, free from daily life's constraints.

In place of the usual gratifying lunch, a larger than usual spread of baklava and halvah adorned the tea and coffee tray and promised more than just a pleasantly spirited get-together.

We settled into our chairs and waited for my wife to finish the last touches on the table. She lingered on. *What is she up to?* I wondered. She had claimed to be too busy to prepare lunch but now was wasting time without concern.

As though she had read my mind, she turned around, fixed her eyes on the floor, and said, "The wives would like to know what you are doing. We don't want to interfere or join your group. But could you give us a presentation? Any time, really."

We all looked at her as if someone from an extinct canopied world had just appeared in the basement.

"We thought we could have our own discussion group," she continued.

"That'll be the day!" Solon said, almost inaudibly.

"What?" She looked in Solon's direction.

He leaned as far back into the chair as he could, shook his head, and said, "Nothing. I said … I said that'll be the way."

Everyone tried hard not to laugh.

She stared at our contorted faces and then put her hands on her hips, shot a disgusted look around the room, and left briskly.

We all knew we had seen the last plate of baklava and halvah in the basement for a while and perhaps would have no lunch for a few more weeks.

Arjuna eyed Solon coldly and said, "I don't want to criticize. I myself come from a culture that pays little attention to women, but—"

"I meant no disrespect," Solon said innocently.

Arjuna shook his head. "It has nothing to do with respect, love, or friendship. It has to do with sharing. Why are we so averse to telling our women what we are discovering? Why isn't there any woman among us?"

Khufu grinned and said, "First, to tell the wives would be to declare ourselves crazy. They'd never allow us to meet again. Second, you of all people—are you the one who will tell the wives about Osiris sticking his phallus into Isis?" His eyes bulged. Then he laughed uncontrollably, and we joined him.

After the laughter died down, Arjuna wiped his eyes and muttered, "But it is a problem. What are we going to do?"

George said, "We can prepare some sort of a seminar. It'd even be good practice for the future. You know, when we're sure of our findings, we'll have to say something to the universities or the publishers."

Arjuna nodded. "I like that. All those in favor of a seminar?"

All heads nodded in unison.

In the back of my mind, I knew no such seminar would ever come about. I loved my wife, but I also knew that men and women were socially conditioned to be different, often radically. They behaved as different beings, almost different species.

My wife saw life as a game of golf—predetermined paths; steady movement from one position to the next and calculated, premeditated actions at each; little deviation from the course when you knew how to play the game. Only one chance to act. No room for mistakes. Serious penalties for errors.

For me, life was a game of tennis—fast-paced and mistake-filled but allowing for recovery from mistakes and the chance to hit another shot and make another mistake, never knowing from where and how hard the next ball was going to come.

Our conversations often started and ended as if we knowingly exchanged the golf club for the tennis racket. Neither of us could make sense of the other's preference for a different game. Fighting on the sideline was frequently the norm. Neither of us ever won decisively.

Deep in thought, I caught a look of mischief in Solon's eyes and locked onto it. He smiled and nodded as if reading my thoughts, fully agreeing with everything.

Arjuna brought us back to the current moment. "What are we going to do today?"

We had spent several weeks on ancient records, and most were willing to spend even more, but the time was ripe for a redirect. The ancient records were about to meet the modern records.

The cometary canopy had poured down on ancients, burying them in the majesty of a colossal unknown, but the cometary swarm had not visited Earth only. In the solar system, besides Earth, another planet had received a celestial canopy. One other planet could claim to have been canopied as much as, if not more than, Earth.

I was about to take my friends on a celestial journey to visit the swarm's footprints in the solar system. Would it be as exciting as the footprints left behind in the sacred texts and myths? I wondered.

George said, "I love to focus on science. I bet there is more in science than all the sacred texts and myths put together." He was serious and nodded at length to affirm it.

I didn't want to dash his hopes but had to say, "It's not just science. There are also other records, older than science but a lot younger than the *Rig-veda*, the Torah, the Pyramid Texts, or *Theogony*."

George persisted. "But the majority has to come from science."

"Yes," I replied aversely.

I had selected two stories showing the comet's footprints. They lay at the core of science and had puzzled scientists for some time. The recognition of a cometary swarm would soon accommodate both.

I asked George, if Earth had intercepted the cometary swarm and passed through it, could Mars have done the same? He did not react verbally. Rather, he looked through his pile of books, picked one up, and looked through the index. Once he had found the page he wanted, he turned the book around so that we all could see a chart of planetary orbits.

"This is a chart of the planets orbiting the sun. Note Earth's orbit. It is inside the Mars orbit. From everything we have learned, we know the Earth–swarm encounter was soft, not hard. If it had been hard, we'd be extinct. For it to have been soft, the orbits of Earth and the swarm would have to have been nearly parallel at the points of intercept."

"Slow down!" Arjuna said. "What is this hard, soft, and near-parallel stuff?"

George hesitated for a moment, thinking, and then asked, "You've seen football on television?"

"Do you mean soccer?" Khufu asked.

"No. I mean the one played with the oval ball!"

Khufu chuckled. "Yes, I have occasionally watched it, though it would be more apt to call it wrestle-ball. How did the name 'football' get attached to that sport?"

"Forget that, will you? Just focus on the ball being passed from the quarterback to a receiver."

"I have seen that too," Khufu said. "It reminds me of dropping a loaf of bread into a basket."

"Exactly!" George exclaimed triumphantly. "The reason it lands so easily in the receiver's arms is that at the very moment it's caught, the speeds and trajectories of the ball and the receiver match. They are nearly parallel."

"Not a good example," Solon objected. "The trajectories of the ball and the receiver are not parallel, but I know what you want to say. Some portions of Earth's orbit, especially near the interception points, kind of overlap the swarm's orbit."

"Right. Not the whole orbit, but some segments nearly overlapped. Otherwise, a hard collision. Your ass would be toast."

"I have seen that too," Khufu said quietly. "The defenders on the other team hit the receiver so hard, they ruin the catch. Stupid! They have to do it all over again. I have seen them try it three times. Then they get so mad, they kick the ball to the other side and tell them, 'Okay, you don't want to play? Then *you* throw, and we'll ruin your catch.' What a game! And the crowd doesn't like it. They yell and scream all the time."

George was ready to pull his hair, and Solon howled with laughter.

"Just tell me you've got the picture," George begged.

Khufu nodded cautiously.

George drew something on the chart, wrote a couple of words, and again held up the book. He had drawn an ellipse and labeled it "swarm orbit." It intercepted Earth's orbit at its outer edge, where the two curves were almost parallel.

George pointed at the orbits and said, "Note how the swarm intercepts Mars."

Enoch looked at the chart, then at George, and back to the chart. "A wider angle for Mars. It means they are not moving parallel. A chance they might hit each other hard?"

George nodded in approval. "It doesn't mean they will definitely hit each other, but there's a higher probability they will."

"How frigging big is that probability?"

"I don't know," George said. "That's why I compared the orbits. If Earth passed through the swarm's periphery, Mars might have done just a bit worse, hitting a few large pieces. However, if Earth went through the swarm and picked up a number of big chunks, then Mars had a good chance of hitting a lot of big pieces. There's a good chance there would have been a hard, head-on collision."

The picture George had drawn implied that Mars could have been hit hard enough to cause destruction, a superb lead-in to what I was going to say about the swarm's Martian footprints.

"Assume Mars plowed through the swarm's core," I said. "What footprints would we find?"

George's eyes opened wide. He loved it. "The footprints? A canopy. No, we won't find a canopy there. It would have collapsed by now, the same as on Earth, but we'll find craters where fragments hit."

"Give me a break!" Solon moaned. "How can you tell a crater made by a cometary fragment from one made by an asteroid?"

"Can't from Earth. But you could do so on Mars. On Mars we could check the crater material and see if it resembles the cometary matter. But through telescopes from the surface of Earth, they'd look the same."

"You're not thinking hard," I said, teasing George.

Solon said, "You heard George. No way to distinguish comet collisions from others."

I asked, "Is there any difference in crater shape when a large chunk of ice creates it?"

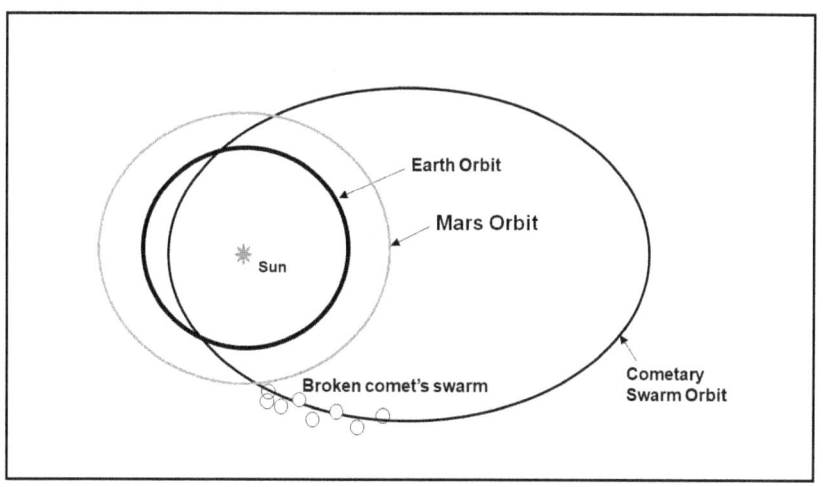

The size of the swarm meant a number of planetary intercepts. The intercept with Mars could have produced a canopy similar to Earth's. Because of the angle of intercept, Mars could have had an almost head-on encounter with the cometary fragments, resulting in a large number of impact craters on the Martian surface.

—George

"Not that I can think of," George said. "Both asteroids and comet fragments are solid matter moving at high velocities. Perhaps the crater of an icy fragment would have softer edges, but I can't be sure."

Arjuna said, "If you know something, please tell us. Don't force George to write a paper he hasn't researched."

I obeyed and took two pictures out of a folder and passed them around. "Have a look at these Martian features. They are called 'outflow channels.' Science says outflow channels formed from a sudden, huge outpouring of water from holes in the Martian surface."

Enoch looked up from the picture and said, "Not unusual. On Earth we have geysers. Water shoots out like a jet. The same could have been present on Mars. All you need is an underground reservoir."

I nodded and said, "Except for one problem: the fountain of water that shot out of Mars was many times the size of the Mississippi."

"*The river*?"

"Yes. Imagine a fountain many times the size of the Mississippi suddenly exploding out and ending as suddenly as it started. Imagine it creating the teardrop shape you see in the pictures. Does this inform us of our canopy-building comet?"

The Martian outflow channels puzzled science for a number of reasons. First, the Martian atmosphere did not accommodate liquid water. Any surface water evaporated quickly. There were no lakes or oceans on Mars to feed and maintain an underground reservoir. Science could not explain such a huge amount of water accumulating under the Martian surface. The reservoir had to have been gigantic to explode out like a punctured balloon.

The problem was complicated further because science knew that the Martian outflow channels had resulted from the most massive and sudden release of water anywhere in the solar system. In terms of volume and explosive release, nothing on any other planet came close.

Solon pondered for a moment. "I'm sorry, man. I see no relevance to a swarm footprint. Those are not even impact craters. They are ..." He froze and then murmured, "Damned icy fragments."

George repeated, "Damned *icy fragments.*"

I smiled. I had known they could solve the riddle. But soon, George, Solon, and I were the only ones smiling.

Khufu and Arjuna seemed displeased. "What's going on?" said Khufu. "You want to tell us?"

George said, "An outflow channel would not make a teardrop-shaped outline. What we see is the outline of an impact crater where a cosmic water balloon fell onto Mars. You see, an icy fragm1ent hitting the Martian surface is a better explanation than some gargantuan accumulation of water in a high-pressure reservoir exploding out and flooding the surface."

"It doesn't need a high-pressure reservoir," added Solon. "Needs no explosive force to push out. All you need is a whopping icy fragment hitting the damned surface. The swarm provides that."

We had resolved the first footprint quickly. The swarm had hit Mars hard. "Outflow channels" were there because large icy fragments had hit the surface. The swarm had been full of large icy fragments, and as the pieces neared the surface, Martian tidal forces had pulverized everything. When the fragments hit the surface, especially at an angle, they had caused extensive flow of ice, water, and dirt from the point of impact, like a massive river. The teardrop shape was born as the water rapidly evaporated into the thin Martian atmosphere. By the end of the teardrop, no water remained, only the solid debris brought by the cometary ice or dug from the Martian surface.

Arjuna and Khufu listened. They imagined huge snowballs landing on Mars, splashing sideways like celestial water balloons. George and Solon talked quietly. I had enjoyed taking them to a distant planet. Now I had to bring them back.

"Are you ready for another footprint?" I asked.

They were not. They preferred snacks. The mood was pure celebration. No one was in a rush.

Arjuna munched the last of halva and asked, "What is the next footprint?"

It was not on the other planets, I explained, but on Earth.

I sensed a slight disappointment. They were acting like veteran space travelers. Earth was home. Only space promised adventure. But I was about to prove them wrong. The footprint left on Earth by the polar downflow was as impressive as any outflow channel.

I reminded them that Earth had encountered the cometary swarm repeatedly. Each occasion had renewed chaos in the canopy. After incorporation of new fragments, the canopy would be temporarily overloaded and could not retain its material content in orbit around Earth. It had to dump the excess at the poles, and thus, large polar downflows had occurred, reducing the canopy's overload and bringing it back into balance.

Arjuna picked up his copy of the *Rig-veda* and muttered, "This is odd, but let me pursue it. Let me read a verse about the god Indra, one of the most powerful gods, closest to what we may know as a supreme being. Among his deeds two stand out: first, the restoration of world stability; second, the release of large floods."

He paused to study a page and then went on. "Indra constantly fights instabilities. He battles intruding dragons and serpents but brings stability back to the world. Here! This is from Book 2, Hymn 12, Verse 2: 'He who fixed fast and firm the earth that staggered, / and set at rest the agitated mountains, / Who measured out the air's wide middle region and gave / the heaven support, He, men, is Indra.'"[19]

Arjuna looked at us as I picked up my book to reread the same verse. He smiled faintly and went on. "After restoring stability," Arjuna said, "Indra's next feat was the release of floods. Listen to Book 2, Hymn 11, Verse 2: 'Floods great and many, compassed by the Dragon, / thou badest swell and settest free, O Hero.'"[20]

Solon broke in. "Let me summarize. Indra encounters the swarm, smothers the dragon of cometary fragments, and dumps the extra material down the polar opening, flooding the pole. Right? We already know this from the canopy geometry. Who needs Indra's divine testimony?"

Arjuna seemed hurt and looked at Solon with contempt but continued. "Here is some more to help you—Book 1, Hymn 30, Verse 5: 'Thou, Indra, without effort hast let loose the floods / to run their free course down.'[21] It again emphasizes that Indra releases floods *downward*."

I had planned to present the canopy footprint through scientific records, but Arjuna had found the *Rig-veda* parallels, though to some in our group, the two paths of discovery diverged. Logical knowledge of the canopy's rudiments had already turned Solon into a renegade. He no longer had time to consider a canopy feature modeled in the *Rig-veda*, and he said so aloud.

Arjuna took offense. "Now all of a sudden you side with science! Something superior to sacred texts? You forget—if it weren't for the sacred texts, your science would know nothing about the canopy."

Enoch looked at both and said, "You two are acting like kids. With my luck we'll probably spend the next two years studying Indra in this basement, and you are already fighting over a couple of verses. Is this how we are going to dig into details? Must we see science and sacred texts as sworn enemies? I tell you, without one another, neither would get very far."

Enoch was both right and wrong, but he had said nothing new. We already had thousands of years of history to prove his latter point wrong. Science and religion had never walked arm in arm. We the few were forcing them together by obscure traces of affinity. We had not bridged the ancient and the modern, and we were not bringing religion and science into union.

"We all know Solon," I muttered, looking at Enoch. "If he doesn't say something derogatory, he's not alive. Ignore him."

As for Indra, we had yet to study him to know what canopy feature he represented, but the verses Arjuna read were utterly clear. In the *Rig-veda*, Indra definitely played a key role in releasing the polar floods. He represented the stabilizing force in the canopy.

Solon smiled and offered an apology.

"I also apologize," Arjuna said. "We were talking about scientific footprints. I shouldn't have brought the *Rig-veda* into it. Please, forget about Indra. We'll look at him at a later time."

Enoch sensed the need for a break. "What about refreshing our cups?"

We applied ourselves to the little tea and coffee that remained. The cookies were mostly gone.

Soon we were back in our chairs. We had had a friendly fight, neither the first nor the last. Our friendships had emerged intact, perhaps even stronger.

Arjuna motioned for me to continue.

I reviewed Earth's encounters with the swarm. The encounters had not been alike; not all had captured the same amount of matter. At times, a lot had been captured, overloading the canopy and causing a large polar downflow. Massive rivers of cometary material had flowed into the oceans at the poles.

"Some very large and extremely cold cometary rivers poured into the ocean. The ocean water immediately turned to ice and formed icebergs that floated away to melt in the warmer water beyond the poles."

"Hel-lo!" Solon looked at me in feigned amazement. "You yourself just said they melted. What kind of a footprint is an iceberg turned to piss thousands of years ago?"

"The footprint isn't water," I said, speaking without emotion. "The footprint is cometary dust and debris."

Enoch asked, "How do you get the dust and debris into this?"

I explained. The downflow was a slushy mix of ice and dirt. The cometary swarm had created a canopy full of dirty ice around the planet. It then drained at the pole, flowing down. The massive downflow formed a celestial river of powdery ice and debris that poured into the ocean and converted the seawater into large chunks of ice. The cometary dust and debris got trapped in the icebergs.

"I see," George murmured. "The cometary downflow was like the supply line for the icebergs to deliver celestial garbage to the far reaches of the earth."

As they considered the image of icebergs moving one after another into the ocean, Enoch said, "I don't get it. I expect the ice to form on land in sheets, not in the ocean as icebergs. What's going on?"

George tried to explain. The polar downflow was made of pulverized ice and dirt, not water. It would fall onto the polar land and sea. Even when the downflow fell on Earth's surface, its volume forced a river-like flow. When it fell into the sea, the extremely cold cometary matter directly formed icebergs. The new cometary material flowing into the ocean forced the icebergs to move away to create room for formation of new ones.

"The surface did not warm the pulverized ice and dirt much before it reached the ocean. No ice sheets formed on land, and when the cold celestial river poured into the ocean, it displaced the coastal waters. Away from the coast, the water changed to ice and aggregated into icebergs. At the North Pole, depending on the size of the polar circle and the direction of the polar downflow, the cometary material could have fallen directly into the ocean to form the icebergs."

The cometary material would have continued to pour into the ocean and create more new icebergs that pushed the previous ones out. So long as the cometary material flowed, the iceberg train formed in deep water and floated away. It all would have ceased when the downflow diminished and then stopped. When the canopy had unloaded its excess material, the iceberg train died.

Enoch said, "At the coasts, it would be like a wharf. The icy river pouring into the ocean would first form a wharf. The rest of the river would slide over the icy wharf, pour into the deeper ocean, and form icebergs that floated away like loaded ships."

"I like that!" Arjuna said, slapping the arm of his chair. "Makes it easy to understand. At the icy wharf, pieces of floating ice clump together, form larger pieces, and move out like a train of icebergs."

"Exactly," George said, nodding. "And trapped inside each were dust and debris and perhaps terrestrial matter scraped from the riverbed." He turned toward me and asked, "Which is the footprint? The wharf or the iceberg train?"

"If you were to guess," I asked, "which would you say?"

George said, "I can't see much remaining from Enoch's wharf, so it's the icebergs. They melt in the ocean and deposit dust and debris on the ocean floor. Did somebody by chance come across their track?"

"What do you think?"

Arjuna spoke before George could. "It is not just dust and debris. These were the gigantic floods released by the god Indra. Perhaps they would have left a long, wide gravel road on the ocean floor. That would be noticed—a divine road."

Solon smiled at Arjuna. "The wharf is significant for launching some of the icebergs but has no footprint of its own. Shores are erosive. If they preserved anything, it'd be piss-poor. So it's the iceberg train."

Massive downflows were rare. When they occurred, the iceberg train took off from the polar sea and deposited a long stretch of debris on the ocean floor. Science had observed the footprint and even given it the name "Heinrich event" but could not explain it.[22] It needed to know about the canopied earth but did not.

The puzzle was not just the strange debris on the ocean floor but the equally baffling repeated and abrupt cooling and warming of the ocean's surface water over a period stretching tens of thousands of years.[23] Nothing in science's experience could explain Earth becoming cooler or warmer abruptly or laying a stretch of debris on the ocean floor—unless Earth had been canopied.

After every swarm encounter, the polar circle would be covered with debris and would close almost instantaneously. The polar sun would suddenly shut off, and Earth would cool. But most of the cooling would take place where the cometary material fell on Earth. The cometary river dumping material into the sea would cool the ocean's top layer.

"I can see it happening," George said. "Once the canopy stabilizes, the polar circle opens, the sun shines, and the climate quickly warms back to normal. Today no mechanism for such quick cooling and warming exists. There's no way to use the models of today's Earth to explain sudden cooling and warming or iceberg trains."

It was time to throw my friends back into space. "What about getting away from Earth?" I said. "How about another Martian footprint?"

They liked that. Space seemed more captivating than Earth. Logic had nothing to do with it. Rationally, it should have been the other way around. Earth always should have been first.

I grinned and said, "*This* footprint, science does not like."

George sneered, "There is no such thing."

I said, "This footprint is from the fringes of science, outside the scientific community, from a dedicated group that seeks to decipher the data buried in ancient myths."

"Sounds like us."

I nodded and went on. "This group seeks to demonstrate that at some time in the past, Mars was as big and bright as the sun."[24]

Visibly annoyed, George said, "No wonder science doesn't like that. How could Mars be as big and bright as the sun?" Then he paused, thought, and said, "I'm sorry. Where the hell do I get this habit of compulsive rejection before hearing the facts?"

We knew Mars. Today's Mars shined like a bright star. At times, it outshined Jupiter. Yet though it might be as bright as a star, it could not possibly shine like the sun.

Could the comet's swarm and a canopy have done the trick? We knew that Mars's orbit lay outside Earth's. Like Earth, it could have intercepted the swarm and captured fragments—even formed a Martian canopy.

George said, "You told us about the outflow channels, so plausibly the swarm did hit Mars. But there are no Martian texts to tell us if the Martian day and night reversed or if a thirty-thousand-mile-long dick pounded the polar opening. So we cannot be sure that a Martian canopy formed or ever existed."

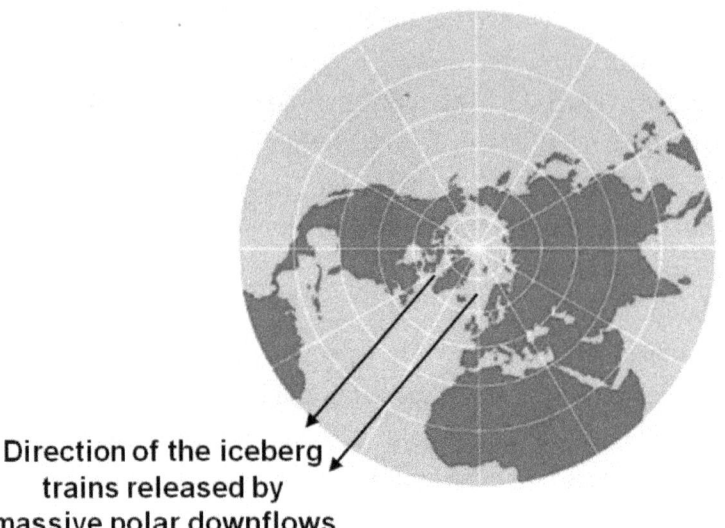

**Direction of the iceberg
trains released by
massive polar downflows**

Much of the polar downflow in the Northern Hemisphere would fall into the Arctic Ocean and directly form icebergs. The outlet into the Pacific Ocean is a narrow and shallow channel. As such, the iceberg trains primarily moved through the much wider outlet connecting the Arctic Ocean to the Atlantic Ocean.

—George

Solon nodded in agreement. Then he seemed to have a change of mind. "We've already accepted that Earth and Mars passed through the swarm. We know that Earth captured fragments and that Mars got hit by fragments. We know the swarm finally pissed itself into oblivion, and the canopy exhausted itself and collapsed. So why now a pissing contest over whether or not Mars had a canopy? We can assume its canopy formed and then collapsed, just like on Earth."

George shook his head. "That is just an assumption. Sacred texts may validate it for Earth, but that's not an option for Mars."

Khufu said, "Perhaps there are canopy remnants in Earth's skies? Or around Mars? Has anyone looked?"

"That's exactly my point." George wanted to end the conversation. "Just because we don't see anything in our sky doesn't mean canopies formed on other planets or that every canopy would collapse totally. Clear skies are not evidence of a canopy."

My voice betrayed my eagerness. "Assume lots of fragments hit Mars, and many big ones were captured. Assume a canopy—a big, thick one. Assume it collapsed. What would you expect to see as evidence of a Martian canopy?"

George gave me a look that seemed to say, *You know and won't tell!* Then he said, "Martian craters and the outflow channels leave no doubt. Very large fragments hit Mars. Yet it is credible to assume the canopy formation. Perhaps a few large pieces remained intact and were not incorporated into the canopy. Such loners may not have collapsed with the canopy. Instead ..." He paused again.

"Instead?" Khufu could not stand the suspense.

"And instead they became Martian moons. Hmm. How did I overlook the moons?"

Solon said, "If you are saying what I think you are, science will kick your ass to kingdom come."

Until that moment the canopy and the Martian moons had not come together in George's mind, but slowly they did now. He described the two Martian moons. Science saw them as captured asteroids, though they were not like asteroids. They had the look and density of comet material. One even had been briefly observed to emit gas like a comet would.

Were they cometary fragments? Were they swarm remnants? George did not know, but for the first time he had some logical, concrete reasons to consider such a remote possibility. Assuming a canopied Mars, there was a good chance the moons of Mars were stragglers among captured fragments. They had survived the canopy's collapse. They had remained Martian satellites. The same had not happened for Earth because it had never had Mars's hard encounter with the swarm.

"It sounds logical. It's as plausible as captured asteroids. If you're right, we'll rename the damned moons after you!"

Everyone laughed.

Arjuna shook his head, looked at me, and said, "We digressed to the Martian moons from your story of Mars shining like a sun. What did you mean?"

We were solving the canopy puzzle. The pieces of this celestial jigsaw reinforced each other. One piece built on the ones before. To make Mars shine like a sun, I needed a canopied Mars. The bigger it got, the brighter it would be. The planet alone could at best be as bright as a star, I explained. A canopied Mars, however, could compete with the sun.

"That's right!" George exclaimed, jumping in passionately. "The Martian canopy could have been five to ten times, or even more, the size of the planet itself."

Solon took noisy exception. "But the size shouldn't matter. Didn't you say Jupiter is larger than Mars but from the surface of Earth seems no brighter than Mars?"

George nodded. "Yes and no. Yes, Jupiter and Mars seem equally bright from Earth. No, size does count. Brightness is a combination of surface properties *and* size. If the canopy surface were like the Martian surface, its relative brightness would be proportional to its size. But a canopy's reflective properties differ markedly from those of the Martian surface. A canopy would have an icy surface, and ice is a good reflector. Comparing Mars to canopied Mars is like replacing a piece of paper with a mirror ten times as big. Which one would be brighter in the sunlight? The mirror or the piece of paper?"

"It's a no-brainer," Enoch agreed. "The canopy would be full of ice crystals. It would certainly outshine the dusty surface of Mars. So the larger the canopy and the icier its surface, the more substantial the increase in apparent size and brightness."

Solon concurred.

"So canopied Mars was bigger and brighter. I accept that," Khufu boomed. "But how could anyone see anything from the earth?"

We looked at each other, perplexed. That was a serious problem.

Arjuna smiled serenely and murmured, "They could because of god Vishnu's three steps." He paused for effect and then added, "The *Rig-veda* says the whole world came into existence after Vishnu took three dusty steps. Obviously, Earth's first two encounters were glancing confrontations with the swarm. The first two times, Earth got only a thin, dusty canopy through which people could see the heavens. They saw Mars under a canopy. They noted its exceptional brightness. A few recorded it in texts that have reached us as myths."

The large, ice-rich Martian canopy had reflected the sunlight. From Earth men had gazed upon canopied Mars, many times the original planet's size. For the ancients, questions abounded. How had it ceased to be just a bright star? How did it shine so like a small sun in the sky? Perhaps during the day it could not compete with the sun, but at night, it would have ruled the skies, turning the night into day.

Enoch fixed his eyes on me. "You said others have worked on the idea of the Martian sun. Who are they? Have they also found the canopied earth?"

"They have rejected the canopy model," I said. "They are looking at other alternatives."

"Such as?"

"Such as a new theory of an electrical universe."

Solon said, "Perhaps we should give them a call. Perhaps when … after we know the canopy a bit better."

Arjuna agreed. "We should talk to them. I am sure they are like us, with few resources. We all need every bit of support we can get."

He then got up slowly, every bone creaking, and went to the window. The silhouette of his head glowed against the tiny patch of sky visible through the glass. This signaled the end of another afternoon, one more journey completed.

Could we claim success?

Throughout the journey, few had stopped to marvel at how small and fragile we were, how easily we could get lost in things we sought to discover.

16

The Return of the Watchers

John knew the Watchers' surveillance car had to return to the neighborhood to listen to the basement conversation. It would be parked within a mile or two of Roughie's house. Any farther, and interference with other electronic signals would make reception impossible. He could not ignore the Watchers' tactical positioning. They were a key component of the struggle he faced, and he had to know what they were up to.

He went through the box where he kept souvenirs from his days as an undercover cop and took out a fake mustache, a hat, and dark glasses. He put on the hat and the glasses and pressed the mustache onto his upper lip. It did not stick as firmly as he would have liked. The adhesive had aged, but it would stay on for a couple of hours—and that was more than he needed.

He almost ran from the house to the car, afraid one of the neighbors might spot him. On a map he had drawn the tightening spiral of the route he would take to cover every street in the area within a two-mile radius. After almost an hour of driving, he had covered the first mile but had found nothing resembling a surveillance car. Yet he was positive he would find the new location soon.

As the spiral tightened to within a few blocks of his house, he became despondent. The surveillance car was nowhere to be found. "I must have missed it," he said to himself.

He wanted to run the route again, but he was hungry. He decided to go home. As he passed Jenny's Gardens, his heart skipped a beat. The Watchers' car was parked in the same place as before. "How stupid can you get?"

He drove by and recognized the driver as the man he had talked to briefly a few weeks earlier. "These stupid bastards know nothing about surveillance," he said.

Then it dawned on him. "Oh shit," he groaned, "it's a trap. The sons of bitches want me to try to question someone again. I bet a protection unit is just a few seconds away."

As he circled the playground, he saw an odd car at the far end of the Jewish temple parking lot. He didn't need to guess who its occupants were. One was the man he'd beaten up.

He went home and called a buddy at police headquarters. "I need a little help with community watch."

"What can I do?"

"Couple of guys are sitting in a parked car at the temple a few blocks from my house. Can you send a squad car to see who they are and what they are doing?"

"Will do."

Half an hour later, John's friend called back and said, "They're private eyes. Their licenses checked out. A woman hired them to watch her husband, who is fooling around. They wouldn't give any information on their client."

Excellent cover.

John thanked his friend, ended the call, and began contemplating his alternatives.

He could try to surprise the protection unit, but that would be risky. The first time they hadn't been ready, but this time they were ready and waiting. From what he had learned from Pasha, he knew they were fanatically loyal. At best, he would get another medallion and a password seal. His best current bet was to avoid them. So long as they did not know who he was, he had the upper hand.

He went back to listening to the garbled meeting. His biggest challenge was to find a way to place a microphone in the basement. He hated the idea of doing it himself.

17

The Ladder of God

Oddly, I sensed the weekend's arrival as normal. Had the canopy afternoons become routine?

I was reminded of the tennis I played with friends: every Tuesday, seven thirty, routine but fun. Nothing out of the ordinary, but good exercise. Had we unknowingly reached the same stage with our canopy investigation? It was not physically demanding like tennis, but rather an intense mental exercise, and it was fun also, creating the same moments of pain and joy as tennis when someone missed an important shot or an opponent hit a better winning shot.

The moment of victory or instance of resolution caused pain for one and brought joy for another. How did the canopy game and tennis produce the same ups and downs?

As we sank into chairs and arranged our books and notes around us, Khufu spoke first. "We have looked at the sacred texts. We have looked at scars on planets. What about spending some time on the physical artifacts of the ancients?"

"Such as?" Solon asked.

Khufu said, "I know I am prejudiced about humanity's most amazing monuments, the pyramids. Inevitably, in some way, the pyramids are linked to the canopy."

"They must be!" Arjuna affirmed.

Solon sneered, "You guys have a screwed-up way of proposing theories. Do I get the whip and chain if I don't bow before your majesties?"

Khufu grinned and said, "You dare miss the canopy's link to the pyramids, and you'll see what majestic wrath means."

Solon feigned fear and chattered, "Ooh! I already see a cometary pyramid forming around Earth."

Enoch quietly intervened to stop the mock battle of wits and get us back on track. He described the programs he had seen about the pyramids on public television. According to him, the smooth, streamlined appearance of the Giza pyramids was deceptive. It hid the fact that the first attempts at pyramid construction had begun with step pyramids. Initially, the sculpted surface had sat on a foundation of steps.

Enoch and Khufu took turns telling the story of the first days of pyramid building, when Pharaoh Djoser had laid tiers atop one another to build six terraces, two hundred feet high. The stepped surface was then encased in smooth white limestone, to make the sunlight reflection more impressive. Later, at Giza, the Egyptians learned to build the smooth pyramids directly out of stone blocks rather than in steps.

Solon asked, "What is the significance of pyramids originating as step structures? It's a logical design progression for pyramid building. On the first try, the society of the time didn't have the engineering skills to build out of stone blocks."

"I agree with Solon," George said. "The goal was a pyramid. That's why they put a stone casing on a stepped pyramid. If the intent had been a stepped pyramid, they would have kept the steps and not added the casing."

Enoch shook his head. "But the Egyptians were not the only pyramid builders. Americans also built pyramids, and they kept the stepped appearance."

Arjuna suggested, "Perhaps they learned from the Egyptians. Didn't I read something about that?"

"We need to remain open-minded," Enoch said. "It is possible that all over the world, some aspect of the canopy was seen like a pyramid, perhaps like a stepped pyramid."

Khufu added, "The smooth pyramid could be another canopy aspect. The canopy did change with time."

George and Solon believed the steps had more to do with the building process than with something inspired by the canopy. Enoch and Khufu took the opposite view. Arjuna and I tried to remain neutral and objective.

Enoch asked simply, "What canopy aspect resembles a pyramid? Can we focus on that?"

George and Solon said nothing.

Arjuna had listened carefully to both sides. "The canopy itself can be seen as a pyramid. It is sort of wide in the middle, narrows toward the pole, and gets flat at the top, at the polar circle."

"If that's the frigging picture," Solon said mockingly, "then next you'll claim the canopy bands are pyramid steps. You definitely have a Model T mind."

"Model T?" Arjuna looked at George stealthily and murmured, "Is that good or bad?"

George winked at Solon and then said, "Good! Definitely good."

Satisfied with the slang use, Arjuna said, "It is all in perception. It all depends on how you see the bands. They could be seen as celestial steps set at an angle. In that case they would resemble a stepped pyramid. Or they could be seen as tiers smoothly set on each other. In that case they would resemble a smooth pyramid."

"You may have something there," George said cautiously. "The bands are not always distinctly visible. The canopy can become chaotic. When it does, its surface would be more smooth than stepped."

George reached into his stack of books, picked one up, looked through the index, and held up the book, showing what he had found, a picture of Jupiter. "Here is one example of a banded canopy. How do you see it? Like a pyramid? Smooth or stepped?"

Arjuna looked disapprovingly. "You surprise me. You are a scientist. You should know the difference."

George closed the book. He and Arjuna stared at each other.

Arjuna tried to change the tone and said softly, "The picture you showed is from a human looking at a planet millions of miles away through a telescope, which could never capture the perspective of someone on Earth looking directly up at the canopy only thousands of miles away. In your picture, all we see is light reflecting from the surface. In a canopied earth, we would see sunlight shining through the bands. They are not the same. They cannot be the same." He paused for a moment and then asked, "Have you ever been inside a cathedral when the sun shines through the stained glass windows? I have. I can tell you, it is a totally different world from the one you see when standing outside, looking at the cathedral walls."

"You're right," George conceded. "We cannot make a judgment about the stepped pyramid from looking at a Jupiter picture. I just wondered if it would help."

Solon raised his hand as though he had just discovered something new. "I am not buying any of the canopy-pyramid shit. But somehow you reminded me of the name the Greeks gave to the Cyclopses. They called them wall builders."[25]

"Wall builders?" George repeated, intrigued.

"Yes. They were also called 'belly-hands' or 'hand-bellies' or something like that."[26]

"Belly-hands?" George asked, as though he thought he had misheard.

Solon murmured, "Damn! I should have remembered the belly-hands when we talked about the cyclonic vortices. Obviously, the Greeks saw the cyclonic eye as a belly button and the spiraling cyclonic arms as hands."

"That's a nice model," George said with a smile.

"But why did they see the cyclonic vortices as wall builders? Makes no sense. As a wall, the canopy was already there. The cyclonic vortices just roamed around the canopy face."

"But the ordered bands came later," George replied. "Perhaps your ancestors saw the banding as wall building."

Enoch's face came alive. "Remember George saying the middle of the canopy was less chaotic? That's where the band formation started. When bands formed in the middle, the cyclonic vortices were limited to chaotic areas outside the bands and closer to the polar circle."

Arjuna looked around and asked, "Do you all see it?"

"Imagine this," Enoch continued. "At first, there are cyclonic vortices everywhere. Then the first band forms in the middle of the canopy. No cyclonic vortices are in the band. They're all outside it. Then the second and third bands form. Again there are no vortices in them."

George muttered, "It would look like the vortices were building a wall of bands in the canopy as they backed away from the ordered bands."

Enoch concluded, "By the time the canopy is fully banded, no cyclonic vortex remains. The job of wall building is done."

"I am a disgrace to my Greek heritage," Solon mumbled. "A moron like you has to explain to me why the Cyclopses built walls."

With that Arjuna noted that perhaps the pyramids also might have been built not as steps but as walls. He wondered aloud whether the stacking of tiers on each other to build a wall to reach heaven had been an attempt to replicate the canopy. Had the replication process eventually produce the pyramid?

He asked Khufu where the term "step pyramid" had come from. Was it new scientific terminology? Or was it in the language the ancient Egyptians had used? Khufu did not know.

Arjuna surprised us by remembering something band-like from the *Rig-veda*. He recalled that the description of the god Rbhus resembled bands.

He pulled out the *Rig-veda* and found the Rbhus hymn. "I was wrong," he said. "Not bands. Not walls. Listen to Book 4, Hymn 33, Verse 1: 'Wind-sped, the Skillful Ones in rapid motion have in an instant / compassed round the heaven.'"[27]

The Greeks saw the cyclonic vortices as *wall-builders*. Initially they roamed everywhere on the chaotic canopy.

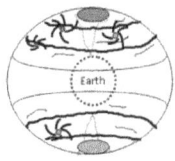

The first bands formed in the less chaotic middle part of the canopy. The Greeks saw the bands as strips of canopy wall built by cyclonic vortices.

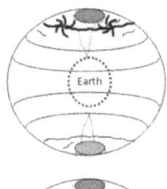

The Greeks saw the cyclonic vortices moving back toward the poles as they completed more of the banded canopy wall. The polar circle was the last piece of the wall built.

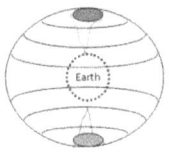

Finally, the work of the cyclonic vortices was done. The Greeks saw that the vortices disappeared with the completion of the banded canopy.

George said, "I'll be darned. They saw the canopy's vortical motion. They didn't use scientific language but simply described it as something that went round the canopy rapidly. That's superb!"

Arjuna said, "For the *Rig-veda* describing the bands as vortical motion, I'll give it a B. But for Greeks describing the banded canopy as a wall built by the Cyclops, that's an A."

"Amen to that," Solon said approvingly.

Arjuna smiled. "Given your interest, I will tell you another Rbhus story. You see, Rbhus had the power to make his parents young. Listen to Book 4, Hymn 36, Verse 3: 'In that your aged Parents, worn with length of Days, you wrought / again to youth so that they moved at will.'"[28]

Solon threw up his hands. "I give you *one damned inch*, and you take a frigging yard. I give the nod to Rbhus as canopy band, and you claim he owns the fountain of youth."

"I don't like what you just said," Arjuna replied. He hesitated and then said, "And I am about to climb the wall."

"You old fart!" Solon shouted, smiling. "You just used slang! Climbing the wall." Mimicking Arjuna's accent and way of talking, he said, "What does that mean? Why can't you just say you are frantic with frustration and anxiety?"

When the laughter died down, George said, "I am amazed how often we act immaturely, especially after all we have learned about the canopy. My first reaction to the verse Arjuna read was to say 'impossible,' even 'bullshit.' Instead I should have asked what canopy feature it might be … I haven't learned a thing."

Solon said, "First, you ain't as bright as me. Second, you have such a damned orthodox idea of scientific righteousness, you make us hear the birdies sing."

"Some habits die hard," George said, smiling.

"Yes, they do."

George turned to Arjuna and said, "So how did Rbhus make his parents young?"

Solon asked, "What is the parent of a band anyhow?"

Enoch joined in. "Or better yet, what are bands born out of?"

We all thought about how a band came to life.

I thought about the canopy. The canopy was the parent of every band. Before I could say so aloud, Enoch came up with the same answer. He said, "Every band is born in the chaotic canopy's lap. So the parents of a band must be the chaotic canopy. The bands are children born to the chaotic canopy."

The chaotic canopy was bigger and older than the bands.

George thought for a moment. "There is more to it. The chaotic canopy wasn't just old. It *looked* old."

Arjuna asked, "What do you mean?"

"Just imagine the chaotic canopy. It would have had ill-defined lines and features, unstable pieces that regularly fell down. Its surface was not tight and smooth. But then came the children, the bands. They brought well-defined lines to the canopy, and the surface now became smooth and stable. Few things fell down. The conclusion was inevitable. The bands were making their parents—the canopy—young. A banded canopy is a young canopy. A chaotic canopy is an old canopy. See?"

"The banded canopy," Enoch repeated excitedly, "is young because it has well-defined lines and features."

George added that the act of "making the parents young" was not a one-time event. The bands repeated it every time Earth encountered the swarm. The rejuvenation was most evident during the major encounters, when the bands became highly chaotic and even disappeared. The parent canopy would age, becoming wavy and ill-defined. Pieces would fall down. But after the encounter, the children, the bands, would restore the canopy's youth, giving it well-defined lines and a smooth surface. Nothing would fall down.

Solon grumbled, "Wall building and restoring parents to youth. Are these the grand stories we want to tell?"

"The best," Arjuna replied almost inaudibly.

We had followed a tortuous path. The canopy bands had brought the step pyramid to life in our minds. Who were those who had seen the banded canopy as a step pyramid? Had they sought to replicate the pyramidal heaven on earth?

Who had looked at cyclonic vortices roaming the face of the canopy and modeled them as Cyclopic wall builders?

Then came those who had sought to reward their parents. They had looked at the canopy gods and wished they could do the same—make their parents young again.

The path of our discoveries in prehistory seemed endless. Wherever one sought to draw a line, call it an end, the horizon of prehistory moved a bit farther away.

Now it was Khufu's turn. He opened a book to a marked page and said, "I have to admit, I have not fully thought about this, but it fits our discussion. Here is Utterance 7 from the Pyramid Texts. It is a definition of the goddess Nut. She is one of the oldest Egyptian gods: 'Nut, the great, (who is) within the encircled mansion.'"[29]

George shook his head and said, "I'm not sure." He then muttered, "Sorry. Go on."

Solon said, "'Encircled mansion' sounds like the canopy, but it's not as clear as the images of wall builders or giving elixir to your parents."

Khufu nodded. "Fair enough. Listen to another definition of Nut in Utterance 432: 'Great Lady, who didst become heaven, thou didst become (physically) mighty, ... / thou encompassest the earth and all things (therein) in thine arms.'"[30]

George said, "That sounds a bit more like the canopy."

Solon asked, "Doesn't it describe the bands as Nut's arms? If we take the bands as arms, they do surround the earth."

Enoch murmured, "It is not as good a model as wall builders or resurrecting aged parents, but it *is* another model."

Khufu shrugged. "This one is from Utterance 474. Oh, in reading this, when I say *N*, it stands for the deceased, the one for whom the utterance is written." He paused and looked up. "Did I tell you all spells and utterances were written for the dead?" Returning his gaze to the book, he read aloud: "N. goes therewith to his mother Nut; / N. climbs upon her, in this her name of 'Ladder.'"[31]

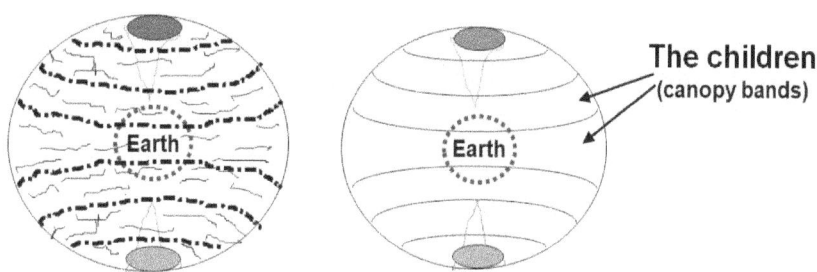

The children
(canopy bands)

Aged Parent
(chaotic canopy)

Young Parent
(regularly-banded canopy)

The attributes of every society's gods reflect its ideals. In the bands, the
Indians saw the ideal child, strongly linked to the parent, the canopy.
The bands were so dedicated to their parent that they constantly made
it young, reversing the effects of old age. The rejuvenation of the parent
was most evident after major encounters with the swarm. The parent
aged and became chaotic. Its surface became ill-defined. Pieces of its
body fell off. But as soon as the encounter was over, the children, the
bands, restored the canopy's youth, giving it well-defined lines and a
smooth surface. Nothing fell off. Only a god could treat his parent so.
To the Indians this was an example to imitate.

—Arjuna

He paused for effect and, getting no response, said, "This is how I see it now. My ancestors modeled the banded canopy as a ladder. It could be climbed in the afterlife when one went to the canopy heaven."

"In a sense," Solon muttered, "climbing the ladder parallels the wall building. I can readily see the damned wall builders as ladder climbers."

Enoch said, "We're back to the step pyramid. If they saw the canopy as a celestial ladder, each pyramid step would be the rung of a ladder that took the person—or more appropriately, the spirit of the dead—to heaven."

Solon nodded agreement. He now believed the builders of step pyramids had sought to replicate the canopy on Earth. "Assume we go with your ladder model. How do you explain the addition of the stone facing to change the step pyramid to a smooth one?"

Enoch spoke before Khufu could reply. "We know the Egyptians were bright. They knew the ladder model was one way of looking at the canopy but not the only way. They knew the canopy also had a smooth, reflective surface. In fact, that's how the earth received the light of the polar sun. Perhaps the combination of the smooth-faced stones and the step pyramid was an attempt to combine both the ladder and the reflective features into one physical model."

This was progress. We now saw the pyramid as a physical model of the canopy bands. Everyone was satisfied with Khufu's pyramid-building logic.

Solon winked at George and said, "Today we've come across so many models of canopy bands—Greek, Indian, Egyptian. But nothing from the damned Hebrews."

George winked back. "Boy, what a crying shame."

Enoch fell into the trap. "I don't have anything now, but the time will come."

George muttered, "Later is later."

Solon joined the challenge. "What can you say now when it counts?"

Arjuna pleaded, "People! That's enough. Please stop it!"

"I don't mind," Enoch said.

I joined the fray on Enoch's side and said, "What about Joshua making the sun stand still?"

I enjoyed the deafening silence that followed.

The well-known Torah story told of a time when for a while the sun had stood still. Because our meeting was nearing its end, I gave them a clue. The sun standing still was the same as the day lasting longer than normal.

George immediately said, "Let's say that here in town, today, the sun shines for ten hours. If the next day the sunlight somehow lasted for thirty-six hours, then you could say the sun stood still for an extra twenty-six hours. How could that happen?"

"Before I answer," I said, "let's see if we have a consensus on the normal day. What do we mean by a normal day?"

On Earth, the normal day varied quite a bit by location. It also varied relative to Earth's position in its orbit around the sun. Earth's orbital position was not the only determinant of the day's length. There were other factors.

When people spoke of a normal day, their point of reference was the Earth location where *they* lived. Thus, if a person lived in the tropics, the normal day would be about twelve hours throughout the year. If that person lived in New York, the normal day would probably vary from eight to fourteen hours, depending on the time of the year. For someone living at the pole, the normal day would be twenty-four hours long for months.

"I don't get it." Arjuna seemed puzzled. "How does the length of day vary with Earth's orbit? Is it because we get close to the sun, then move away from it?"

"Earth's axis is tilted relative to its orbit," George said. "Earth maintains the tilt as it travels in its orbit around the sun. It is like a person who always leans to one side, for example to the left, regardless of where he is. So, that person, walking on the right sidewalk of a street would lean *away* from the buildings. On the left sidewalk of the street, going the same direction, he would always lean *toward* the buildings."

Arjuna nodded. "I can picture the person, but what about the day?"

"One year is one Earth orbit around the sun. Can you imagine Earth tilting to one side all the time? Okay! Now its inclination relative to the sun would change along the orbit, so the amount of sunlight received by different locations would change."

Arjuna shook his head. "That is the part I still don't get."

"Imagine you are at the pole."

"Okay."

"During the part of the orbit where the Northern Hemisphere leans toward the sun, what would you expect?"

"Leaning toward the sun, I will get more sunshine."

"Now you get to the other part of the orbit, where the Northern Hemisphere is tilting away from the sun. What do you expect then?"

"More darkness?" Arjuna muttered, not sure of his answer. "It seems that Earth's body would block some of the light."

"That is right." George continued. "Earth always tilts the same way, about twenty-three degrees. During half of its orbit around the sun, the North Pole tilts toward the sun. On other half, the north tilts away from the sun. With the change in tilt relative to the sun, the length of the day at each location changes. So a normal day varies between zero and twenty-four hours on different parts of the planet."

Solon wanted to reach a quick conclusion. "Look! When the North Pole tilts toward the sun, the Northern Hemisphere receives much sunlight. Normal days are damned long. It is called summer. When the North Pole tilts away from the sun, it gets a hell of a lot less sunlight, so normal days become short. It is winter. The more you move away from the equator, the more noticeable this annual variation becomes in the length of days. Kapeesh?"

I waved my hand to calm things down. "Okay! You now know a normal day. It's time to relate it to the sun standing still. We can start with the normal day of any location on Earth. Under the canopy and under the right circumstances, how can a day last in multiples of the normal? That is the question."

All signaled their unspoken desire to know more.

I posed the problem with new questions. How would it be possible to live in New York and see that Monday, Monday night, Tuesday, and Tuesday night are all one long sunny day, the darkness of night returning only Wednesday evening? How could the sun shine continuously from Monday morning through Wednesday afternoon? How could the sun stand still for two whole days?

"I can't see it," George said, shaking his head. "How can the polar sun appear to be in the sky continuously for more than a day? It's fixed at the pole. Earth rotates every twenty-four hours. There's no way the reddish polar light would shine on canopy's night side. So surprise me, if you can."

Two things affected the length of a canopy day, I explained. First, a longer than normal day could come about if the canopy became unstable. Instability arrived in full force during major encounters with the swarm or when the canopy was collapsing. When the canopy became unstable, the vortical bands could not hold together, and the vortical motion that defined each band would become irregular. Some bands would move apart for a moment, others longer. The band separation acted like a crack in the canopy shell, and through the crack the sun could shine directly into the canopy's interior.

George smiled and said, "Wow! Two canopy suns. One shining through the polar circle, the other through breaks between the bands."

"Two distinct suns?" said Enoch. "Okay, I see it. One shining during the regular canopy day, the other shining through the cracked canopy at night, turning the night into day."

"With the right crack in the canopy," George said, "you could get an abnormally long day. As Earth rotates, the polar sun illuminates the day side. Then the sun disk would directly light up the night side through the canopy cracks and turn it into day. The length of day could vary widely, depending on the size and duration of the crack between the bands."

George had finally gotten it, but I reminded him he was only half right. Two suns shining together would have been rare, not common.

The cracks in the canopy would come with instability or collapse, when there would be much dust and debris at the polar circle. Often the polar sun shined when the polar circle was relatively free of debris. That was normally at the end of instability, which also meant the end of cracks in the canopy shell. Again, two suns in an unstable canopy would be rare.

Similarly, if sunlight were to turn night into day, the canopy crack had to be large and free of dust and debris. Only then would there be no night on the night side of the canopy. The sun would shine directly through the crack, but if the crack closed soon or was full of dust and debris, little sunlight would get through. Nonetheless, on rare occasions, both suns shined at the same time through the polar circle and the breaks in the bands and gave rise to a longer than normal day. The sun would not set as normal but rather seem to stand still.

Even then, not everyone on Earth would have been able to see it. The cracks between the bands would be narrow and highly directional. As such, the extended day would not exist everywhere. Only a certain swath across the face of the earth would have a longer than normal day. It was the reverse of an eclipse. During an eclipse, there would be a band of shadow across the planet. When the canopy cracked, a band of light was superimposed across the darkness of night.

"Then the Hebrews lucked out to observe and record this ... this Joshua story," Solon said.

Khufu added, "The cracked canopy resolves another ancient paradox. You see, in the Egyptian sacred texts, the sun disk is the god Re. I always wondered why in some spells Re is said to shine at night. How could the sun disk shine at night? Until now, I considered it a mistake or something impossible."

He picked up two books from the floor and said, "I had already marked the spells and meant to bring them up. Listen to Spell 106 from the Coffin Texts. It describes the sun disk feature of Re: 'Re who is in his disk.'[32] Now listen to Verse 1098: 'It is Re who shines in the night.'[33] It's the same as the Joshua phenomenon, though I prefer the Joshua model.

It gives a composite of day and night and a measure of the length of the longer than normal day."

George thought for a moment and said, "But the Egyptian model says sun disk. The Joshua model is silent on what shines in the night to make it a day. True, it focuses on the length of the day, but it doesn't say how the day got lengthened. I prefer the Egyptian model. It is concise. The sun disk shined at canopy night."

Actually, both the Egyptian and Hebrew perspectives were valuable. The idea of the length of day as a multiple of normal and the sun disk shining at night were different but complementary models. Without different sacred records, it would have taken longer to arrive at this understanding of the canopied earth.

Different prehistoric models spoke to human diversity across time. Humans did not have to, perhaps did not want to, and maybe, by natural design were mentally incapable of seeing everything the same.

"I wonder how many records were thrown away," Khufu mused, "because they didn't make sense or were changed to force them to make sense. It is a sad commentary. I know it firsthand. Many times I asked myself why somebody hadn't changed the verse 'Re shines at night.' For so many years I *knew* the Coffin Texts had a wrong verse. Think about it. How often did the redactors and translators listen to themselves and make changes?"

Arjuna said, "We are often so sure of what we know. We treat everything else as wrong. In such behavior lies so much bias, so much human suffering."

It was getting late. Everyone seemed pleased with what we had discovered, but the story of the longer than normal day was not finished. I had to keep their interest alive a bit longer. There was another type of "continuous day" that lasted many twenty-four days. The Indians had observed it.

The Hebrews and Egyptians had seen a relatively global canopy feature. On the contrary, the Indians had observed something local. It happened only in the polar region. The Hebrews and Egyptians had seen the lengthening of day during instability or when the canopy was collapsing. The Indians had seen a "continuous day" when the canopy was stable. This condition was visible at high latitudes when the polar circle was large and the top canopy bands had narrowed out. It implies the presence of Indian observers located at or near the pole.

Arjuna asked anxiously, "Where have you seen that? Is it somewhere in the *Rig-veda*?"

I nodded and said, "Book 1, Hymn 88, Verse 4. It—"

"No, no, no. Let *me* read it."

Arjuna hurriedly found the verse and read it aloud: "The days went round you and came back."[34]

Solon shrugged. "It says the same thing."

George said, "It says the same. Continuous repetition of the day." He turned to me and said, "You said it was local, only at the poles. I see nothing local in the verse."

George was right. The information about the locality came from other verses. One source was the Marut hymns. The Maruts were gods identified with polar clouds. They had come to prominence when the canopy was stable. Toward the end of the canopy life, when the cometary swarm had weakened, Earth would have picked up little material during encounters, yet the polar downflow would have continued.

Gradually, with the aging of the swarm, the polar circle would become large, and the continual loss of material to downflows would reduce the width of the canopy's top bands. When the polar circle was large and the top bands narrow, the polar region received sunlight from two sources. The reflected light of the polar sun illuminated the canopy's day side, while the sun disk shined directly on the pole over the top of the bands. It changed the night side of canopy into day. At the pole, direct sunlight shining above the canopy edge combined with the reflected sunlight from the canopy shell to light the polar region continuously.

Solon said, "We should have seen that possibility. It's inevitable. The mature canopy would become more and more like a single band. It could not stay a spherical shell. The more the edges of the polar circle drop down, the wider it would get and the more sunlight would reach the pole directly."

"Yep. Should have seen it coming," George lamented. "Fascinating. A lighting phenomenon that happens only at the poles. For the way the sun stood still for Joshua, there was no such restriction. It could happen anywhere. The 'Joshua day' only needed cracks in the canopy. The polar continuous day needs the lowering of the top band."

"There is another difference," Enoch said. "The phenomenon you call 'Joshua day' was rare. It happened when the canopy was unstable or collapsing and only under certain preconditions. The polar circle had to be free of dust and debris. The breaks between the bands had to be large and free of dust and debris. Otherwise, there could be no Joshua day with two suns shining simultaneously. It was a rare event. But the continuous day at the poles would be commonplace and last for months at a time, as long as the polar circle was large, the top band low, and the canopy stable. The continuous polar day would be a regular event, though only for people living near the pole. Only they could live in a continuous day. But to see it you had to have observers at the pole. It seems the Indians had a research station set up at the pole to study the polar phenomena in canopied earth."

Arjuna had already walked halfway to the top of the stairs. He waved his hand and smiled, tired and pleased at the same time. The next weekend seemed far away.

18

The Break-In

It was Tuesday morning, and John was already sweating profusely. He was scared. He had never been a burglar before, never done anything so illegal. He felt like thousands of cops were watching him. He tried to relax and found it impossible.

He knew the movement pattern well—who went to work and who went shopping. But it was not an exact science. There were always variants. Sometime one would stay in, perhaps sick or choosing to shop another day. Others would return for something left behind, perhaps a wallet or a coupon. He tried hard not to think of the variants. They scared him even more.

Roughie's wife was off schedule. She was late, or was he imagining? Then she too was gone, and it was the time to act.

He froze. He had planned to just walk to the other side of the street, up the driveway, and to the back door. But suddenly, he thought of taking a car. Why hadn't he thought of renting a car? It would have been easier to pull into the driveway in a rental car, perhaps a white van.

"Should I do it next week?" he asked himself seriously. No, he had to do it at once. He couldn't just sit back and listen to another week of "can OP."

He checked the small bag he was taking along. The microphones were there, as was the Zap-Checker meter to find any microphones the Watchers might have planted. He checked the flashlight. He thought he might need one in the basement.

"Come on, you dummy!" he said, trying to pump himself up. "Let's go!"

He picked up the bag, walked out of the house, and crossed the street as casually as if he were delivering a bag of cookies to a neighbor.

"Damn," he moaned. "I should have brought some cookies just in case." It would have been an excellent excuse, but his feet were moving and he was already at the back of the driveway, right next to the back door.

He stopped at the door momentarily, thinking his racing heart would fail at any instant. He looked around to see if anyone was watching, even though his mind was too fuddled to notice anything. He reached into his pocket and got out his lock-picking set, but when he turned the knob, just in case, he learned the door was open.

What did this mean? Was someone still in the house? He panicked. He desperately wanted to turn back, but he opened the door and stepped in.

"Hurry up!" he growled at himself. He had seen how quickly the Watchers removed three microphones. He had to be just as good and get out in a few minutes. The thought of finishing energized him. He went through the kitchen, took out the Zap-Checker, turned it on, and moved it in an arc as he read the meter. There was a signal from the direction of a guest room. As he moved, the signal amplified toward the couch. He located the source and found a microphone taped underneath, near a back corner. He had dreamed of this moment! He would take the microphones, and then on Sunday when he was sure the Watchers were listening, he would smash them with a hammer and give them a taste of what they had done to him earlier.

As he was about to pull the microphone out, he had a second thought. "They would know," he moaned. They would realize their microphones were gone. They would come back not only to install them again, but also to remove and destroy his. A game of tag was not what he wanted. "I'd better leave them where they are."

He put his microphone by the other one and secured it with the duct tape. Then he hurried upstairs, listening for the slightest suspicious sound that might mean someone was in the house. He located the second microphone under a bed in a slit in the mattress. He nudged his microphone in next to it.

As he walked downstairs and headed for the basement door, an impression forming in his mind surprised him. The house was clean. The furniture was practically and pleasantly arranged. Until now he had imagined the house as a pigsty. Where he had gotten such an idea, he didn't know.

At the basement door, he stopped, as if he were about to enter a very special place. He shook the feeling off, opened the door, and started down the stairs. The steps were narrow and the basement darker than he had expected. A few chairs and a small sofa sat in a circle around a large, low, square table. His surveillance meter located the third microphone at once in a pile of broken things stored in a corner. He could not find the exact location and did not want to move things around. He chose a spot for his own microphone, taped it in, and sighed in relief.

He was done.

As he walked up the stairs, he heard a loud knock on the back door and almost fell back down the steps. The knock reminded him of the way police would knock at a suspect's door. He moved back down into the basement, not knowing what to do.

"Mrs. Zadeh," a voice called, "I am here to read the gas meter in the basement. Can I come in?"

John looked around for the gas meter. It was in the corner, near the top of the stairs. *He won't come in with no one in the house*, John told himself. He tried to remain calm.

But he had guessed wrong. He heard the back door open and a man's footsteps approaching the basement. Instinct took over, and he dove behind the sofa, trying to make himself as small as he could. He cursed himself for not bringing the ski mask with him. If the man discovered him, he could have knocked him out and left without showing his face. But it was too late.

The man opened the basement door but did not walk down the stairs. He knelt at the top of the stairs, looked at the meter, recorded the numbers on a handheld device, and left. It took no more than thirty seconds, but John felt as if time had stopped.

The man was gone, but John could not move. He took a few minutes to regain control of his leg muscles. As he climbed the stairs and left the house, he felt a new sense of respect for burglars. It was not an easy profession.

At home he sat impatiently in front of the window and waited for Roughie and his wife to come home. Roughie's wife returned, and John could hear her moving around the guest room. Then Roughie arrived home from work, and John heard every word they said in the bedroom about the weekend's luncheon arrangement.

For the first time in months, John felt a sense of comfort and accomplishment. He was finally a member of the basement group. He even thought he had become an uninvited member of the Watchers. All that pleased him no end.

19

The Risk of Being Misunderstood

The week did not pass quickly, though Earth's rotation guaranteed the weekend's arrival. John waited impatiently for his first audible words from the basement. He didn't know and could not know that across the street, another man searched impatiently for lessons hidden in his experience, but nothing profound came to his mind. John could not know and may never know that, for the other man, discovering the celestial origin of prehistory no longer seemed radical.

Through binoculars John watched someone carrying two full briefcases. He guessed they contained books and documents. He wondered about the others. Was this how they got ready for the meeting? Did the books in every hand signal readiness? Or had it become a habit, a routine, no different from the rest of life? If they had not feared the host or perhaps the wife, he wondered, would they have hauled in more books?

"Why are you guys so quiet?" John wondered as he strained through his binoculars to see the details of facial expressions. All he heard was the occasional murmur of compliments to the cook. *Have they detected the microphones?* he wondered.

There was no way for John to know until the group retired to the basement. Then, from the body language, he sensed the approach of the meeting. In his mind he saw six combatants rearing to go to their battleground, the basement.

He shook his head. "What the hell am I doing? Why did I just think of them as combatants? They're terrorists."

In all meetings Enoch had been the most bashful, rarely taking the lead. He surprised the group by speaking first. "History is a teacher, though we often ignore it. Those that offer radical ideas, for years, try hard to reach the establishment and the masses. But the established channels of communication rarely carry new, radical information to others. Society never shows any interest in listening to radical views."

Khufu cut in. "I think I know what you are talking about." Then he turned to me and asked, "Tell me, how long ago did you start on your theory of the canopied earth? How long? How long did it take to develop a reasonable understanding of prehistory? How long did it take to dare to share your experience with others ... with us?"

At that moment I felt uneasy.

John felt as if he had tuned into another planet in a different galaxy. He couldn't believe his ears; he couldn't believe that the group was talking about prehistory and addressing one among them as if he were the bringer of a radical view of the past that could change the whole society. The thought horrified him.

The way my friends were talking did not seem right. My unease emanated from an absence of canopy conversation. With all the books lying around, why were they not discussing another canopy feature? Had they planned this digression? In our very first meeting we had already covered what they were talking about. What would cause this sudden return to the beginning, to the fate of the one with a radical view of humanity?

I tried to turn them back to the canopy, but to no avail. Had they met behind my back to set an agenda of their own? Would I again have to describe my initial concerns about a radical theory of prehistory? They had heard it all, months ago.

Had my wife said something?

I hoped for a break, but Arjuna was summarizing the earlier conversation. "The man who wants to deliver a radical social message takes a huge risk," he said.

I was lost.

John was lost even more.

Sitting in two different rooms in houses across the street, they both wondered if they were watching a foreign film. To both the basement group had the appearances of a normal group of humans, but they talked in an esoteric language. The subtitles were in another foreign language still. From his vantage point, John could not see that every so often they unified their focus to stare at one individual, expecting him to confirm that he understood it all.

John heard Arjuna's voice: "People! You are scaring him."

Everyone laughed. None laughed for real. *Bad actors*, I thought. Now I was sure. They did have a secret agenda.

Did they want to tell me the canopy model was incomplete? Or that there was no canopied earth, only an intuition that did not pass scientific muster? Were they suffering from some sort of panic? After all, I had taken them on this prehistoric adventure. They knew as much as I did. If it all became public, they were as exposed as I was.

"Let us take it one step at a time," George began. "First, how to get the word out. You can find communicators, like salesmen. It works. They would propagate the idea of your model of prehistory. Or even better, you can become a storyteller. The story must be interesting. This often works well. For example, people with no interest in prehistory might be interested in the story of an exceptional comet."

John was totally lost. He looked at his equipment, tested a few plugs for firmness, and wondered if he was getting signals from somewhere else. He had not heard a single mention of the "can OP" that had been repeated so often in previous meetings, only an occasional "canopy."

What the hell is a canopy? he thought. *And what does it have to do with anything?* Was it possible that the words "canopy" and "canopied earth" were what he had earlier heard as "can OP"? Part of his mind found it logical, but he was totally unwilling to accept it. Worse, there were no signs of preparation for terrorism. Instead they appeared to be a lunatic group talking about one of them having conceived a radical model of prehistory. Had he wasted his time, chasing after this group? If he had, what about the Watchers? Were they as gullible?

Arjuna touched my arm and said, "A story has always been a powerful vehicle to get a message to the masses. If the story has a hero, a little bit of sex, and some action, most people would love to hear it. You can take the time to write a story. Find a publisher. Let them print it and publish it."

All eyes were on me. Arjuna gave my arm a squeeze and asked, "Can you tell a children's story?"

John felt like taking his headphones and slamming them against the window. Why was he listening to a group of non-American-looking people talking about publishing children's stories?

I felt like a stranger, like the neighbor across the street that I could not feel or see. I felt like throwing something at someone, but I did not have anything to throw.

Whenever I heard UFO stories, I wondered how someone abducted by aliens would feel. At that moment, for the first time, I knew. My friends had turned into aliens. They might as well have been space travelers who had brought the canopy-building comet into the solar system.

I shook my head in confusion and muttered, "I don't know how. I am a businessman, not a storyteller. All I have is a tiny yet exceptional model of prehistory. The rest, you know as much as I do. You have deciphered as much as I have. To tell it as an exciting story? To tell it as a children's story? I don't know."

"Telling a story in business language, you'd put everyone to sleep," Solon said, laughing heartily.

"History is on your side as a storyteller," said Arjuna. "Your model of prehistory is ultimately about the origin of myth and religious thought, even if you put it in children's language. Just look at any sacred text. They are full of stories that children love."

"But his situation is more difficult," Enoch said. "He is not telling a children's story about gods. He is telling a story of the destruction of *all* gods. Though ... yes, he could make everything fictional, tell the story of a planet in a galaxy far, far away. He could mask the world's religions and myths, their origin a single celestial phenomenon on a fictional world. He doesn't even have to start with an earthlike planet or humans. He could start with a Mars-like planet and green Martians."

"That doesn't make it any more interesting. You still have to have gods of sort in that galaxy. Then you have to veil the reference to myths and sacred texts to make it exotic and foreign. Otherwise, parents buying the book for their children will go nuts if they find parallels to their own cherished beliefs. Consider this. Your true model of prehistory is about a celestial phenomenon that people observed and assumed to be the presence of God. The story can still be about an exceptional comet. Even its recording in every society's myths and sacred texts can be retained. It can even be told in a way that brings the science and religion of that faraway planet together, achieving a merger of sacred texts and science. But the context within which these facts take shape has to be fictional, distant. Yes."

Arjuna forced a smile. "You can tell your experience to children with fictional characters. They will get the gist of canopied prehistory. I am sure they will. Generations from now, people will be ready to discover your true story and find that the fictional characters have a real place on Earth. Then, without any adverse reaction, they can start to see life from the point of view of an earthly cometary experience. In the process, they will start to learn about God gradually, from scratch. It will be slow but nonviolent. It will be ambiguous in the short run but clear and certain in the long term."

"Anything else could be a scary proposition," Enoch said gently.

"The gods we have known for thousands of years and relied upon every day suddenly disappear and become pieces of a comet. It proves everyone wrong about many conceptions of God. It will force everyone to start all over. Not easy. Many could not face such an ordeal. They'll get violent."

For the first time a picture started to form in John's head. He was listening to a revolutionary group, but not one bent on acts of terrorism. It sounded as if they had found a model of prehistory that shed a new light on the origin of the world's myths and religions.

"Listen," Khufu said, "any change is scary. But using Solon's immortal words, yours is a shitload. I am not saying being wrong about God is not a grave mistake. There must be the right God-to-human connection. Wrong views of God *must be* corrected. Your canopied model of prehistory has the potential to act as a foundation stone for such correction, but correcting too fast is an equally grave mistake." He paused, touched me tenderly on the arm, and muttered, "The worst that can happen is we'll remain stuck in a historical mistake for another decade or two. That is much better than the chaos of trying to correct every religion in a matter of months. It would be like trying to build a house in two hours. If we have never done it in that manner before, the effort will only produce a heap of rubble. But if we spend a year building it, it will be a solid house, good for years."

John's head was spinning.

My head was spinning with the abrupt turnaround. It was overwhelming. Yet I found the group utterly rational. The world was constantly beset by man's inhumanity to man. Men needed only the slightest excuse to strike out against others. Religious excuses were among the favorites. My friends wanted no part of that, either for themselves or for me. They were aware that much societal filth came from a disconnect with God, but the filth was already here. If God did not do anything about it, why should a handful of men in a basement?

The most they were willing to risk was to get a semblance of the canopied earth to children. They felt no obligation to adults or their gods, but children were different. They were born free of gods. They were forced to learn to accept the adults' gods. Someone had to tell the children a story of a distant canopied land, hoping that someday, they would see the story as their own.

I now knew what the group wanted to do. They did not know that I knew. I now understood how everyone had played the game. "Until a while ago," I said, "you were asking me to tell a good story. Now you tell me I can't tell the story to adults, only to children, only in a fictional setting. You are worried about the grown-ups being shocked by the news of a radically different prehistory created by a cometary phenomenon."

John was furious.

There were so many things he did not know.

He knew what a comet was, but what was the comet that could challenge the origin of religious thought? That seemed an impossible proposition, but the men in the basement talked as if it were a fact.

Solon said, "Don't make a big deal out of this. The majority don't give a fart about prehistory. They'd welcome not being burdened with a new search to replace the things already established."

The others nodded their agreement. Solon went on. "Rapid change has always been fanatical. People totally resist it. So what's the difference if the truth about the canopied earth enters the religious mainstream two centuries from now? True, we won't be around to see it, but that's the way it is. Holding back might hurt a small percentage that want to see God for real, right now. But the majority is tired of reality. They are comfortable with the current mix of imagined and real in their lives. They are happy with what they have. For their children, some may buy your fictional book. That's how change comes about—slowly."

"So we all agree," George said. "We do see, in the long run, the unifying significance of the canopied prehistory. Within a fictional setting, and as a children's book, the truth about the canopied earth can be presented logically. It could bring together religious and scientific thought all over the world. ... Are we done? Anything else?"

For the first time I saw the group differently. They all looked abandoned and defeated. Who or what had led them to take this position?

Until today, they had been the ones who wanted to know every detail of Earth's cometary experience. Last week they did not want science, centuries from now, to discover what was already known or could be known. They loved the chance to read through the ancient records describing the cometary event's path through religions and myths. Yet they now acted as if to walk away was the right choice—to ignore, forget, or at most fictionalize what we had learned for those who needed a story of a distant land.

How could they have changed so quickly?

"A children's book is the best way," Arjuna murmured assuredly. "Anything else will be difficult. Just consider the *Rig-veda*, the oldest Indian sacred text. Who among us has read it or can read it in its original language? Books get translated. So you also must be sure that the translation will not produce the imagery of a canopied earth accidentally."

"I would agree with that," Khufu said. "Who among us has read the originals of Egypt's sacred writings? How do we know the translations correspond to the original records?"

John finally had a physical picture of the canopied earth. The comet must have left a covering around the earth with significant effect on human behavior and social structure. But that did not make sense. From what he had heard, this sounded like an event from thousands if not tens of thousands of years ago.

The basement, reconfigured, was creating a different set of problems. Mired in the new setting, they were asking the wrong questions.

They should have known it but could not. How many had read the original records was immaterial, as was how many wanted to learn to read them in the original language. Few people ever had such desires. The masses could find out about the canopied earth only through scholars, translators, interpreters, and similar others.

Perhaps the notion of a children's book was not so naive. People were like children when it came to their readiness to know about the canopied earth. Few if any knew much about the diverse heritage of the canopied past. Everyone had a strong language bias and even stronger reading preferences. No one read everything. The rare person familiar with the *Rig-veda* probably knew less about Greek mythology and even less about the Jewish Torah. The one who excelled at the Torah probably knew nothing about the Pyramid and Coffin Texts. Who would act as the bridge? Who could focus all minds on the subject of the canopied earth? It was not just a religion problem, limited to the past. The writings of science presented the same problem.

Reading the findings of science on the structure, motion, and properties of comets was as difficult as reading any ancient text. The solar system's cometary footprints were observed and recorded so obscurely that the religious texts seemed easy reading in comparison. Who wanted to open his eyes to so many intellectual barriers, logical dimensions, and rational preferences?

A few years back, none of my friends had even thought about the possibility of a radical prehistory concept. Was I lost in what I perceived to be the significance of the canopied model of prehistory? How naive to assume that if I gathered evidence from science and the sacred texts, others would see the same.

When I noticed the concerned stares, I smiled and said, "I know I can put together an exceptional story to tell the children. Assume I can do it—tell a good story, a fiction based on science, sacred texts, and myths but without directly referring to any of them. Easy. Readable. Able to be retold for centuries. Where would I go from there? Would my work as a model-builder be done? Write, publish the children's book, and get back to normal?"

"You're going too fast, dear friend," George said. "Your story might be exceptional, but every society has gatekeepers. Galileo had an exceptional story. Too bad it was factual. The gatekeepers did not allow its release. Today, publishers are the gatekeepers. They decide what can or cannot reach the masses. They have to approve whatever you write before it becomes available as a book for the masses."

John was bored.

I felt boredom. The game of convincing the convinced no longer excited me. The discussion to persuade me continued for another half hour.

John had understood little. This was his first time listening to the basement meeting. There was so much that he did not know, and there was no way for him to catch up. Though he had listened to the group only today, he believed he understood the dynamics well. Someone had discovered something and had shared the discovery with friends. Bad idea. Friendship wouldn't let them be blunt. They could not look the friend in the eye and say, "Go piss up a rope! Get a life!" Instead they wanted to redirect him, be nice to him. That sort of approach often ended at advising a person to do something he was not skilled at. They were trying hard to develop an alternative to outright rejection. They were good friends, John felt, but lousy providers of alternatives.

They stood up, ready to leave. John heard the creaking furniture and almost yelled out, "Please don't go." He did not want to let them off the hook. There was so much to learn. They had dragged him in; they could not just kick him out. He eagerly listened to what seemed to be the last words of the basement meetings.

"Here is my final decision," I said. "I have talked with you for weeks. You have helped me immensely. You have tried to make me see all sides of my experience. So I have decided to call it quits. I have much better things to do than worry about prehistory."

"Fucking candy ass!" Solon blurted scornfully, frowning.

"Candy what?" Arjuna demanded.

"He's a wimp. A weakling."

I nodded my head.

Everyone but John was happy.

A radical model of life had come and gone without causing damage.

Would this be the last basement meeting?

Who cares! I read Solon's mind. *Who wants to chitchat with the past?*

But I had not read Solon's mind correctly because instead of leaving, he sat down and hurriedly set up his laptop, navigating for something.

"Here it is," he said. "Let me read it and listen carefully. It is from the movie *World War Z*, an action-horror film about humankind turning into zombies."

"What do zombies have to do with the canopied earth?" Arjuna objected strenuously.

"Listen!" Solon commanded.

Everyone obeyed.

Solon read the script of a dialogue between two characters in the film. It went something like this:

> "The problem with most people is that they don't believe something can happen until it already has. It's not stupidity or weakness. It's just human nature," said Jurgen.
>
> "How did Israel know?" asked Gerry.
>
> "We intercepted a communiqué from an Indian general saying they were fighting the Rakshasha. Translation: zombies. Technically, undead."
>
> "You're Jurgen Von Brunn," said Gerry. "High-ranking official in the Mossad. Described as sober, efficient, not terribly imaginative. And yet you build a wall because you read a communiqué that mentions the word 'zombie'?"
>
> "Well, when put like that, I'd be skeptical as well," said Jurgen. He continued, "In the '30s, Jews refused to believe they could be sent to concentration camps. In '72, we refused to fathom we'd be massacred in the Olympics. In the month before October 1973, we saw Arab troop movements, and we unanimously agreed

they didn't pose a threat. Well, a month later, the Arab attack almost drove us into the sea. So we decided to make a change."

"A change?"

"The Tenth Man. If nine of us look at the same information and arrive at the exact same conclusion, it's the duty of the tenth man to disagree. No matter how improbable it may seem, the tenth man has to start digging on the assumption that the other nine are wrong."

"And you were that tenth man," said Gerry.

"Precisely," Jurgen replied. "Since everyone assumed that this talk of zombies was a cover for something else, I began my investigation on the assumption that when they said 'zombies,' they meant zombies."

Solon paused for effect, looked up at everyone, and then said, "The canopied earth information is no different than the letter sent by an army general from a distant land. These are letters sent from the distant past, letters deemed significant, collected, and labeled as sacred texts. In whatever we have in our current sacred texts or in remnants of previous sacred texts, we face the same dilemma posed by the zombie letter received in the movie. Do we act based on the information received, or do we wait until it happens, at which time we can do nothing but shit our pants?"

I shook my head, got up, and started out of the room.

The others looked around at each other, avoided Solon's gaze, and did the same.

"Holy crap!" Solon yelled in the empty room. "No one cares. No one wants to hear from the past. … Fucking morons."

20

Let Motivation Ring

John could not express the fury he felt. He had gone to such lengths to listen to the basement conversation, only to find it ending. He could not believe it, even though he listened to the tape several times. So he waited for the next weekend, but despite all his hopes, it was true: the meetings were over. The men stayed with the women the whole time, talking about food, the weather, and current events. It was as if there had never been any basement meetings.

In a fit of desperation, John dropped his headphones, put on a jacket, and hurriedly walked to the park, oblivious to the threat of being recognized by the Watchers. He had hoped to see the Watchers' car, but there was none. He rushed to the other side of the park and saw no Watcher car parked in the temple parking lot either.

They had disappeared.

John felt like crying or beating someone up but could do neither. He returned home with shoulders slumped and brow furrowed, like a man who had lost something most dear. He tried not to watch the party across the street and thought about what had happened.

He had learned from Pasha that the Watchers released knowledge according to people's mental capacity, but he could not understand why they had eavesdropped on the meetings that seemed to be discovering new meaning in the scientific literature, sacred texts, and myths that were already available to the masses—some of them for thousands of years.

Had something in the sacred texts been released from the Watcher repositories accidentally? If so, were the Watchers worried about somebody finding something in the sacred texts too soon?

He remembered Pasha saying, "Knowledge changes things. If it comes at the wrong time, it might cause undesirable and even destructive radical change. Are human societies ready for radical change? No. They are fragile structures that collapse before radical change."

When John thought of the basement group, he wondered, *To keep things the same, would the Watchers use violence against someone who accidentally got new knowledge?*

Again he heard Pasha's voice. "They are knowledge keepers, not knowledge destroyers. Perhaps all they want is to better know the depth of the new discovery of ancient knowledge, to streamline it and make it less radical. They may offer the same choice they gave the Templars—turn the basement group into a secret society that would use the knowledge to gain power, to support a better transformation of human societies."

He missed Pasha.

There was so much he could have learned from him. What a powerful mix the basement group and Pasha would have made. But Pasha was dead and gone, his knowledge buried for all eternity.

He thought about the basement group. It was good they had stopped what they were doing. In this world there was so much prejudice directed against change. It did not matter how real the knowledge was. What the people saw was a changing social structure. Many could not take that and would fight to keep things unchanged.

He thought of his favorite bringer of new knowledge, Jesus. Pasha had insisted that Jesus had not been allowed to pass on what he knew. Instead

Paul had become the mouthpiece and had put together something to fit the existing structure rather than change it, as Jesus would have done.

John was going to hate tomorrow. Back to the routine of his first day of retirement, surfing one cable channel after another, hoping to find something new.

Boring!

The something new was in the basement across the street, but except for him, no one wanted any of it. He yearned for canopy talk, but no one spoke it any longer.

He tried to sleep, but all he could see were the corners of a password seal, randomly opening and closing to no effect.

Endnotes

1. Don E. Wilhems and Steven W. Squyres, "The Martian Hemispheric Dichotomy May Be Due to a Giant Impact," *Nature* 309 (May 10, 1984): 138-40.

2. Martin Redfern, "Giant Comet Spells Slow Death for Dinosaurs," *New Scientist* 27 (December 20–27, 1984); Victor Clube and Bill Napier, *The Cosmic Winter* (Basil Blackwell, 1990).

3. Zdenek Sekanina, "Tidal Breakup of the Nucleus of Comet Shoemaker-Levy 9," *The Collision of Comet Shoemaker-Levy 9 and Jupiter* (IAU Colloquium 156, proceedings of the Space Telescope Science Institute Workshop, Baltimore, MD, May 9–12, 1995), ed. K. S. Noll, H. A. Weaver, and P. D. Feldman (New York: Cambridge University Press, 1996), 55-80.

4. James Y-K Cho and Lorenzo M. Polvani, "The Morphogenesis of Bands and Zonal Winds in the Atmospheres of the Giant Outer Planets," *Science* 273 (July 19, 1996): 335–37.

5. All references to pyramid texts are from Samuel A. B. Mercer, ed., *The Pyramid Texts* (New York: Longmans, Green 1952).

6. Mercer, *The Pyramid Texts.*

7. All references to coffin texts are from R. O. Faulkner, *The Ancient Egyptian Coffin Texts, Volume I: Spells 1–354*; *Volume II: Spells 355–787*; and *Volume III: Spells 788-1185 & Indexes* (Aris & Phillips, 1978).

8. All references to the *Rig-veda* are from Ralph T. H. Griffith, trans., *Sacred Writings, Hinduism: The Rig Veda* (New York: Book-of-the-Month Club, 1992).

9. P. Le Page Renouf and E. Naville, *The Egyptian Book of the Dead* (London: Society of Biblical Archeology, 1904).

10. Mercer, *The Pyramid Texts.*

11. Griffith, *Sacred Writings, Hinduism.*

12. Griffith, *Sacred Writings, Hinduism.*

13. Griffith, *Sacred Writings, Hinduism.*

14. Griffith, *Sacred Writings, Hinduism.*

15. Griffith, *Sacred Writings, Hinduism.*

16 Griffith, *Sacred Writings, Hinduism.*

17 Holy Bible, New King James Version (Thomas Nelson Publishers, 1979).

18 Holy Bible.

19 Griffith, *Sacred Writings, Hinduism.*

20 Griffith, *Sacred Writings, Hinduism.*

21 Griffith, *Sacred Writings, Hinduism.*

22 Gerard Bond et al., "Evidence for Massive Discharges of Icebergs into the North Atlantic Ocean during the Last Glacial Period," *Nature* 360 (November 19, 1992): 245–49.

23 Michael Bender et al., "Climate Correlations between Greenland and Antarctica during the Past 100,000 Years," *Nature* 372 (December 15, 1994): 663–66.

24 David Talbott, *Saturn Myth* (Doubleday, 1980).

25 Mott T. Greene, *Natural Knowledge in Preclassical Antiquity* (Johns Hopkins University Press, 1992), 75–76.

26 Greene, *Natural Knowledge*, 75–76.

27 Griffith, *Sacred Writings, Hinduism.*

28 Griffith, *Sacred Writings, Hinduism.*

29 Mercer, *The Pyramid Texts.*

30 Mercer, *The Pyramid Texts.*

31 Mercer, *The Pyramid Texts.*

32 Faulkner, *The Ancient Egyptian Coffin Texts.*

33 Faulkner, *The Ancient Egyptian Coffin Texts.*

34 Griffith, *Sacred Writings, Hinduism.*

Printed in the USA
CPSIA information can be obtained
at www.ICGtesting.com
LVHW041811160324
774662LV00037B/424